HILL, PAMELA.
MARJORIE OF
P9-AEW-807
COUNTY
1956
37565002327954   CENT
LIBRARY

MARJORIE OF SCOTLAND

By the Same Author

*

THE KING'S VIXEN
THE CROWN AND THE SHADOW

CS

MARJORIE
OF SCOTLAND

Pamela Hill

1956
G. P. PUTNAM'S SONS
NEW YORK

Printed in Great Britain

WOMEN'S part in war is of recent definition, if one speaks of a recognized active share. Chance played into the hands of Black Agnes of Dunbar, Lady Buchan, Joan of Arc; they are remembered because they were not only brave but spectacular. In that latter clause lies their exception, but there are many women as brave who have never been heard of. Advertisement was denied them; on the whole, before suffrage and after the Olympians came, the female lot was to endure passively, without striking a blow; often without seeing a blow struck, and this, for ardent spirits, could be as hard as seeing too many. On reading of the stirring events of history, it is easy to forget those who lived among them quietly, maintaining as far as it could be done the ordinary gentle way of life; or, if this was taken from them, suffering by deprivation, by a course run unseen, without the compensation of glory.

By far the greater number of such women are un-heard of, and Bruce's daughter might never have been remembered if she had not been royal and—by the kind of black mischance that followed her descendants, the Stewart Kings, always—had not ended, in a way that appeals to the macabre pens of historians, in the very act of founding that unlucky house. Nevertheless it is sad, as someone remarked of the Princess Charlotte of Wales, to be remembered merely for one's exit, and on putting together the meagre information available about Marjorie one finds nothing but what is courageous.

5

It is, therefore, with this particular brand of feminine courage that I have dealt; not the showy kind; no boiling pitch is poured on enemies by her hand, and even the sounds of Bannockburn are far distant, as she was in prison. In her short life, almost every opportunity to be flamboyant was denied her; even the cage was so, although Edward I obviously intended that she should be hung in it and his instructions, related by Palgrave, may be clearly read to-day. Nevertheless, the household accounts in Bain's *Calendar* show that Marjorie was in fact taken to Walton at the time I have mentioned, and kept there from All Souls' Day, 1306.

CONTENTS

*

7

GENEALOGICAL TREE

*

Robert de Brus of Annandale

Robert, *m.* Marjorie, Countess of Carrick

ROBERT BRUCE,   Others
KING OF SCOTS
  m. (1) Isobel of Mar
   m. (2) Elizabeth de Burgh

Marjorie *m.* Walter   DAVID II, o.s.p.
k. 1316   the Steward   *b.* 1324

ROBERT II

THE STEWART KINGS

A*

Part One

SCOTLAND,
showing the journeys
of Marjorie

ROSS
Tain
Elgin
BUCHAN
MAR · Kildrummie
Aberdeen
Methven· Perth
·Gasconhall
LORN
Stirling Kinghorn
Bannockburn
Falkirk
Cambuskenneth
Paisley· Glasgow Edinburgh
Dundonald
Douglas
Turnberry CARRICK Roxburgh
Glen GALLOWAY Lochmaben
Trool Dumfries
Carlisle Chester-le-Street
Durham
FIRTH OF CLYDE
FIRTH OF FORTH
Berwick
Dundalk
York
Walton

SCOTLAND
Stirling
Edinburgh
IRELAND Dundalk
York
WALES
ENGLAND
London

THE KING OF MAY

I

"MARJORIE!"
She heard the light voice clearly, with its
suggestion of a lilt that showed that the Lady Egidia,
after all, came from Ireland. The accent was so
familiar now that she did not even wonder at it, or
make great haste to go down. The new toy that she
had found, this mirror, was of such fascination that she
could not put it back at once even to go to Walter's
mother, whom she loved. The mirror was of silver, flat
and clear, and in its surface she saw her own face reflected, and the dark soft hair that curled at the ends
slightly but was so fine that it would not grow much
past her shoulders; and her eyes, which were grey and
set squarely.

This was herself, the Demoiselle de Brus, only
daughter of the Earl of Carrick. Much intrigued, she
tilted her head, so that the head in the mirror tilted also;
smiled, laughed, venturing at last, slowly and with care,
the tongue out between its teeth.

The Lady Egidia had other smooth luxurious things
besides this mirror. There was a comb of carven horn
that had come out of Norway as a bride-gift, that would
be in the time of the little dead queen who had never
reached Scottish shores. There was a box made of
alabaster from the land of France, elaborately wrought
with tiny castles, kings and saints upon it. The Lady
Egidia's lord, who was James, the High Steward of
Scotland, had brought it for his wife when he last re-

13

turned from across seas. Other things she had had when she came as a bride out of Ulster, the sister of the Red Earl.

"Marjorie!"

It was necessary to go, now, or they would come looking for her and find her here, in the Lady Egidia's chamber. She would not have meddled with the beautiful things to harm them, but she had wanted, very much wanted, to see her own face in the silver mirror. Only it was not the same here as at Turnberry or Lochmaben, Father's own castles where she could do as she liked, so perhaps . . .

"*Marjorie!* Where in the world has the child got to?"

There were her fingermarks on the mirror, warm and damp, a little. Hastily she breathed over the silver to clear its surface, and her reflection and the marks merged and vanished together in a cloud. She replaced the mirror carefully on its chest (how unthinkable to have dropped and dinted it, as she had done with the baby's French toy yesterday!) and stole out of the room towards the stairs. As she slipped past the hanging, she met her cousin Walter, sent to look for her.

"What were you doing in Mother's room?" he said curiously. "Everyone has been searching for you. You'd better come down."

He grasped her hand firmly and led her down the twisting stairs. Marjorie went obediently enough, but in her heart burned a little flame of rebellion. Walter was almost four years older than she and thought himself important on that account and because he was a boy; his voice just now had held a slight officiousness which she resented. "He's not the heir, anyway," she muttered. That was Cousin Andrew, who was too tall and thin and too grand to notice girls, and had a cough and was often ailing. Marjorie, who had never ailed in her life, considered it curiously. Why were some people sick and others well? Walter and she were as strong as horses. Walter could wrestle and tilt. She had tried to cajole him to teach her to tilt also, but he would not. "It's not a pastime for ladies," he had said. Marjorie's mouth set mutinously. She did not want to be a lady. How much better pleased everyone, including herself, would have been if she had been born a boy!

"Where were you, I said?" pursued Walter. His tone was kind but determined; if his cousin, Earl Robert of Carrick, whom he greatly admired and who would in due course take him to be his esquire, had ordered Walter to have an eye to his wild small daughter whilst he, the Earl, was busied with affairs on his English estates, that Walter would conscientiously do. Besides, it gave him a pleasurable sensation to order about someone smaller than he was, but not so small as baby John and little Egidia, who were too young to understand. He looked down with tolerance at his cousin's stubborn dark head; she was good sport, Cousin Marjorie, although it would have been better, he also thought, if she had been a boy. He talked on, never noticing that Marjorie had not in fact answered; he was pleasantly aware of the sound of his own voice.

"We're going out with the ponies. You're to come with me."

"I can ride a pony by myself," said Marjorie.

"Well, you can't ride alone here, while you're in Mother's charge. It isn't safe with so many vagrants about still, after the fighting."

15

"The fighting's been over three years."

Walter took refuge in condescension. "What can you know about it, when you were too young to remember? *I* remember the news of Falkirk fight, and Uncle John. . . ." He bit his lip, remembering the young uncle who had been killed fighting for Wallace, the Guardian of Scotland, defeated at last in that battle by the English seven years ago. Walter denied the angry pricking of his eyes, caution asserting itself in him; Earl Robert, Marjorie's father, had not been on the side of Wallace and Uncle John at Falkirk, as they supported the Bruce's hereditary enemies, the Comyns. It would not be safe maybe to talk before the child, even though it might be long enough before Earl Robert came north.

Walter spoke persuasively of other things. "You'll come with me, now. We'll go by the burn and the little hill—do you remember I told you about the thrush's nest there? The young ones are still learning to fly, I saw them yesterday."

"Here's your mother." Marjorie wriggled free of his hand and ran out before him into the sunlight. Walter followed slowly, uncertain whether he had cajoled her or not. Helplessly, he looked out towards where his mother stood, with her back towards them, inspecting her green garden of English herbs. It was so like Mother to have called and called, and then to have forgotten what she wanted.

"Why, there you are, both my children," said the Lady Egidia absently. Her short-sighted eyes focused at last on the two young people, and she tried to remember what it was she had had in mind to say to them. Human beings were like plants, she thought, pleased with her fancy; prune them occasionally, water them after the day's heat was gone, and otherwise leave them alone. There was no sense in nagging continually, as James always did. Egidia thrust down a sense of faint relief that her lord was from home. Such a fuss, such uncertainty, wherever James was! And all one had to do was wait and be patient, as when growing fennel. "Seeds are so expensive now since the English peace," murmured Egidia. "In the days of war one simply did without." Her hands caressed her cousin's child's dark hair.

"Dearest Marjorie, put a hood on before you ride abroad," she said. "It's cold in spite of the sun." Still with her mind running on the garden, she took leisure to wonder if Robert of Carrick, when next he rode north to Dundonald from Westminster, would think to bring some Spanish carraway for her. Everyone was using it down south since Edward Longshanks' first queen, the one that was dead now, Eleanor, had first brought some with her from Castile. It had a delightful tang in baked bread. . . . Dear Robert. He would remember, she thought, although James would certainly have forgotten; for one thing, he was obliged to her, Egidia, for her care of Marjorie. But Marjorie was no trouble, and had in any case been with them on and off since she was a baby and her own mother died. Egidia sighed, and wondered if she had been right to foster Robert's second marriage with her own niece, Elizabeth de Burgh, three years ago now. But how was she to have foretold that Elizabeth would find this child a burden? Willing and pleasant enough she had seemed, at first mention of a step-daughter. "And so she ought to have been, with Robert handsome enough for anybody, and the wealthiest widower in two kingdoms, excepting possibly Edward Longshanks himself, and *he's* turned sixty! But they say his new young French queen thinks a great deal of him for all that," murmured Egidia. Well, in any case, no doubt Robert would be due north again soon; his Carrick estates needed attention as much as his English ones in Hertford and Essex, and he had never been one of those who left their Scottish possessions to care for themselves while they danced attendance on Edward four seasons of the year. "Elizabeth, no doubt, prefers the south, and the English Court, to settling here, and giving an heir to Carrick," thought Egidia. Yet in so failing to do her niece was cutting off her nose to spite her face, for surely a son of hers and Robert's would wrest the heirship from Marjorie?

"Well, well, all will fall out as God wills, no doubt," said the Steward's wife aloud. "Off with you, now," and as the children's figures retreated she watched them and calculated, as she had done ever since Marjorie was born, her chances of marriage with one of the Steward's sons. For this had been growing in Egidia's mind long before the day seven years ago when Robert, in great haste and with harassed tired eyes, had brought her his dark-haired, chubby girl-baby to tend, with warning that Edward of England had a mind to her keeping also.

"Edward had his suspicions of Robert at that time, and he'd not allay them by refusing to send Marjorie south as hostage in Percy's charge, as was demanded," thought Egidia. Had Edward—who they said forgot nothing, forgave nothing, and stored up details in his lawyer's mind to be recalled years later—had Edward really lulled all doubts of Robert, whom now he appeared to favour? "He hunts by his side, kneels in chapel by him, even rode to the siege of Berwick by him—no one has ever heard what he thought of *that*— and yet, and yet, has Edward forgotten, or *he* forgotten, who some say Robert is?"

Egidia bit her lip. To think of that took one back, very far back, back to the shores of Ireland, where she had lived when she was a child. Even there there had been felt the shock of grief and change when the great, golden, generous King of Scots, Alexander the Third, had been found dead one morning at the foot of a cliff in Fife, after riding all night through storm. That had been the beginning of other storms, sweeping in greater and fiercer intensity till they engulfed the whole land. For there had been nobody to succeed Alexander but a baby girl, his dead daughter's child, in Norway; and on the way home to Scotland she, too, had died.

"I remember that," thought Egidia, "and the way the lawyers' noses burrowed everywhere for three years after, trying to prove the claims to the Scottish throne." It had been a case of ferreting back among the twisted roots of dead Alexander's ancestors, to find the nearest of kin that might now succeed; and after every lawyer's argument under the sun, fourteen claimants, no less, remained. Egidia had been a bride then, and she re- membered hearing her solemn young husband talk of it, for although he himself was not a direct claimant his kinsman, old Robert de Brus of Annandale, was.

"The late King Alexander, when his queen was barren and he had no heirs—that is the second Alex- ander I am speaking of, Egidia, not the third—" and she had tried to stop him with laughter and her arms about his neck, but James had disengaged her and gone weightily on with his own speech, which was when she first learned that he hated to be interrupted "—the *late* King Alexander made a charter wherein Robert de Brus of Annandale, who was a young man then—later his son married Marjorie of Carrick and became the father of Robert, whom you know—wherein Robert de Brus of Annandale should succeed him to the crown, by reason of their both being descended from King David. But later Prince, that was afterwards King, Alexander, was born; and so there was no need for the charter any more at that time. But old Annandale has not forgotten, and neither will any of his clan, that some say they should be Kings of Scotland."

And so, and so . . . the child Marjorie was heir to all that. If Andrew or Walter should marry Marjorie, for that reason and for old friendship's sake, it might be as well.

Egidia let her eyes dwell on the small figure of Marjorie, admiring the way the child sat her pony. Gruff, sturdy, outspoken, honest—how little outwardly she resembled her golden father, except for the eyes! As for the young mother, it was difficult to remember; so quiet and unassuming had Isobel of Mar been, and so short a time had she lived as Robert's wife, that no one had ever got to know her very well. She had had Welsh blood, Egidia remembered, from that queer old mother of hers, who was still alive somewhere up in the north, and had herself been a daughter of Llewelyn of Wales. Did Edward Longshanks remember that also, attempting as he had done to stamp out everyone of Welsh royal blood? He would have grudges enough against Robert of Carrick and his daughter, if he cared to recall them.

But perhaps, having himself supported one of the

other claimants to the Scottish throne, Edward would assume that Robert of Carrick thought no more of that old charter.

"And perhaps he does not," thought Egidia. But her eyes narrowed. Robert had shown no great eagerness to acknowledge John Baliol, Edward's choice, as king. ... Toom Tabard,* everyone had called Baliol, who had been Edward's creature and accepted the Scottish throne from him as a fief of England, and done homage for it. Then at last even the Tabard had rebelled at the humiliations Edward had imposed on him, and Edward had marched north and soaked Scotland in blood. Ah ... Berwick was a charred ruin now, that had once been the greatest port of the east, and there was neither crown nor monument in the Abbey of Scone . . . and Baliol had lost in the end and finished, at last, in France as Edward's pensioner.

"And now we have no king," thought Egidia, "for none since has dared lay claim."

Something hurt her, remotely, difficult of location at first while her thoughts ranged so far. Then she saw; it was the stalk of the herb she had pulled, twisted and wound tightly about her own fingers. She caught her breath a little at her own folly, released the stem and dropped it on the ground. Plants . . . men, kings, thrones! Leave a seed where it had fallen into the ground, and it would thrive; force it, and it would die. Not one of all the nobles of Scotland who had in the end sworn fealty to Edward had done so willingly. . . . Robert least of all.

Marjorie and Walter and the two grooms rode at a

* Empty Coat.

21

pleasant pace out through the arched gateway and along
the path that led to the moors. Walter had a heron's
feather in his hood and his hair showed beneath it in a
heavy square fringe of gold. Marjorie clenched her
hands on the reins, feeling their nakedness by contrast
with Walter's elegance, gloved in Portugal leather.
How like Walter to have worn his gloves on this un-
important ride, because they had been a gift from Sir
Henry Percy, the English lieutenant, and he wanted
to show off!

She tossed her hair back, thinking how Walter
annoyed her at times. How like a girl he was, in spite of
his strength that he was always demonstrating, with
that hood-plume and his care for his nails, like a lady!
Yet no one was prouder of being descended from Alexander the Fighting Regent than he, or listened more
avidly to stories about the Battle of Largs, where old
Alexander had helped defeat the Norsemen. How often
they had listened to those tales at Rothesay Castle, with
the grey sea washing below in the bay, and the firelight
shining on the old Regent's studded leather shield, and
his sword that was too heavy now for most men to lift,
except Marjorie's father!

"I don't want to think of father now," thought
Marjorie. Returning to Walter, she remembered that
in any case he could fight when he had to; yet she herself had seen him downing young Umfraville once for
ill-treating a dog. Walter had made Umfraville bleed
from the nose and then Cousin James had had him
whipped, because Umfraville was a guest and in any
case it was not, the Steward said, a nobleman's way of
fighting, or a nobleman's reason. Walter had borne the
beating very white about the mouth with anger, and

had not cried at all and only said afterwards that
Umfraville was an Englishman and deserved to have
his nose bled . . . which made it all the more curious
that he should be wearing Percy's gloves now.

"Why are you wearing those?" she said.

Walter turned his head. "Because I like the feel of
them," he said reasonably. "Why shouldn't I?"

"There are too many up here who take presents from
Englishmen. Everyone knows Sir Henry Percy is
Edward's man and sends reports on us all twice a year
to Westminster."

She heard the pertness of her own voice, repeating
words she had heard someone else use . . . who? Egidia?
The serving-women? It would not be Cousin James, he
would have shuffled and doubted, while he talked, if it
was indeed so. . . . She had spoken thoughtlessly, less
aware of the meaning of the words than of their high-
sounding phrases, signifying that she understood more
than in fact she did. She was surprised and dismayed at
the dark flush that rose beneath Walter's fair skin,
spreading from the roots of his hair to the lines of his
throat-linen. She had not meant to make him really
angry.

"You're a baby and you don't know what you're
talking about," he said. "That kind of thing isn't safe
to say, even in jest."

Bewilderment at his rare harshness came to her. And
he had called her a baby! Her underlip thrust out.

"I wasn't jesting, Walter Stewart," she told him.
"The English King put Henry Percy over Father's
castle of Turnberry when it was forfeit."

She screwed up her eyes against the sun, triumphant.
Where had she dislodged that piece of information,

hidden in her mind till now? All that had happened years ago, when she was too small to remember anything; and Father had got Turnberry back afterwards.

Walter was talking still, with his first flush of anger gone; he bore the tone of one determined to instruct her. Marjorie listened, half against her will, aware that his voice had grown gentle again, as when he would talk to sick animals he tended. What was it about Walter that was so different from other people? She caught her lip in her teeth, uncertainly.

"Your father held out long enough, but in the end he had to bow the knee to Edward with the rest of the Scots lords. What else could they do? They're all at feud here in the north, Comyn and Baliol and Bruce and Fife. No one leader can rally them all. The English *have* a leader, and in that way they have been able to subdue us . . . for now. But even old Edward'll not live for ever, and his son's no soldier. When there's a change of king in England, there'll be a change of state in Scotland. But until then it's only good blood spilled to attempt it, and we can do little except wait—and sharpen our swords."

His eyes, blue against the sunlight, gazed ahead; she had the feeling that he did not talk to her any more, but rather to himself. The words, which seemed so like those she had often heard over the High Steward's table, wearied her; she did not grasp their significance or follow the names. Comyn, she knew, was her father's enemy, because he and her father both wanted the same thing. . . . Egidia had told her that. But old Edward? Young Edward? Change of state? What did it mean except that Walter had forgotten she was here? Weary

24

of the whole business, she spurred ahead and flung
back at him, crying over her shoulder,

"You make a great deal of talk with the fine names
you've heard, Walter Stewart. All it means is that you
think more of yourself and your English gloves than
anything," and digging her knees into her pony's sides
she beat sharply at it with her small whip. She could
ride faster than Walter, she was certain. It would do his
tiresome nonsense good if she could get away from him
—and how delicious to ride free and alone, at speed, as
she had been used to do, in the days when the Earl
was north!

"Marjorie!"

She felt the summer wind lift her hair and heard
Walter's voice calling as the Lady Egidia's had done,
but now she need pay no heed. Giving the pony his
head, taking pleasure in the way the little beast responded to her urging, she jolted, jolted, across the
ground's scars and hollows. Soon, at this rate, she
would be free of Walter and his grooms. Soon! Why
should it be such joy to be alone, even for the space of a
bird's flight between stone and tree? Everyone was kind
back there, but she wanted for an hour to be by herself,
herself, herself. . . .

"Marjorie! Come back at once . . . do you hear,
Marjorie!"

A clump of birches had come into view as she topped
the rise. She would make for them; Walter's voice
sounded far off now, and she could lead him a chase. In
the end the pony would find his way home again.

Stones tumbled and clattered beneath the pony's
hooves. Among the yellowing height of bracken
Marjorie was soon lost; it pressed in close like a forest.

A guilty joy possessed her, and she let the pony scramble on down the incline, laughing as she went. Walter's voice, sharp now with anxiety, faded. Let him call, she thought wickedly. How good to be by herself, with the beast's flanks gripped securely between her thighs and her seat firm, the way father himself had taught her, starting almost before she could walk . . . in the days before the Lady Elizabeth came. Marjorie's lips trembled. Well . . . no one could take away what the Earl had taught, even if he had less time to ride with her now.

When would he come again? Would he ever come again?

Why, she was crying . . . here on the pony's back, with the world a shifting mass of grey and green about her. How stupid people were! If she had cried on her pillow at night, someone would have heard, and come to try and comfort her . . . and she did not want comfort. No . . . nobody could alter what had happened, or make things the same again.

Father, Father, Father. . . .

"Fool," she thought fiercely. Not even last summer, but the one before that, she had been out among the brambles and come in with juice on her face and hands and her gown torn. And in the Earl's hall a cool strange woman had been sitting, and Marjorie could see she did not want to kiss her at all, only must do so for the sake of ceremony. Her cheek had smelled of flowers, and was smooth and cold. Then she had laughed with a high silvery sound, and said something about Marjorie's stained hands and face, and looked at her from her feet to her head, and back. And then Father, who had been standing by the cool woman's chair, had laughed also.

"She's been allowed to run wild, so that now she's a hoyden," he said. "With a new mother, she'll soon become like other young ladies, and sew and spin."

It was not the words so much as the glance, not for her at all but for the new woman who sat there, slim and graceful in English camlet, that hurt. . . .

"And I still can't sew, or spin either," thought Marjorie with a fierce satisfaction.

The pony gave a sudden lurch downwards into a clearing. There were the twisted trunks of birch-trees and men there, talking. Marjorie saw them and heard the murmur of their voices in the same instant that she knew, with the sudden jolt and cessation of speed, that she would fall. She braced herself, and then went flaccid; panic had risen, been fought down, and she remembered the Earl's voice again, from that time long ago; loosen your muscles, loosen, loosen, when you fall.

The ground and sky whirled about her. She was thrown violently, over and down, striking the ground heavily, rolling over and lying still. Silence, fear of feeling, then pain, and a rush of talk; the sound of her own most shameful crying, and the awareness of hands about her, and a voice.

"She's not hurt badly. Only, there'll be some bruising."

The voice was matter-of-fact, young and with humour in it. Marjorie opened her eyes; a man was kneeling on the ground by her. His hands, which were deft and gentle, examined her arms and legs, flexing them, and ran round her skull beneath her hair. Marjorie stopped crying and fixed her gaze on his face.

He was speaking, she noted, to someone who stood behind them, over by the pony's head. She did not turn to look, partly because the movement hurt her, but also because the speaking man's face intrigued her so that she could not look away. She could not explain what it was that held her gaze. He was not a handsome man, or richly dressed, like her father and his acquaintance, whose surcoats were embroidered with coloured silks over their mail and their sleeves lined with furs and their linen perfumed. This man wore a rough leather jerkin such as common soldiers had. His casque and scabbard were old and dark with rust, and his hair, lint-coloured and dry with the sun, hung unkempt about his face. His skin was bronzed, as though he lived always in the open; against it the blue of his eyes seemed light and strange. They looked as though they saw beyond her, although he was looking directly at her. Although there were lines on his face, he was young. He might be the same age as her father.

He smiled, seeing her watching him. "You've stopped crying! That's good." When he smiled, the far-seeing eyes deepened in colour and seemed to focus their gaze. She could not explain the feeling the eyes gave her; it was a kind of shyness, and she found herself unable to speak. But the young man himself was kind, she thought. She eased her body upwards, not wanting to be thought a cry-baby.

"That was a fair toss you took. Have you often fallen?" said the young man. Marjorie nodded, and straightway a second man, the one she had not turned to see, came forward, leaving the pony; it was as though he did not wish the first man to have longer speech. "Have you no one with you that you were riding alone at speed, over this bad ground?" he asked her. He had a long, lined face and Marjorie thought, from his looks and the way he chided, that he might be a priest. Priests often, she knew, and bishops also, rode abroad now attired in leather and mail, especially after the late wars when they had had to defend themselves like the next man. This man's hair, which was grey, had thinned over the top of his head; there was nothing there to tell whether he was a priest or not. She left him, turning again to the younger man, who still knelt by her.

"Not very safe ground, indeed," he said, "but where is safe?" Although his hands held her and he spoke as though to her alone, Marjorie felt that the words were intended also for the priest-man, as a kind of jest. But the speaker did not laugh. Perhaps he was not a person who laughed often. She pondered on it, still unable to take her eyes from his face.

But now he had become aware of her watching and again she saw his eyes change, showing for an instant a light, wary gleam, like an animal's. He set her gently on her feet, and rose.

"Who are you, my child?" he said. Standing, she was aware of his great height, which topped even her father's.

"I am the Demoiselle Marjorie de Brus, and my father is the Earl of Carrick." Eagerly, glad that she had found her tongue again, she tumbled out the words; how she was staying at Dundonald with the Lady Egidia, how she had been with Walter, and his two grooms, and had run away.

Why was she so eager to tell the man? He had no horse and he bore no device, and he had no followers who wore his livery. Who was he? Not an earl, like her father; nor a seneschal, like Cousin James. Not a king, for the King of Scotland (other than poor Toom Tabard) was dead. Yet if there had been a king, Marjorie was certain that he would have looked as this man did now.

She could not ask, as though he had been a servant, who he was. Would he tell her, now that she had told him her name?

She stared up at him. When she had spoken of her father his face had changed. It was as though a vizor had slipped over it. Then, in the same courtly way in which he had come to her aid, he raised her hand and kissed it.

"I cannot take the Demoiselle de Brus back to her cousin's castle, but I can set her on her way again."

"Have a care to yourself!" said the priest-man in a low voice. But the other turned to him and answered quickly. "John, John, can you not trust my discretion, even yet?"

"Not on your own behalf, God knows!"

"Well . . . for weightier reasons."

"And what are those? None, for me . . . and a thousand others."

The young man shrugged a little, and smiled. "*Your* discretion has gaps in it!" Then he turned and took hold of the bridle of Marjorie's pony. "Come, *ma demoiselle*, I'll lead your mount so far, till we get on the smooth turf again."

But on that instant there was a swift indrawing of breath from the man called John, and at once the other loosened his grip on her bridle and laid his hand on his sword. "It's only Walter," said Marjorie. She saw, above, the single rider, poised above the slope; then rider and horse hurtled down, with a clatter of loosened stones, and arrived among them.

Walter was panting and looked flushed and angry. Marjorie heard his quick breathing with guilt. She had forgotten Walter! Oddly, in this clearing where the four of them stood, she could see her late actions plainly; saw herself now as petulant, spoiled; a naughty child.

"Oh, Walter, . . ." she began. Perhaps she ought to beg his pardon. If she did so at once, and he forgave her, he might say nothing of this at home. She wondered which way he had sent the grooms; they must be still searching over the moor. "Walter, . . ." she said again, and turned to him where he sat in the saddle.

But Walter had no eyes for her. Walter was acting in an extraordinary way. He had lighted down off his pony and was kneeling now, among the young springing grass and new fronds of bracken that curled, thin and green, in the shade of the trees. He had taken the stranger's hand and laid his cheek against it. Marjorie watched, bewildered.

Was this a king? Walter, with the high rank he bore, would kneel only to someone very great. To his own father; to hers, as his esquire who owed him service. To his overlord . . . during this peace, to Edward of England. To his God, at the altar or in the confessional. To . . .

"Save that for the King, lad," said the stranger very kindly. Then he raised Walter with two hands beneath his elbows and led him towards his pony again; Marjorie heard words pass between them. It all sounded odd, because Walter's officious certainty had quite

31

deserted him, and he even stammered a little as he spoke. One phrase she remembered, partly because it was so close to the things in her mind; partly, also, because of what happened later. But that she could not have known then.

"The King?" had said Walter. And then, almost sobbing, "*Which* King?"

Then the stranger's face grew bleak and his eyes remote as when she had first seen them, as though they saw beyond the clearing to matters long past, or still to come. "Whichever it is," she thought, "is more real to him than we are, standing here." Her thoughts had an odd clarity which she remembered afterwards. But the stranger's voice when it came again was normal, light and rather amused.

"At any rate, you may be sure" it said, "which King it is not."

"I don't want you riding off again," said Walter.

He did not sound angry. Back on the moor, the movement of the saddle had made her aware of the bruises on her flesh. She bit her lip, resolved not to cry again. "A fair toss!" Yes, but without it she would never have seen the strange man.

"Who was he?" They rode slowly, knee to knee. She had given Walter the reins passively; if she was quiet, perhaps he would tell her. She felt older for the last hour; ready to wait, obey and listen.

"Oh, Walter. . . ." She watched his profile, young and stern in the severe confines of the hood. He had not answered. Marjorie's eyes filled; she felt hurt and tired. Why should Walter tease her always? Then he turned his head.

"Why, you've hurt yourself," he said. "Why *did* you run off like that? We'll tell Mother and she'll put unguent on the place. Not far to go now."

"I don't want unguent. Tell me who the man was. I found him first."

"You found him?" His voice displayed tolerant amusement. "A queer manner of finding! There, don't cry, for pity's sake! We're almost home."

She evaded his grasp. "I *will* know . . . if you won't tell me, I'll ask others. Someone's bound to have known of him, back on the moor."

"You'll not." The face he turned to her was white. "You'll *not* tell, Marjorie. If you do. . . ."

"Well, if?" Now they were quarrelling again. It was Walter's fault. Tiredness and misery made her tears flow faster; she turned away so that he should not see them. As if she would have told if he had not been so stupid! But to be treated like a child so. . . .

"Tell me, then." She wheeled round suddenly and fixed her eyes on his hands. They were bare. In the urgency of the moment she scarcely noticed it.

"Promise, then . . . promise you'll say nothing of it to any soul."

"I promise. When have I ever given you away, Walter Stewart? Did I tell about your nose-bleed? Or the time you turned the sword's edge and said nothing at all? And when Gilbert beat you at the vault and you said he hadn't?"

"No, you didn't tell. But this is different. This may mean a man's life, Marjorie." He looked at her, and something reassured him in the small stocky figure sitting so bravely astride its saddle, with short dark hair and grey eyes straight-set. When he spoke again it was as to an adult; his eyes looked through and beyond her.

"The English have set a price on his head of three hundred marks. That way, it's not safe or right to tell even trusted servants of him; it's so much money and they are poor. If your father were never to come home, Marjorie, you'd grieve; but every honest man in Scotland would feel that same grief if William Wallace of Elderslie were taken. He's been father and leader to them, poor and rich, for nine bitter years. He won a great victory for us against the English at Stirling Bridge, then later he was defeated at Falkirk, as you've heard. Since then he's been a fugitive, now here, now there. *He*'s never bowed the knee to Edward, nor sworn him allegiance, as every other leader in Scotland has done, out of sheer necessity. Necessity means little to Wallace, in that way; he's lost too much. They hanged his wife, the English, in Lanark, and burned his house to ashes; when Will heard of that, he never rested till the man who gave the order was dead. Now he's an outlaw, made so by one who's not our king and has no right to our country. If I were a man myself, I'd follow him. I pray that I shall."

She stared at Walter, thinking that she had never heard him speak so passionately. Listening, she felt a child again, groping for words. What could she say that would show she could understand?

"You said . . . you said we'd no strong leader." She remembered Walter's speech of an hour ago.

"I said we'd no leader that all men would follow. The nobles put up with Wallace, who's a poor knight's son, as long as he had claim to be a wizard, undefeated. It suited them well enough to have him fight for them at Stirling Bridge, or lead forays over the Tweed to harry the English in Carlisle. They raised him to be one of themselves after he routed Surrey's cavalry; Guardian of Scotland, he's been, like your father and the Comyn. But after old Edward came north and defeated Wallace at Falkirk they remembered that he was humbly born and they were high, and they fell to squabbling among themselves again as they have always done, and had no heed to Will and would have betrayed him to save their own skins. But the poor men love and guard him." Walter paused, thinking of the tales and minstrels' songs that already had the quality of legend although the subject still lived; stories of strength more than human, of one man killing seven, one man saving five; of escapes in woman's guise, of forays and burnings, and bravery and pain. "Oh, Marjorie, he's set fire to more than towns. You've seen the heather smoulder. There's no great blaze, but it goes on smoking away, spreading underground . . . until one day the heat comes to a dry patch, and the wind's right, and it's up and roaring flame, with the heat of it felt for a mile and no stopping it till it burns out. That's what Wallace has done for Scotland. Face down, we were, when Edward came trampling north into a land without a king worthy of it, and took away everything that made it a kingdom, its sacred things and its pride and honour, and marched them back to England, even the stone where the Kings were crowned. It would have been easy enough to do as some did, and let him take all, and settle down, comfortably enough, no doubt, as dependants of him and his lieutenants that he sent up here . . . and with so many of our nobles owning land also in England for which they must do Edward homage, that made it simpler. But Wallace owns no English land, and wishes none. Please God he'll lead us again."

Marjorie saw an appalling thing; Walter was crying. For a boy to cry! She must never let him know she had seen. . . . Fear of betraying her knowledge made her search for small, familiar matters again; her eyes fell on Walter's hands.

"What have you done with your gloves?" she said. Her voice was still shaky with her own late tears; in a rush of revulsion from taut feelings, she wanted to tease and be teased, hear his laughter, even anger, again. But he neither laughed nor answered sharply, and did not loosen his grasp on her reins; he might scarcely have heard her, but his voice when he replied was light, as Wallace's had been when it spoke of Edward of England. "I threw them away," he said. "It's cooler without them."

Marjorie watched him, finding him changed.

11

Remembering that meeting later, and what followed, she always felt as though one happening led directly to the other, although it was not so; and followed hard upon the other, although it could not have been so. For the young thrushes Walter had found to show her that day would have learned to fly by the time her father came, which was in summer.

Often Marjorie had heard him speak of the summers in the south, that came early and stayed late, with their lush blossom and golden light and the sound of bees harvesting. But for some reason there was nothing lovelier, the Earl said, than this brief Scottish summer,

36

fickle and late-born, often swept with rain. But there
was a clear sky on this day, when beyond the heather
still in bud the hills of Arran showed plainly, blue and
shimmering a little in the close heat of June. If her
father had diced for all the days of the year to ride to
the west, he could not have thrown better.

Long before the banners showed her his device,
Marjorie had seen the dust of riders far down the road.
She lingered a little at the tower window, hugging her
hope to herself. Last year she would have run down to
tell them, shouting that after all it might be the Earl;
how much older she was now! Count ten and wait, and
look again; by the time they had ridden forward a long
arrow-shot from a bow, she would be certain. An arrow
could be fitted in its shaft in the window here . . . how
little she had seen of the late wars! Always guarded,
sheltered, with Egidia and the Steward, at Rothesay
where the sea called night and day, or here . . . guarded
especially from Sir Henry Percy, whose orders it had
been to take her into England long ago. And still
Father would pretend that that was why it was not safe
for her to go south with him now, although everyone
knew it was really because the Lady Elizabeth did not
want so old a step-child.

Marjorie shifted her weight from one foot to the
other. Would the Lady Elizabeth have come on this
ride? She was always about Father, hanging on his arm
and making him laugh. . . . Father was good at laughing. Always where he was everything was gay, and he
could handle a lute and string rhymes and tell stories,
and advise ladies as to what to wear and what jewels to
buy. Why, hadn't everyone talked for years of the
trousseau he had chosen for Aunt Isobel, his sister,

37

who had gone overseas to wed King Eirik of Norway? Golden crowns and silver plate, samite and jewels and furs. It had been very grand even for a royal wedding, but now King Eirik was dead and Aunt Isobel was only the Dowager Queen.

"Marjorie!"

They were calling her now to tell her to go and get ready. Why must she always share Father with the rest? If she went down to the courtyard now, that was the way it would be, watching him ride in to where the others stood round her, and then alight and embrace Egidia and the ladies and among them herself, and come in laughing. . . .

"But here I can see him alone," she thought. She would not go down.

Soon the riders came in. Among them was a tall figure, very erect in the saddle, his vizor down and a swirl of blue, which was his cloak, borne behind him. His train, with banner-poles strapped by their saddles, clattered behind his splendid horse; everywhere were gleaming bright colours against the sky. She was suddenly glad to be watching from above, here, secretly. The Lady Elizabeth had not come with him.

She stole down the turret stairs before they should call for her again, and was in time to see the Earl alight from his horse and greet Lady Egidia, who went to him with both hands extended and her light Irish voice crying welcome. But Robert ignored the outstretched hands and took and kissed her on both cheeks.

"You never change," he said. He smiled, put her from him, and the grey eyes turned with a curious steady gaze from one to another, and then to the stairs. "But another has," and he held a hand out, almost shyly, Marjorie thought, as though he guessed already that she was different from the child who would have run to meet him a year ago. She picked up her skirts and jumped down, feeling suddenly gauche in face of this splendid courtier and his train. "It's because I was standing on the step," she muttered, hearing him say she was taller.

The Earl kissed her and she smelled the essence he used on his beard, and suddenly clung to him. She had to finger everything; the stuff of his cloak, the plain burnished metal of his armour that was jointed after the new usage and no longer made all of mail, which rusted quickly. He was a shining man, she thought. Irrelevantly the remembrance came to her of the time he had stood in the hall of Rothesay Castle and lifted up the old Regent's sword, that so few now could hold, balancing it, laughing, with the sunlight from the doorway shining in his hair. She had thought then that he was of silver and gold, and now. . . .

"Well?" said Robert of Carrick. Jerking a glance at the face below the upthrust vizor, she saw that although the voice teased her his eyes were grave. What had happened? Would he tell her? Would he take her back with him?

"You've come for me?" Standing with her face against the embroidered surface of his surcoat, she could feel the separate, small cold surface of metal thread among the silk. It was as though she were sensible of tiniest things, like an ant must be in grass. Everything was so important and yet needless; Father could fight as well as anybody with a plain broadsword and no embroidery, and had done so at Lochmaben three years since, when the English came.

"Not this time, sweetheart. In a little while." That was for no one but herself to hear; and now he was giving her an answer out loud and saying how graceless she was to want to leave Egidia, who had been kind, and then Egidia and all of them were laughing and everyone was saying how wild she, Marjorie, was and would never stitch, or spin, but only sit in the saddle in all weathers as if she had been a boy. But no one was really angry, and in the end they all went in together to the great hall, because in the Steward's absence nobody bothered about precedence, and at the high table all the children and herself and Walter and Egidia clustered round the Earl and listened and talked and stuffed meat in their mouths, and drank wine. But although the meat was unsalted and very good, Marjorie forgot to eat heartily, seeing instead clearly how when the Earl's casque was removed his hair curled brightly, its locks flowing to meet the short essenced beard that was so fashionable now in England. Thinking of that, she scowled; *there* there would be brilliant talk, not like the story Andrew Stewart was telling now about his pony, drawling over it in his nasal voice that was so like the High Steward's. Why did Father pretend to like listening, courteously as though it had been one of King Edward's ladies, with their pert painted faces and perfumes from Spain, and their gloves and songs and greyhounds, that were talking?

But when supper was long over she still had not gone to bed, remaining curled up at the Earl's feet beside Cousin James's wolf-hound, which lay by them. The glow of the fire and the heat of the sputtering torches made her sleepy, but she would not for worlds have moved, or drawn attention to herself in order to be sent upstairs after the others because she disturbed the talk. How different talk could be, she thought; not now like a brilliant game of coloured balls, flung swiftly to and fro and caught, and flung again. That was what Father's tales at the supper table had been like at last, so that young Andrew's narrow face had flushed with laughter and he stopped being such a bore, and Walter had shining eyes and listened always, and Egidia . . . Egidia had not said much, only watched with her heavy lidded eyes that were liquid and dark, like a deer's. She was watching now, seated as she was in the lamplight, sewing at one of Cousin James's shifts. He was absent again to-night, and Marjorie was glad; with his uncertain kindnesses and abrupt fidgeting ways, as though he were afraid of something over his shoulder, the talk could not have run on as it was doing now, murmurous and slow, like a sleepy burn. The sense of the words was lost to her as she listened and stared at the fire.

There on the floor, she closed her eyes for an instant. If one were blind it should still be possible to live, a little. . . . The faint, foreign perfumed smell that came from the Earl's high boots of leather mingled with the warm odour of the wolf-hound's coat. It would be lying with its great head sunk on its paws, seeing with eyes that were the colour of fire into the logs that burned with their own tarry scent. Yes, a blind man could know of certain things. . . . Father had said that in England the fires of poor folk were banked secretly with black, foul matter dug deep from the earth, though there had been a law made against this because of the neglect of wood-burning it led to. How could anyone be so poor as to forgo the sweet aromatic smoke of birch, reminding one of forest rides last autumn when the Kyle charcoal-burners' fires had drifted this same scent on the wind? That, here, and also the late satisfying smell of roasted meat, from the carcases that had turned and dripped above the great hall-fire that now was glowing ashes.

Roast meat . . . roast flesh.

Marjorie shivered. Why had she let *that* come now, when she had been thinking only of pleasant things? It was so long since the horror of that tale had come to her in dreams at night after the nurse at Turnberry had told it to her, but she had never told anyone of it and for a long time it had gone.

Roast flesh. Running blood, about the gutters of Berwick.

"No one obeys Edward of England willingly."

Was it only now that she had heard it, or had the words been spoken already in her mind? She crouched on between the great dog's form and the hearth; once the logs fell and the pictures shifted, a little shower of ash floating down.

Berwick. The King of England had ridden north. Berwick had been so rich a town that in golden King Alexander's time Italian merchants came and begged the King to let them sell pearls and gold there, cunningly set. That was in the days when any man rode south or north without hindrance, and one King rode to another's crowning or his wedding. But Edward had not come north to that wedding of King Alexander's to his pretty French bride, or seen the skeleton they said had danced at Ferniehirst among the marriage guests. No, Edward had waited till the King was dead before he had come, and sacked Berwick; burning the Flemish merchants alive in their guildhall, slaying women and children in the streets, even a woman who had been in the act of giving birth to a child, when, her father said, he made them stop. . . .

"I was with Edward at Berwick."

Yes, it was the Earl that spoke. Had he been talking so for long, while she dreamt by the fire? Had he talked of Berwick, of Edward? He had told her before that the English King was a very tall man, so long and lean of leg that they called him Longshanks, though not to his face, and that he was a lawyer and had drafted laws for England, and that he was pious and took two shrines wherever he might go. Had he had his shrines in Berwick? He was a strange old man. Once at the siege of Stirling Castle he had devised a great engine of war called the Wolf and fired it after the surrender of the garrison so that his queen and her ladies who watched from a window in the town might have entertainment from the size of the showering stones.

The Earl was leaning forward, chin on hand. The Lady Egidia sewed silently. A little lamp set by her in the wall sputtered with a rush-wick in oil, after the manner of lamps since the Romans came. Its warm light fell on her smooth cheek, veiled eyes and busy hands. The thread went in and out, in and out, ceaselessly. Marjorie's father watched the thread.

"I can tell you so much, Egidia, that's not for your lord or my wife." The words were like a shrug; he did not turn or move. Marjorie waited still, like a stone; they had forgotten her. Robert talked on.

"It comes so often to me, to reproach me, now, again as I am in Edward's peace."

43

"But who is not?" said Egidia. She raised her head, lips parted slightly. A glance passed between them that held many things; once and again this would happen, as though the years that should have befallen differently had slipped back, for an hour, a second. Why struggle against hopeless odds? the look said. Is there any now alive that does so, except one man? "You've been out against Edward," said Egidia, "oftener than many in Scotland; too much so for your own safety, holding lands in England as you do."

"Lands!" said Robert, "what are lands?" He spread out his hands in a small bitter gesture. "There's too much thought for lands in England by men whose hearts should be here . . . haven't I erred as greatly as any? I've been out against Edward, as you say, true, but have I struck a blow for other than my own? Did I starve in Stirling, with Oliphant and his garrison that held out for three months? No, I sent engines to Edward to aid him in reducing the siege!"

"How could you disobey his order openly without doing your cause more harm than good? And even Oliphant is in the service of England now."

"Ay . . . and wherefore? Because, save one, there's not a soul to care for the name that used to be called Scotland, and in fifty years we'll be absorbed as a province of the south."

"Unless the tide turns," said Egidia.

"The tide? Can one man build a wall to stem it? That needs an army . . . an army without division, without dissension, without feuds. Who is to say what might not have befallen four years ago had I been for Wallace and not against him? Together we might have driven them out."

"How could you do so, when he supported Baliol and the Comyns?"

Wallace. Twice now the Earl had mentioned him. Marjorie sat still and fearful, hardly drawing breath. There was change in the air; her father had changed. His eyes as he sat there, chin on hand, brooded darkly into the fire. No gaiety, no lutes now, or laughter; what did it all mean? And the Lady Elizabeth was elsewhere. . . .

Egidia bent swiftly over her seam, holding it close as if her short-sighted eyes were straining in the lamplight. "Baliol, in such time as he was King, took away your lands and gave them to Comyn. They would have beggared you because you had a rival claim. How then could you have joined them? And you hate the Comyn, Rob."

"Hate—possessions—rival claims! That old decision of Edward's at Norham thirteen summers since has sown as much harm as dragon's teeth . . . perhaps he intended it so. *He* knows, the lawyer, well enough, that they who are united stand, and they who are divided fall . . . and so he gave the crown to Tabard, who he knew could not hold it a twelvemonth without aid."

Egidia was silent. She knew well enough that no Bruce had ever recognized the Tabard's claim, regarding themselves as prior not only by reason of the old Scots charter but by Tanist rights. She waited until Robert should speak again, knowing that, perhaps, it would be months before he could so open his heart to anyone; he was safe here, with no spies about him who would send his words to the south.

He spoke now, suddenly, as if the words were wrung from him. "I'd rather be a landless knight, with my

45

sword in my hand, and Wallace by me, and my cause my own, than riding at the stirrup of the world's craftiest king, receiving grants of land in favour from him instead of my own land, which is Scotland."

The Steward's wife looked up as if to speak. A gesture of Robert's hand stopped her.

"Listen," he said, "listen. I met with Lamberton two days ago."

"Bishop Lamberton of St Andrews? Wallace's ally? Then that means . . ."

A little silence hung on the air. For the first time Robert turned his head, as if sensible that this, the very kernel of danger, might be guessed at if any heard him speak. But the half-dark of the hall was still.

"There's no one," he assured Egidia. "But the time's not come for open talk, nor open deeds, as yet." He smiled; suddenly, for the first time since supper, he looked again the young golden man, the courtier whom Marjorie and Edward knew. "Wallace has been brought to see," he murmured, "that the Tabard is a broken reed. He gave his loyalty long enough, God knows."

"To the country, may be, more than the man."

"To what he was convinced was the king of our country. What was he to know but what he heard, and how can any but ourselves know how we Bruces regard that claim? But now Wallace sees and has been persuaded; Lamberton is wise. Also, he sees that Will can be the right arm and I the head. When the old wolf's dead, there will be confusion for a while in England; his heir, young Edward of Caernarvon, is a weakling and governed always by his favourites. Then we'll strike, but until then. . . ."

46

The silence quivered strangely. "Until?" said Egidia. "There is all the danger in the world."

"Whatever's done now will be done in my name."

He talked on, gesticulating lightly; it was as if the burden had been lifted from his mind by speaking of it. His speech became rapid and precise, in the French that had more of Breton in it than the Norman spoken in England. "We met, Lamberton and I, two days since in Cambuskenneth nave," he said. "You remember how when the council of Churchmen assembled at St Andrews our friend Edward had a candidate of his own choosing ready to be elected, but Will Wallace and his men stood over the meeting with their swords and made the delegates elect Lamberton instead?" The Earl threw back his head and laughed. "That was a nine days' tale. . . . I tell you, this dream of Edward's that Scotland is his vassal has so long eaten into the old man's brain that he believes it himself, and would kill any man that denies it. Toom Tabard knelt to him, but so now will not I—for any other reason than the due one. Ah, it may suit Edward to confuse my homage for English and Galloway lands, but I'm not so confused. Nor is Bishop Lamberton—now. He and I, together against all men, Egidia—and that third with us, who has the commons of Scotland behind him! When the old wolf's dead, we'll rise."

"Then you will be King," said the Steward's wife, and rose and trimmed the lamp. Marjorie saw from where she sat the tears overflow and run down Egidia's face. "Rob, Rob, my dear, have a care! There's so much can happen ill!"

Later still, Marjorie lay in bed and heard beyond the

narrow window the cry of an owl in the June night, making the darkness haunted and strange. The things in her mind stayed with her, making her awareness sharp so that sleep would not come. Everything now seemed awake, rustling and no longer still; the stirring of leaves in the light wind that had arisen, cooling the ground after sunset; the scurry of a mouse in the tower; her own quiet breaths. Everything waited, awake; for what? Where was Wallace lying to-night, with his head pillowed on grass? Did he sleep, and if so, what were his dreams? Did he think of the dead woman, his wife, who had been hanged? Did he remember ruined Berwick? Or did he only dream of what was still to do, the blows still to strike, the cities still to recapture? Did he feel the wreath of prayer woven round him by a hundred poor men, many without homes? She would pray too . . . for that third, together with her father and Lamberton, his friend, against all men. King, Church and commons, as it had been in old days.

"It would have been easy enough to do as some did, and let Edward take all . . . and settle down as dependants of him and his lieutenants that he sent up here . . . and with so many of our nobles owning land also in England for which they must do homage. . . ."

Walter's words. Walter must have been thinking of her father as he spoke. She was glad that Father now had cast off his allegiance to Edward, not yet openly but in secret. Perhaps he never had bowed the knee in secret. Perhaps. . . .

Edward. The old wolf. When the old wolf's dead. . . .

Against all men!

She slept.

III

The Countess of Carrick came at last to reside in Gasconhall, her husband's place near Perth, and as they were again north of the border there was no reason not to send for her step-daughter. Word came accordingly by one of the Earl's riders into the west, and Marjorie said good-bye to the Lady Egidia and the children and set off. In the bustle of departure she had no time to think, and it was only when the familiar castle was out of sight, and the sound of her escort's hooves grown louder than the voices crying after her, that she found time to feel at all strange.

What would it be like, with the Earl and Elizabeth again? It was over two years since she had lived with them, and then only for a spell. Her mind cast back to that time, almost a year ago now, when Earl Robert had ridden to the west and talked of himself and Lamberton and Wallace. Since then she had heard nothing of the last two, and very little of the Earl. Everyone was waiting for the wolf to die. Yet the wolf still lived, and that was one reason why Marjorie was riding to Perth now, for old Edward had sent up north for representatives to come from Scotland to his Parliament at Westminster, and Earl Robert was one of the commissioners sent to oversee this. Marjorie stared ahead of her beyond the escort's banners and wondered how her father must have felt this past year, riding and hawking with Edward in England again, to all appearances his vassal as formerly. There were so many Scots noblemen down there, like the young Earl of Fife, who had been taken south when he was only a boy, and the

Earl of Buchan, whom Edward kept by him always and in fact used on errands abroad as his ambassador. And Buchan's kinsman, the Comyn, her father's enemy, was Edward's man also.

Several of those living in the south would have ridden to Perth now for the elections, and Marjorie felt a quickening of interest at the thought of seeing them. At the same time she felt hesitant, remembering Elizabeth's laughter at her gaucherie two years ago. "I'm ugly and awkward to her," she thought. Would they laugh likewise, the Earl's grand English friends?

Yet she was not sorry to go to Perth when all was said and done. Back at Dundonald she had heard nothing, and surely in the town there would be some talk of Wallace and what he had done this year. His face was still vivid before her, as it had been that first day, although the more recent talk over Egidia's fire had faded now almost to unreality. It was only the thought of Wallace that kept it at all real; she and Walter had not dreamt that meeting among the trees last spring.

They rode inland, with the bright colours of the outriders' livery smirred at times with rain. Marjorie raised her head to sniff the damp May air; blossom, delicate and white as foam, cast its heady scent from trees and thickets on the wind as they rode. Some old woman who sat in Egidia's hall had said that hawthorn was unlucky if set in a bowl, otherwise she would have liked to stop and pick it. . . . Why was it that so many lovely things were touched by the devil? The creamy petals scattered like little flakes of snow as they rode by, shaking the branches.

At last over a rise they saw Perth, rising like a fairy city out of the mound of its high old walls. Perth had

once been the king's place in the days when there still
was a real king. Even now it had the air of being set
apart, different from other towns. Riding under the
gateway and into the narrow streets, Marjorie saw
square houses of wood, so weathered that it had become
the colour of pitch. Out of the windows people leaned,
curious to see who came riding in; she felt uncomfortable with so many unaccustomed eyes on her. The town
air was stuffy and close after the fresh hill winds; everything seemed to close in about her. A grey church,
solidly built of stone, loomed up; that must be Saint
John the Baptist's Kirk, where dead King Alexander
had been used to go to Mass and fling alms to beggars
as he emerged, and hear poor men's petitions as they
brought them to him openly in the street. She wished
she had known that big-boned King, with the bright
hair and kindly countenance. Riding now through the
shadowed streets of Perth, the thought came of how
Alexander must have ridden out along here to English
Edward's coronation at Westminster, with all his train
mounted alike on horses of great strength and beauty,
richly caparisoned in studded leather. Then when the
English King had been crowned, the Scots, to show
their magnificence, had each one turned his beautiful
horse loose among the London crowds, as a gift to
whomsoever might first lay hands on its bridle. Those
had been splendid and open-hearted days; her father
might have acted like that if he were King. Perhaps he
still would do so.

Marjorie stared ahead of her, brought with a jerk
back to the present. Mounted men rode the streets here,
clearing the way with swords; they drove back the
townsfolk in their sober garments and also, sometimes,

the yellow-shirted whiskered men from the north hills, who came to Perth at this season to trade hides for wool. The high voices of the armed men came to her; they were English, and she could see the hatred in the dark eyes of the Gaels even though they said nothing and allowed themselves to be herded back against the doorways. The Lowland townspeople themselves were calmer, elbowing each other placidly; some of them even avoided the Gaels to make little groups with the Englishmen. But on the whole there was small friendliness in the streets, and Marjorie felt sudden resentment rise. Was it a right thing for every man to have to walk as though a hand were about to be laid on his shoulder?

The English garrison showed her escort respect and made way for it in the crowded street; she saw their faces gape over at her from below their round casques. They did not look unfriendly, she thought; probably they had no real idea why they were stationed here. She saw one man glance at her escort's banners and explain to another who she was.

Only once did they pass another concourse of riders; it was midday and everyone except chance travellers would be indoors at meat. This escort rode leisurely, making way neither to right nor to left; it was as though it owned the causeway. Marjorie could see the two chief riders, who were in citizens' dress; one was a churchman, stout and attired in furred violet camlet, with a broad hat shading his eyes. The other was taller, and his hair was red. He wore no hat and the sun shone on it. His eyes were beady and dark, and as they turned in his lean face and assessed her Marjorie was conscious of a chill, as though someone had ill-wished her. She did not care for the man's face and glanced up swiftly at the device which his riders bore; it was a fosse of three sheaves, the arms of Comyn.

"There goes the little sprig of Carrick," she heard someone say.

She held herself erect then and looked neither to right nor left. These were the sons of Black John, who had been a claimant for the Scottish throne together with her great-grandfather, old Annandale. That was the Red Comyn who had looked at her just now and spoken. She did not like his speech or the tales she had heard of him; once, Egidia had said, he had flown at Earl Robert's throat in the old days and the two of them had to be forced apart with swords. . . .

The Comyn men thrust heedlessly by and left her train to make its own way up the street. Marjorie rode on, her cheeks flaming. If she had been a man, and able to maintain her right to the middle of the way equally with *them*, and set her men on them! How dared they take for granted that no word would be said, and no blow struck, because the English were policing Perth streets?

"The devil fly with all Comyns."

She heard the muttered cursing of her own men and saw their side-glances, which showed that it was because she, the little lady of Carrick, was under their guardianship that they could not fight. She fell silent with rage and humiliation. In her mind, as though the bitterness of the year in which she was born had lain dormant till now, hearsay rose and clamoured. Perth a prisoner, chained . . . and out of these streets Edward had ridden, as the Comyn rode now, bearing with him the Honours of Scotland and leaving in the sky a glow of

53

fire from the burning of such charters as he could not take. He had left nothing, nothing but hatred and sullen acceptance behind him. If she had been a man, if she had been a man!

Gasconhall was full of brilliant chattering people, friends of the Lady Elizabeth and of her father, the Ulster Earl. Among the high drawl of their voices Marjorie fell silent, withdrawing herself into the shadows of the background, watching and listening. Quite early she realized that she had no part with anyone here; if she had been pretty or amusing they would have made a pet of her, but she was neither, and so they left her alone. She was glad of this, seeing them all as figures in a tapestry, with no depth, only colour. They were different from the Lady Egidia, and she wondered how the Steward's wife would have fared here after so many years away from towns. Or would Egidia, too, have wound her hair into a multitude of little plaits, stuffing it out with horsehair at the sides, and fixing a square of linen over it with a metal circlet worn well down over the brow? They said that was the fashion brought lately by Edward's young queen from France. They talked a great deal of fashions, these ladies; clustering round Marjorie's step-mother like a flight of pretty bees.

Elizabeth de Brus was also pretty. Marjorie thought that the Countess looked, if anything, younger than when she had first come north three years ago; she was as slim as ever and moved with grace and ease, as though she were a young tree with light winds stirring its branches. She took very little notice of Marjorie, and the blue eyes fluttered vaguely, occasionally, to the

girl's face and then away again. Sometimes the ladies
would dance for their own diversion, and then the
young Countess's tinkling laugh would ring out,
silvery and shallow, or her voice call languidly for a
tune. There was a new minstrel named Will whom
someone had brought north from England; he was a
tall pale fat man and handled a lute with skill. Most
of his tunes were different from those that the bards
used here; deeper and more intensely stirring, with
queer melodies and little unexpected trills. It was said
he had learned them in Spain, and Marjorie one day
heard two of the ladies giggling because, they said,
Will had been taken prisoner when he was a child by
the infidels, the Moors, and although they had taught
him to play the lute and also a certain lore of herbs, they
had taken away what he prized much more.

"And what was that?" asked Marjorie, glad to be
able to think of something to say to the ladies, who
must often think that she was unable to speak at all.
But they only screamed and laughed in a superior way,
and she saw them whisper later to her step-mother and
point at her and all three shake with mirth. She scowled
to hide the fact that her eyelids pricked, and did not
speak of it again. Altogether in those days they made
her feel foolish, overgrown and ignorant in all of the
arts that they knew.

Thinking of it at night in the bed where she slept
with two of the women, she would try to assemble the
things she had learnt that were new. They added up to
very little; among them was the fact that even with hard
riding it took two months to reach London, where she
did not want to go; that King Edward's new queen had
nursed him through his late illness so tenderly that he

was as well as ever he had been, and that although now
over seventy he had every tooth in his head as good as
new. Everyone here seemed to love King Edward, and
related with pride the tale of how on the morning of the
Battle of Falkirk his horse, by which he lay asleep, had
kicked him in the side and broken two of his ribs, but
he leapt into the saddle and rode to fight without assist-
ance. It seemed certain that the wolf was brave and
pious, and that those who knew him loved him; how
was it then that he could do the things he had done?

But always the simile of the tapestry figures remained with her. Among them moved her father,
the Earl, richly clad in red and white as betokened
Edward's commissioner. He did not seem like the same
person who had brooded last year over Egidia's hearth;
Marjorie began to wonder if she had indeed dreamt
all she heard then. By day the Earl would be much
abroad, but at night he would come to where the ladies
sat; as the summer lengthened, this was often in the
garden, where flowers bloomed and pigeons rose and
fluttered against the sky. There, with jewels on his long
hands, he would play the lute and sing or tell French
tales, and make everyone laugh. Marjorie watched him,
remembering another summer's day in the west; and
the face of Wallace the outlaw, and the expression in
his eyes.

One day Marjorie came in to find a young girl seated
beside the Lady Elizabeth, watching the grey pigeons
as they cooed and postured about the windows. She was
made known as the Countess of Buchan, and Marjorie,
recalling the Comyn encounter in Perth streets, was
startled. Why was the wife of Buchan, a Comyn, so

welcome here? She surveyed the Countess with the faint scorn of the robust for anything fragile; the young lady's face had the brittleness of alabaster, with a faint flush deepening on lips and cheeks as the Earl of Carrick came in. Her hair, which hung in soft pale curls beneath her English hat, fell forward about her face as she curtsied; her mouth trembled, as though she would like to cry. Marjorie noticed the chivalrous and tender manner of the Earl's raising of her, seeming more marked than for other ladies, even Egidia. The Lady Elizabeth watched from her corner, saying nothing, lips closed and smiling.

"So they meet again," murmured a woman's voice, low with amusement. Marjorie did not turn; there were always whispers and innuendoes about Gasconhall, it seemed to be the fashion among Elizabeth's friends. "Lovers' meeting!" said another. "They say he saw a good deal of her in Warwickshire."

"In the absence of her lord."

"Oh, her lord's hardly ever present," drawled the first woman. "He's been away lately, on Edward's embassy to France."

"And made little enough of it, so I've heard."

"Well, that'll not drive him to the arms of his wife."

They sniggered, but quietly; and Marjorie saw them move towards where the young Countess and the Earl of Carrick sat, he talking to her in a low voice with head bent. Scraps of their words floated back along the hall; the women's high voices praised and flattered. They said much the same as they had said before, only with a different emphasis. Isobel of Buchan answered shyly, twisting her hands like a schoolgirl.

"My lord? Yes, he's still in the south. No, he does

not ride north to the bidding for the parliament."

"King Edward can ill spare the Earl of Buchan, likely?"

"After his embassy. . . ."

"The King desires to keep my husband near him," said Isobel. She spoke with sweetness, even humour, but a shadow crossed her face at mention of her husband. Marjorie heard later that he was a moody brutal man who was a good deal older than Isobel, and had been married to her for convenience at the request of the English King.

The Earl interposed smoothly, sheltering Isobel from the prying tongues. He began to speak of her brother, the young Earl of Fife, whose marriage to a granddaughter of King Edward had lately been concluded.

"The festivities would be very grand, I don't doubt," said Isobel. She sighed a little. "Oh, Duncan's completely an Englishman now. Small wonder, having been south since the age of nine! He does not remember our father at all . . . and would not come back here, I believe, for anything."

She raised her head and looked full at the Earl of Carrick and for the first time Marjorie saw her eyes. They were pale and queerly luminous, as though a lamp burned behind them. It might have been a spoken message that passed between the Earl and herself.

Robert gave a slight, almost unnoticeable inclination of the head. A stout woman, wife of one of the assessors whom Edward had sent north, interposed at that point; her eyes held curiosity and a kind of malice. "Changed days, aren't they, when the Thane of Fife won't come north at all? My husband says the Fifes used to crown all the kings here, when they had kings. It was part of the ceremony, like the crown and the block of stone they sat on." She tittered. "A fair task the English bearers must have had, carrying that weight south into England. I saw it in Westminster Abbey, where they've placed it now. Is it true it was once Jacob's pillow? At all events, it's south, and likely to remain there—with the Earl of Fife and the rest of the gear." She surveyed the girl. "Oh, you're better where you are, as I daresay you know. Warwickshire, your husband's place, isn't it?"

"Yes. . . ."

The little, whispered word broke the silence that had arisen. Everyone began to talk again, leisurely and calm. A little vein, which had been throbbing in Carrick's temple, subsided; colour ceased to ebb and flow in Isobel's throat. Yet something had been glossed over as though it had never been; something was wrong and a little current of resentment trickled through the assembly like blood escaping from a tightly stanched wound. Voices sounded again, Isobel's among them, soft and calm. Yes, she had been in Warwickshire these four years past . . . yes, now she was going north.

"To Buchan, madame," she said to the woman who had accosted her. "As you say, I may find it—a change."

With a little, courteous gesture, she soon took her leave. Marjorie watched her ride away, seeing the garnished trappings on her palfrey, the care her men were at to lift her into the saddle so that her light skirts avoided the mud of the yard. She still felt scorn for the delicate, almost childlike young woman; the implications of what had been unspoken were beyond her. The assessor's wife, who seemingly disliked the young

Countess, was droning on behind her about how much colder it would be even at this time of year in the north. "She'll not bide there long, my fine young lady! Oh, they've done themselves well enough, those Fifes, with King Edward—orphans as they were, he's seen that they never missed their father. Kindness does a deal more than force, when all's said; he's tamed them. The boy will be half-royal now, wed into the King's own circle."

"So many hostages in England," yawned Elizabeth. "King Edward must find it an expense to clothe and feed them all."

The Earl said nothing. Marjorie surprised a hooded cold look in his eyes, like that of a hawk.

At the end of May the representatives rode south again to Westminster, the Earl of Carrick among them. To everyone's surprise he would not permit Elizabeth to accompany him, and it was arranged that she and Marjorie should ride to the west.

"He says that matters are unsettled," pouted the Countess of Carrick, "but when were they ever otherwise here?" The blue eyes surveyed her step-daughter, mounted on her pony and thus on a slightly greater height than Elizabeth's litter. Without doubt she was wasting her time in attempting to make conversation with Marjorie, who was so silent that Elizabeth wondered often if she were not a half-wit, although she kept the supposition to herself. She moved a little, impatiently, on her cushions. Forty miles to go, along these roads and with Marjorie of Carrick for company! The only diversion would be to try and think what had got into Robert's head lately that he should have suggested it. He had been—how could one put it?—a trifle *distrait*, less aware of her for some time than he had been. Elizabeth wondered if there were another woman. She had never been fool enough to suppose that that milk-and-water puss of a Fife child had intrigued Carrick in England, in spite of all that was said . . . men like to see themselves as protectors, and Buchan, no one could deny, was a sullen-eyed brute. There had never been any children of that marriage. "That's as God sends," thought Elizabeth, and shrugged lightly. She was sufficiently grateful to Providence for sending none of her own; Robert desired them, but she did not. And now they were to go west into the Stewartry, and the months would pass with no company but that of Aunt Egidia, who had grown very dowdy since she married that bore, the High Steward. How could one help it in the country—this country? Elizabeth prayed that Robert would not be long.

The road along which Marjorie had come when the trees were in blossom was darkened now with the season of heavy leaf. Seeing the branches shadowed and dull with the dust that had blown up from a thousand riders, she felt a sense of fear oppress her for no reason. The air was loaded and heavy; there had been no rain for weeks. Ahead, the sky seemed leaden, and sounds were intensified; the running of water unseen among grass, the rustle of a bird, the creak of girth-leather. All were magnified queerly, sudden as a word shouted, or a clap of thunder. "Or the Loup de Guerre," thought Marjorie. Old Edward's showering stones, even, would bring relief; or a storm breaking, the sky and earth drenched together in blinding sheets of rain. But no one spoke except, now and then, the Countess from her litter; the querulous voice complained of the heat always, her head ached, she said, and it was time they were home.

"Home!" She laughed a little, and Marjorie knew that she was thinking of the southern manors, in Huntingdon and Middlesex, that were home to her as the Earl's castles here would never be. How long would they all continue thus, so near by circumstance, so different by desire? "She'd never have me at Huntingdon," Marjorie thought. "She told me my skin was too sallow and my hands and feet too big." How they would laugh, the white-skinned Frenchwomen who were about Edward's young queen, if they could see her! They were all, Elizabeth said, skilled with the needle and the distaff to the intent that they should make purposeful wives, as well as being gay and pretty and ready with songs or laughter, or the dance. "But *I* can't put in a stitch without cobbling, for all Egidia's patience, and I don't laugh and can't sing, and dances confuse me."

She stared ahead forlornly. What use was she to anyone? It was true that if the Frenchwomen had been here, shaken down these worsening roads where bogs and stones jostled one another, they would have complained more loudly than she, but that was a boy's gift, not to complain, and women were expected to be soft and clinging, like kittens, and to cry out at danger.

They were nearing the west now. She saw the landscape change and grow familiar, and yet in the oppressive heat more desolate, lacking trees; like Tartarus, she thought suddenly, where the unblest dead walked in a twilight that was neither night nor day. Why had she remembered that song of Will's now, or the country he said he had seen far beyond seas, where the ground was littered with fallen pillars like bleached bones?

She tried to assemble her thoughts. Soon the horses would halt, and the English lieutenant would give them beds for the night and entertain them to food and wine. Marjorie felt as if she could swallow nothing, although her mouth was dry and she should have been glad of a drink of water. How dry and dusty her skin and eyes felt! If there might only be rain to-night it would be cooler to-morrow for the rest of the journey. . . .

"Marjorie, don't slouch in the saddle so. We're nearing a town."

Elizabeth gazed ahead of her without interest. "A town" might have been anywhere in her reckoning; this straggle of wooden buildings on a site that dipped and rose, with a silver river flung in its midst, was Glasgow. They could see the spires of Saint Mungo's Cathedral rising, with its huddle of fever-houses behind, and the great bulk of the Bishop's stone dwelling and, above that, the Castle where they would stay to-night. It was at once humbler and less secret than Perth, and the water did not wind like the Tay. There was activity on the south side of the river, where men were bargaining over hides with the whiskered crew of a long boat from Ireland. Their raised voices floated over the air with the slow broad intonation of the West. They turned their heads as the party of travellers made its way across the ford.

There was a crowd on the far side, near the Bishop's jetty. It held together in little groups and knots, staring idly. Marjorie saw the fleeting interest in their eyes pass

63

over and leave her; there was something they watched, always, above in the town. Curiously, she noticed, there was very little chatter here; the salmon-catch of a fish vendor hung limp in his hand, shining a little in the sun. The sound of their cavalcade's horses came loudly, clearly in the street; they had left earth now and were riding on cobbles.

"What a dead town!" yawned Elizabeth. "What's afoot?" The street wound sharply, sloping upward as they rode towards the outworks of the Castle. Suddenly, rounding, they came on the reason for the crowds' long staring; stationary, waiting for change of horses, an escort of armed men.

They had a prisoner amongst them. He sat erect in the saddle, stiffly a little as with one who could not move for ease; his hands were bound behind his back and his legs secured beneath the horse's belly. His hair was lint-white, and hung about his face limply in the heat. He appeared to notice nothing, not their arrival or the staring of the crowds.

"Can they not move on?" said Elizabeth impatiently. "The way's not clear."

A man in the crowd, a cobbler or fishmonger, still in his leather apron, glanced up at her. His eyes held contempt, and his glance wandered back to the tied figure. "Clear!" they heard him mutter to his neighbour. "Some while since it was clear enough, here at the Bell o' the Brae! Glad enough they would have been to lay hands on him *then*, when he routed the garrison and took the town! Glad enough—but it took nigh on a dozen years to find the traitor who would help them do it!"

"Quiet now," said his neighbour. "What good will talk do?"

"Does he mind that time, now, as he sits there?" said the first man, ignoring the warning. "Does Will Wallace mind the Bell o' the Brae again? Would as many charge now as followed him then, a handful and all as it was, they could still save him."

"And have a head on a pole for their pains, and their living guts drawn from them? Hold your tongue."

Marjorie stared at the tied man, no longer feeling the pain in her clenched fingers. She gripped the reins with both hands; the muscles of her face did not move. In this moment all the foreboding of the long day merged with the grief to come. So large an escort, and all for one man; such utter precaution, the heavy bonds that stopped the blood in twined fingers and bound feet; spears at the ready, the crowd scared into silence; swords drawn, vizors down, three abreast round the prisoner, six deep before and after. Brief, this pause would be, in the town where he might be rescued; change horses with all speed, then make off to the south, to England.

He had not seen her. Even in the colourless void of shock she still knew a remote, dull wound. That bond, surely so strong since that other day, that other year, in the little birch wood in Kyle, should make him turn now! "Let him turn," she prayed, as though it were to be his salvation. She was devoid of other feeling yet.

They led him down towards the river, and as he passed their eyes met for an instant. Out of the lined face, his eyes seemed to smile; it might have been their curious lightness, giving the impression that even in the dark they would shine so. Did he know her? Lacking volition, as though they acted without her numbed brain's access, her hands reached out to him, palms upward; she might have been asking for his blessing as he went by. After he had gone, she was still seated so, her body rigid as though girths bound it.

"They are saying he was taken near Lenzie, by a man of Menteith's. Dear God, Marjorie, don't stare so, as if you had never seen a felon pass by! You'll have to begin to comport yourself as Carrick's daughter."

Elizabeth's face set in lines of disapproval. She ceased to look at Marjorie, with her hair blown loose in the wind and skirts draggled from the ford; the sight made her ashamed, with the prospect she had of presenting a hoyden to the Lady of Menteith. It was true that Sir John de Menteith was no more than a knight, but he was King Edward's man, and who knew what might come of it? In any case the girl looked distrait and peculiar, staring ahead at nothing as she rode.

"The heat's been too much for you," she said stiffly. "When we get indoors lie down, and the women will get rosewater. This is the last day of travel, thank God." She craned her neck to observe the preparations for them in the inner court. "Ah, there's my lady! How like a crow. . . . Menteith must have gone with the escort. I expect the felon must hang in England; it'll be a long ride south."

A little frown creased her forehead, and she caught her breath and jerked her glance towards Marjorie, who was slumped in the saddle, her face white as chalk. During the pause when the Sheriff's servants came running, and offers of cosseting and burnt feathers were offered by my lady, Elizabeth felt her own speech of welcome set aside, and the small fact irked her. How glad she would be to give Marjorie in charge to her aunt Egidia again! If only Robert had not been so strange, she might have been with him now in England. Why had he so set his face against England for them both, so suddenly? Elizabeth felt her bewilderment and annoyance grow, with fear at the back of it.

"She's young to swoon," said the Lady de Menteith. She began to ask audibly and with interest about Marjorie's maturity. "No, no, green as an apple," answered Elizabeth crossly. The idea that Marjorie might have fainted from other than heat came as a reminder of one's own age, and was untimely. "It is only the sultry day, and she is a greedy child and eats too fast. I beg of you not to trouble yourself."

They began to talk in the low courteous manner of two ladies, host to guest, while the servants moved soft-footed to prepare the meal. Marjorie heard it all through the mists of dread and grief, and the knowledge of a great leader on his way to savage death, after the travesty of trial and the mockery of a laurel crown.

IV

She saw the strange man ride in that year with two followers. He bore no colours and rode swiftly; she did not see his face until they met at close hand. Looking now, it seemed that the brightness about her father the Earl had all gone; the gold and red and whiteness, the furs and gems. It was as though a veil of dust had been flung over hair and skin and eyes, but it was not the roads' dust. Under the rim of the casque the eyes looked out, bleak and hard as metal.

He embraced her without speaking, and together

67

they went upstairs to where the Countess kept her bed. She would do this often for days together now they were back in the west, especially since the light had grown shorter and the winds chill before sunset. For there was little news now. Wallace was dead, and the days of chattering over the savage manner of his execution had passed; the Smithfield fires died down and the smell of burnt flesh faded. Perth, Newcastle, Stirling and Berwick bore each a limb, spiked aloft above sewers; the severed head was over Temple Bar. "Who will remember, after all, in a month's time?" yawned the Countess. "Who will be able to forget?" had answered Egidia, who was with them again. All these things had been talked over, and now there was nothing left.

Elizabeth lay among the solace of furred skins. On seeing the Earl she drew an involuntary breath, sat up, and covered her breasts gracefully with one hand. Her face was unpainted and her hair fell about it loosely; she concealed her annoyance that he should have found her thus. "You should have sent us word you were coming," she told him. "I'd a new gown to wear for you." She smiled; he must not be allowed to remember her as peevish. She was almost certain now that there was another woman. What else could have accounted for his behaviour, so erratic, in riding north unheralded now? Had Isobel of Buchan gone south again? If only one knew, instead of waiting two months for news by road out of England . . . no matter.

"My lord." She held up her face for his kiss. Winningly, she endeavoured to tease him; what had happened to make him leave Court? "Are you out of favour?" she laughed, remembering how the old King had used to flatter Carrick and take him to ride by his side almost daily, at the hunt or on progress. "Are you in flight from the royal justice? God's death, it's what you look like, coming in all stained with travel, and no device. How long did it take you to ride north? Have you left the saddle at all since London? Have you had food?"

He did not seem to see her or hear her after the first; gently, he disengaged her, and went to the window and stood looking down.

"That's no king of mine, whether for land in south or north. So he knows now; I doubt he knew before I took the road home. No, I didn't tarry, Bess; it's scarcely advisable that I should be taken now, just after . . ." His hand sought and found the stone rim of the window, held it and tightened. "Could I endure the sight of Edward's face again?" he said. "Could any honest man do so who heard what befell . . . and to one who's not his subject, never promised him allegiance . . . as I did, Bess, as I did, more shame on me, in the pretence that I could hide behind legality like so many others! But now it's all out in the open, now we know him for a devil and ourselves as lost unless we turn from him and towards what Wallace dreamed—and died for, with God knows what despair when he thought of me by Edward's side! But I was not, and have never been, after the sentence of death was pronounced; not in his parliament, not in his hall."

He turned suddenly, spreading out with a little fatal gesture the palms of his hands. "Poor Bess," he said quietly. "Your manors, that you loved so well in the south, we'll not see again."

"What are you saying?" cried Elizabeth. She was staring at him; her eyes showed their whites a little, like a startled animal's. "Wallace? What had you to do with that felon? Have you gone mad? What are you trying to tell me?"

"That I no longer serve Edward in any capacity."

Elizabeth began to laugh. "You?" she taunted him. "Why, he'll crush you like—like Wallace himself!"

"That is a greater fate than I deserve," said Carrick gravely.

v

That had been in autumn. By the time the winter storms set in and the roads were drifted over with snow and sodden leaves, much had befallen although there was still little to tell.

Yule found them at Lochmaben, that Border castle of his own against which Earl Robert had, not so many years back, levelled strength when it was garrisoned by Englishmen, in that brief revolt as a result of which he had been told to put Marjorie in custody as hostage, but had not done so. The castle itself and the land about it still showed the marks of bewildered change; now to England, now to Scotland, now to Carrick the enemy of England, now to Carrick Edward's seeming ally, and now again to Carrick under Edward's known displeasure and, as everyone said, out of England for his health. Motives, foresight, long-headed planning, all were mingled together like the dullness of mud on the bad roads, the shadow of blackened stubble in the fields. No one would be surprised at what could happen any more; all anyone could do was to wait, and be ready.

Many came to the Earl there, that winter. Always Marjorie was conscious of coming and going; the sound

of horsemen nearing the gates, the clatter of hooves
growing fainter in the night hours and dying away.
Messengers came and went from the north, the west
and, even now, from England. The Earl rode out often,
no one asked him where; sometimes he would be gone
for days, or weeks; surrounded, always, by his own
men-at-arms, or those of his brothers.

Marjorie had four uncles. From the first she was
happier at Lochmaben than she had been with her step-
mother. Although Elizabeth was here with them, her
cool personality seemed to have receded since the
change; everywhere the shouting voices, the harsh
sounds and colours and shining of mail, ousted the
things she stood for. Marjorie ran wild among the four
young uncles, who made a pet of her as no one had done
since Dundonald. Certainly Egidia would not have
approved the way she passed her time now, doing
nothing but what she desired to do; riding out with
Thomas, playing at swords with Ned; chased, caught
and tickled by Alexander, when everyone was in the
hall at meat. But best of all she loved Nigel, the youngest, who was gentle and quiet, almost like a girl,
although he could show a fair arm with a sword; teased,
always, by everyone about his long eyelashes and his
pretty face, until he would show the tormentor that he
could nearly always better them with strength. Women
would gape at Nigel, but he never troubled his head
about them; he was a boy, scarcely older than Walter
Stewart, whom she had not seen for so long. Of them
all, Marjorie heard her father say that Nigel was most
like her grandmother, the gay brave pretty Countess of
Carrick, who had once fancied a sleeping knight she
found in her forests so much that she had him carried

off to her castle by her maids, and would not let him go until he married her. And as it happened that that knight was Robert de Brus of Annandale, who had in any case come riding into Carrick to tell the young Countess that she was a widow (her first husband having been killed by his side in the Crusades), that suited everyone excellently, although King Alexander pretended to be angry because his permission for the marriage had not been asked.

"And so we are here in Lochmaben, for it was Annandale land," the story would end; and everyone would try to picture Countess Marjorie's husband as a handsome young knight and never quite manage it, because they had all known him best as a lethargic gentleman in middle age who had died only lately in Norway at the home of his daughter the Dowager Queen.

"Which is as well, for *he*'d no ambition as Robert has," stated Mary Campbell flatly. Mary was one of the Earl's sisters and as plain as Nigel was pretty, which seemed a waste when he was a man and she a lady. Her eyes were grey and intense, with a clear light shining in them that intensified when she said the things that came into her head, which she always did; some people minded, notably Elizabeth, who found Mary a disconcerting person and seldom replied to her statements other than by the flat, blue glance which lately had grown wary. Mary's husband, Campbell of Lochow, a big blond man in dark armour, was at Lochmaben also with his men. Everyone was at Lochmaben.

Uncle Ned rode in and out, with his red head usually bare because he hated to wear a casque. "You're

a fool," Mary told him, "and will be set upon." But
Uncle Ned only laughed, or swore if he was in a temper,
which he so often was that his own wife would not live
with him, and replied that if he was fool enough to let
anyone near enough his head to hit it he deserved what
he got. He had brought a pretty lady down from the
north; her name was Isobel. She was nearly always
smiling, but seldom troubled to speak; she would sit,
graceful and useless, about the hall all day, gazing from
beneath heavy white lids at the men as they burnished
their mail. She and Uncle Ned talked in Gaelic when
they did so at all and its low, soft sounds came strangely
here among the speech of Lothian. Isobel was the Earl
of Ross's sister, and someone said he had been angry
because she was disgraced. Marjorie pondered this
statement, thinking that Isobel did not look as if she
were disgraced at all and in fact seemed very pleased
with herself. But no one was surprised at anything
Uncle Ned might do, and once the pair quarrelled in
the middle of supper, and Isobel threw a leather flagon
in Uncle Ned's face so that its rim cut him over the
right eye. Marjorie waited, expecting that Uncle Ned
would shout and rage, but instead he suddenly burst out
laughing and seized Isobel by the shoulders and kissed
her hard on the mouth, and then rose and carried her
out of the hall with everyone laughing and shouting
also. The cut swelled afterwards and gave Uncle Ned a
rakish appearance for some days, but no one minded.

Then there were the Setons, who came before Yule.
Lady Seton had been Christian Bruce and had been
married first to the Earl of Mar, whose sister had been
Marjorie's mother. So Donald, the little Earl, was a
double cousin, but this did not make Marjorie like him

c*   73

very much; he was a spoilt little boy and screamed for anything he wanted till he got it, which he always did because Aunt Christian would never have him beaten, as Marjorie would certainly have been if she had ever behaved thus. But Aunt Christian loved everybody, apparently, and she also loved her new husband, Sir Christopher Seton, very much. Then Sir Christopher's brother, Sir Alexander, came also, and that meant another retinue to house and feed.

Over Yule they all met, and there was the burning of the log and drinking from the great common bowl which went round the hall from right to left, as the other way brought evil; and kissing all round, and salted meats—fruits in honey, and afterwards nuts brought out of hoard and roasted, and healths drunk in wine for the coming year. In the chapel of Lochmaben the Earl and Countess of Carrick rendered their gifts of gold, in token of God's birthday, and Marjorie also knelt in front of the decked altar which she and the women had garnished with leaves of holly and pine.

"What will the new year bring?" said Isobel of Ross, and there was a little silence, as everyone had been thinking that same thing but no one liked to say it. Only a fool, Marjorie thought, would have voiced it at that moment; the way matters were moving were clear even for her to understand, and she had heard the elders talking when they had forgotten she was there, as in Egidia's castle long ago. For in the south the old wolf, Edward, was drinking warmed wine, and waiting for the spring; but meanwhile, as had been expected, he had annexed the English lands of the Earl of Carrick, whose precipitate action in riding north had not pleased him.

"The family aren't going home again yet," yawned Mar. "Oh, no, not nearly yet. I'm not sorry; it's dull at Kildrummie. No one ever comes."

He stretched himself and nestled down among the covers, shedding his sophistication suddenly and becoming only a small boy ready to go to sleep. He watched his cousin idly. Marjorie was queer, he thought; always watching for something that no one else could see, or listening for what they couldn't hear. It was like Granny, the old Dowager Countess of Mar in the north, whom everyone said was a witch. "Ah, you're a useless stick!" she had said to him, and muttered something in Welsh, when he went to say good-bye, before they all left. "Bide, then, with your mammet, for there are brave men in plenty who don't mind the cold," and then Mar's mother had cosseted the old woman gently and told her she was havering again. But he, Donald, had been offended, and he was bothered if he would trouble the witch any more. Mammet indeed! He hadn't had a mammet since he was a baby. It was true, though, that he did not like the cold. Listen to the wind to-night, howling outside in the snow! Uncle Robert had ridden out in it; he had gone to Dumfries.

"Oh, Marjorie, what *are* you staring at? Do lie down, there's such a draught."

His cousin, with her short dark hair braided into stubby plaits that stuck out on each side of her head, moved restlessly. "Nothing," she answered. Mar smiled in a superior way. "You're a funny girl," he told her. He lay and watched, lazily, while she lay down. If only he were old enough to sleep alone, like a man! Marjorie was no fun to talk to, she simply lay hunched up like a cat and said nothing. He made one or two more efforts at conversation and in the end went to sleep.

Marjorie lay and listened to the rise and fall of his breathing for a while; she felt tense and wakeful, and the cold was bitter. The sough and flicker made by the wind in the fire beckoned; the nurse who tended Donald had gone and there was no one else in the room. Carefully she slipped from the bed, casting a wool plaid round her; she went and knelt down by the hearth, to warm herself. It was useless, because the storm had brought sharp sleet with it, falling slantwise against the ground and walls; it hurled into the chimney, spitting down into the fire with little blackened spurts of water. Perhaps to-night snow would fall and then everyone would be warmer. Marjorie hugged her knees and thought of her father and Thomas and Alexander and Nigel, riding in the storm. Nigel had promised to take her, if the snow grew deep enough, to the field beyond the near farm to make a snow-image. "Then we can knock it down with snowballs," he had said. It was a pity Mar would have to come too. Perhaps he would scorn it as he did other games, saying they were only for children. Who did Donald think he was? He was younger than she.

Oh, she was really thinking things only to drown the other thoughts that came, only they were not thoughts at all but shapes in the mind's darkness. . . . What was happening to-night, now, somewhere?

She moved again, denying the unease that had come. Why should she be this kind of person, seeing, hearing, knowing nothing? Yet she had felt like this before word came that Wallace was taken, before even they had reached town.

She closed her eyes, seeing only blankness where Wallace's face had been. That was because she was afraid; she had heard long ago what they had done with his head, perched eyeless now over Temple Bar. It was better to think of the face as nothing, a dark blank. That was the only way, before things became too horrible to bear. And Wallace was more now than a dead face, a set of withered limbs. He would be remembered as long as there were Scotsmen anywhere, her father had said. No one died because the body was dead. No one. . . .

Think of another face. Any other, to blot out that remembrance and the terrible image that followed. Quite lately, on a day of rare sunshine, she and Nigel had been hawking. They had ridden fast and were watching the flight of the hawks, swift and cruel to pounce, seeing them glide back to the wrist with a gleam of feathers, a grip of slender claw on glove. Seated there again they were silken and gentle, only the blood on their beaks showing bright. Then in a clearing among the trees she had seen a horseman standing; he must have been watching them all for some time, and he held a hand over his casque as though the sun were in his eyes. He dropped the hand and then beckoned, and Nigel flushed a little and said "Comyn," beneath his breath, and did not move forward.

"Tell your brother the Earl we'll meet at Dumfries, as he demands." The high arrogant voice came clearly to them across the space of tufted grass. Then Comyn —she had seen the eyes again, close and narrow, light on her as on that day in Perth—Comyn had turned his steed's head and galloped off the way he had come, leaving Nigel, who flushed easily, crimson.

"Riding over our land as though it was his, as though he owns all Scotland! And indeed he thinks he does," Nigel muttered, and made her turn with him and take back the hawks to Lochmaben, where they brooded in the rafters and often, looking up, she was reminded of Comyn when she saw their sharp beaks.

So Father had ridden now to Dumfries, to that meeting.

She crept back to bed and lay awake with the cold until dawn's coming, and then in the early greyness she heard horsemen ride in.

Feet sounded swiftly in the courtyard, running; the men-at-arms never slept. She heard voices, muffled and cautious, and then someone ascending the stairs. Their footfalls sounded grave and heavy, as though they bore a dead man up.

The women had been roused now; she could hear their little rustlings and gasps as though of pity. Someone cried out, somewhere, and was hushed still.

What had happened to-night?

Marjorie shivered. She felt surrounded by fear, darkness and unknown things. The noises downstairs had subsided to a low constant murmuring, as though every wind and current bore some news through cellar and hall. Everyone knew now, everyone . . . except herself.

In the bed beside her the child Mar still slept, deeply now so that he made no sound. She saw his short dark hair scattered on the pillows; his lips were parted and he slept on his back, fists curled loosely above the coverlet. Sliding past him out on to the floor again, she felt a queer pity rise in her for him because he had no part in this at all and cared nothing.

The stone of the floor was chilly against her bare feet; no one troubled to put down straw in the sleeping-chambers. She found the woollen plaid and wrapped it close again about her body; the smell of the fleece-oil came to her, reminding her that it had not been washed since it was woven, last spring. The Flemings of Aberdeen had sent it to her father because English fleece was scarce now after the late war. Little, unconsidered items of the kind appeared in the forefront of her mind, keeping it away from what might be happening down below.

She stole down the turning stone stairs and saw in the hall the yellow light of wall-flares that had been re-lit. The hall was full, almost as it had been at supper. Several of the women had risen from their beds and were like herself, hair loose and hanging over their hurriedly donned shifts or plaids. The hall was full of men, too, men in armour.

Her uncles were banded together about her father's chair, on the high dais in the hall. The chair was empty. The flaming torch above and behind it seemed to mock its emptiness, and the stillness of the armed figures that waited, waited, while the talk still rose and fell like a wave. Marjorie felt a sick fear clutch and drown her. "Father," she thought. "It's Father."

Hurrying down into their midst, she saw heads turn as she came. No one chided her for being awake or tried to stop her on her way to Nigel. He stood with his young face drawn in the torchlight, casque in hand so that the light fell on his hair. He stood by Thomas Bruce, who was saying something, vociferously, to him with gesturing hands.

"Right?" said Nigel dully, as she reached them

"Ay, right as may be, in that he deserved to die, but at the high altar of God is another matter." Then he turned to Marjorie as though she had questioned him and said in a tired voice, "No, dear, it's not Rob who's dead. It's the Comyn."

"The Red Comyn? Did Father kill him?"

Her child's clear voice fell into a little pocket of silence. Everyone began to talk again, tactfully, suddenly. No one looked at the group on the dais; no one looked at the stairs. On the staircase the Countess of Carrick stood, in her shift with a cloak about her; her face was haggard in the growing light of day. Suddenly she moved, coming down slowly into the crowded hall. The women and the men-at-arms parted respectfully and let her pass; she was not one of them. When she had come before the high dais, she stopped, looking up at Nigel. Raising her hand, she thrust her loose fair hair back from her face.

"Where is my husband?" she said. "What have you done?"

Nigel began to speak. It was a curious thing that he, the youngest, should be the spokesman for all of them. The elder Bruce brothers stood silently, eyes fixed on his face.

"Leave him now," said Nigel quietly. "He'll see no one."

She began to protest, and he checked her quickly with a gesture of the hand. As though he were explaining to the assembled hall and not to her only, his voice rose. He did not look at Elizabeth, or any of them; his eyes were fixed on the far door, through which grey daylight came.

"It was all of us were in it. Not Robert alone. I held

80

the door and Kilpatrick and the rest went in, after the
first blow was struck, and we made sure that Comyn
was dead. We left him there before the high altar by the
Friars' choir in Dumfries. That's his last assignment."

He smiled a little. "Ay, the red fox!" muttered
Thomas. Elizabeth gave a little wail of fright. "In
church?" she screamed. Nigel looked at her wearily.

"Ay, madame, with all the pains and penalties that
follow. Were it allowed to me, I'd do it again. This
feud's bred ill for too many years, ever since Comyn's
sire and our grandsire stood before old Edward at
Norham, in days gone."

Elizabeth's face began to work, and she fell to
sobbing and twisting her hands.

"Ah, dear God, that claim, what is it but a phantom,
and why shed blood for it? Comyn or Bruce, what does
it matter if both think a kingdom's theirs, a kingdom of
dust, of sunbeams? What will befall now except that
the King of England sends his troops north, to avenge
his lieutenant, and the Pope cuts off the sacraments
from us so that we cannot even die in peace? Did I
bargain for this when I married my husband? What is
this madness that's taken you all, since that felon's
death last summer? The King will give Robert's lands
to the Percys, to the Umfravilles. What will we be but
outlaws, homeless? King, does he say he is? King, since
the death of Comyn? The King of May! And I, its
Queen! King and Queen of the May!"

She began to laugh uncontrollably. It was dreadful
to see her, unkempt, her cold aloofness vanished, pale
lips writhing in laughter, face shadowed by her hair.
Nigel and Thomas Bruce came down, and taking each
an arm led her gently from the hall. Everyone stood,

silent, waiting till they should have passed, remembering Elizabeth's late words. Marjorie waited stiffly on the dais where Nigel had left her, still seeming to hear them flung back from the listening stones. Could her father hear also, alone in his chamber?

"The King of May! King and Queen of the May!"

The Earl sent for Marjorie after nightfall.

During the day snow had fallen, taking much of the cold out of the air. Back in Dumfries it would have silted thickly in the streets and byways, covering up the stains of blood about the church doors and drifting over the hoof-marks where the murderers had ridden off. She could see it all, going over the sights in her mind; even the thought "murderers" had its horror softened, as though the snow's thick blanket dulled full impact. Yet she could wonder how the Earl must feel. He had been such a gay, glittering, noble fighter, a man of lutes as well as steel. It was not like what she remembered of him, this huddle of bleeding flesh in a church aisle after violence. It was like that other time when he had ridden in with bruises on his throat that the Comyn had given him in Selkirk Forest. It had seemed wrong then that such a thing should happen to him.

She did not know how she would find the Earl, but to all outward appearance he was the same, seated near his fire in a furred gown of scarlet, with a paper across his knees, and sand and ink and seals near by. The fire glowed on the scarlet, which drew all the light in the room. She herself was a small, creeping shadow, moving towards him across the straw.

"Come," said the Earl, and laid down his quill. She could see an ink-stain still on his hand, between the second and third joints of the long middle finger. The hand was outstretched to her, and she went towards it. She could not keep shyness out of her gait. So short a time ago there had been blood on the hand, not ink. She tried to picture Comyn dead, the malignant eyes glazed like a hare's after slaughter, the flame of the hair dulled, the mouth flaccid.

"Are you afraid of me now?" said the Earl. She could tell from the voice that his mouth smiled, but the eyes were in shadow. The hand never wavered; she went and took it.

"We meet seldom, you and I," said Robert. "There have been so many other things, and now there will be even more."

He drew her within the circle of his arm, near the warmth of the fire. "Will you be King?" asked Marjorie. She laid her fingers carefully on the smooth fur of his sleeve. How soft it was, and beautiful! Like Nigel's hair. Like Egidia's mirror. There were two kinds of things in the world; it was so easy for the one to smash the other. Even now, messengers would be riding south to tell old Edward what had been done in Dumfries.

Robert stared into the fire; he had not moved. "Out of the mouths of babes," he said. She saw that he was still smiling. "Have they come to you with any reason for this killing of mine? Have they tried to make you less or more afraid?"

"No one's said anything." How long the day had been, with all the women cosseting Elizabeth with warmed wine, and for herself nothing to do but watch the snow shake down from the loaded branches in a shower of white feathers!

"As well," said Robert. He turned his head and looked full at her, but she had the feeling that he saw not her but other things. She stayed where she was, making no effort to achieve notice for herself or to do other than listen. "Truth to tell, there was no reason," her father told her. He gave a little shrug. "So many times I might have killed this man—for injury, for assault, for usurping my place as rightful heir! But now there was none, save that in our talk he angered me with his high words and his refusal to band with me against England for my claim, and I drew my sword and stabbed him, there in front of the high altar." He laughed a little. "It was the kind of thing Ned might have done, rather than I; I thought I'd schooled myself. But now, having murdered old Edward's lieutenant, I'm out of the folds of Holy Church and have lost many a powerful arm to fight for me when the time comes, for half Scotland will rise for Comyn."

"They didn't love him, as your men love you. Nobody could, with that fox's face!"

He smiled. "Love? Can one fight with love? Shall I stay, and make a stand against the wolf's thousands that he'll send north now, when he hears—and among them Comyn's allies, who might have been mine? Shall I be hunted as Wallace was hunted, slain as Wallace was slain? Shall I—ah, I've frightened you—die so?" He drew her to him. "Do you know what the Lady Elizabeth says? She says we should all go overseas to your Aunt Isobel, the Dowager Queen, in Norway, and spin out our lives on the buttered fish of charity, and French wine."

He eyed her, quizzing her. She could not follow his mood of wildness, of mockery of himself and his crime,

of laughter in the face of danger. Now, when everything
was at stake, he was like a man without any troubles at
all. He might have decided everything already; *had*
decided. She stared up at him.

"Would you want to go and hide in Norway?" Without reason, she felt tears rise. The Earl laughed aloud,
and went on laughing. He had not heeded her question.
What was she to him but an encumbrance, someone
who could not speak his language? She could see, as the
laughter abated, his grey eyes alight with hard purpose,
his mouth set and firm. After a while he spoke again;
he must have had all his plans laid early. He told her
how to-morrow he would ride west, to confess his crime
to Bishop Wishart of Glasgow. She remembered
Wishart, a broad, squat, kindly dark man, who had
confirmed her. He could wield a sword with the best
and always rode out armed, in the garb of soldiers, not
hiding in towns in soft clerical dress all seasons of the
year. "Wishart . . . ay, and there's more to see him
about than repenting!"

She stared at her father, seeing as so often the light
point and illumine the shining of his beard, the glowing
colours of his scarlet gown. He looked like a king, as
Comyn could never have done. Shyly, she asked him
what else there was for Wishart to do.

Robert answered strangely. "There's no stone now,
Isobel, no ancient crown. We'll get a goldsmith to
hammer a new one."

Why had he called her Isobel? Was it because it had
been her dead mother's name? Then there was Aunt
Isobel across seas, and Ned's lady; and, newly remembered after so long, the little pale-haired Countess of
Buchan, who must be back in England by now. A small

pang of jealousy startled Marjorie; why should her father think now of Lady Buchan? Then the significance of what he had said came and she thought of the crowning, stroking meanwhile his furred sleeve as though it were part of him.

"You must say nothing of it," said Robert. "But then you never do say anything." He smiled; he had remembered her again, and she would never know now which Isobel it had been.

VI

She did not see that crowning of King Robert on Palm Sunday, 1306.

Outside the snow had melted long ago and she stood by the narrow window, watching the pale sunlight gleam on budding trees. After so cruel a winter, everyone said there should be an easy spring.

"Providence is not so reasonable," Elizabeth had answered to that. Everything Elizabeth said nowadays had that same carping bitterness; the night of Comyn's murder had changed her. She had not wished to attend the crowning, which she still looked on as a jest; grim enough, certainly, for what it might entail. Always her mind was turned towards England, what everyone would say there, what Edward would say. How they would laugh in the south when they heard of this pitiful crowning! King Hob, wielding a sceptre like a child's toy, governing over the clouds and the wind in the trees! A matter of time, no more, before the sceptre was wrested and broken in stronger hands, the puff of wind stilled, the clouds scattered.

So she would not ride to Scone. In the present state

of the roads and danger from the Comyns, certainly, it was the safer part to stay at home. There, also, accordingly, Marjorie stayed; how could she attend when the Queen was missing?

She stood idle, therefore, and stared at the day outside, resentment pricking at her. If her father had only married some other woman! Someone brave, like Aunt Mary, who had gone to the crowning at all costs, her husband's men about her. What was the use of that woman who sat there by the fire, sewing always at head-cloths and altar-cloths, as though her soul would be saved thereby?

There would be no fair cloths in the Abbey of Scone this day, all the statues would be shrouded and the crucifix draped in purple for the coming death of God. The Gospel of the day would tell of Christ's Passion; with the great assembly standing, hearing Wishart's voice, while the sun struck in fine shafts through the windows and spilled gold on the floor of the nave and the tall pillars of painted stone. Then after the Mass the old square hands would raise the new crown and place it over her father's brows, and he would be acclaimed King.

If she could see it! "But I'm a girl. Girls stay at home. There's nothing to do but wait, wait, and hear of other people's doings, and sew and gossip." Women weren't brave. She suddenly thought of Walter, for the first time in many weeks since he had been here, for a while, to serve as esquire to her father; grown taller, and much more silent; he was a man now and careful not to be mocked at for speaking to the Princess too often. The Princess; that was herself. She should have been in the Abbey to-day, in a white gown and mantle lined with ermine furs. Princess. The Princess Marjorie. Marjorie of Scotland.

"What are you dawdling for by the window? Don't idle; come and unravel these threads."

Someone was riding down the road in the far distance; could it be the King returning? No, the escort was too small for all that he had taken with him; nowadays he rode abroad with many companions, all of them streaming along the roads like a crusade. This was no crusade; more like the fugitives from a battle, this, for the haste in which they rode. Three men, with staves, and—could it be a woman? Her hair flew loose in the breeze and she rode as if death were after her. Who could it be, coming this way?

"Do as I say," called Elizabeth sharply. Marjorie turned and slouched away from the window, scuffing at the straw with her foot. Whoever it was, the gate-keepers would interrogate them, and if it was anyone to be seen they would send word up. Nothing to do but wait, here, and unravel threads.

The Queen of Scotland stitched, thin-lipped, by the fire. Marjorie avoided looking at her. She went slowly to the linen square which lay unfolded on a stool with the Queen's silks in it. The colours, blue and vermilion and green, danced before her eyes as she knelt down by them.

"How slowly the day passes!" yawned one of the women. A tension was among them, making impossible the free light laughter and chatter that had been theirs from day to day. Elizabeth shifted her position slightly so that she need no longer see the silent group every time she raised her head. The things in her own mind scared and bewildered her. Every loyalty that she had ever known was changed. Ah, there was too much change, madness, following on Robert's own conversion to . . . what? How long had the seeds of this action lain in his mind? At first she had suspected nothing at all, then a little, hearing a word dropped, remembering the tale of that old judgment of Norham that made the Baliol king. Why in God's name could Robert not have learnt his lesson from Baliol that that gift, favour—what could one call it but that?—was nothing at all, not worth fighting for, dying for? Was a scruple worth so much? If a man was left in comfort and the possession of his own estates without let or hindrance, did it hurt him or anyone to call them a province of England, when to call them otherwise meant such retribution as Berwick had had, as Wallace had had?

King and Queen of the May. That saying of hers had been passed from hand to hand by now; she had her answer in the women's silence, her husband's expressionless courtesy when they met, which they now did seldom. God knew that when this crazy summer was past he would see, if he still had eyes to see with, that she had been right. Where to turn for safety then, when all his pretensions were chaff on the wind and all his possessions vanished?

Edward. Once she had been a favourite with the English King. He liked pretty women and laughter about him, and handsome courageous men like Carrick who were not dull, or afraid of him, like his own weak son, or insolent like Gaveston, his son's favourite. But even then one day she'd seen Edward in one of his rages; it had been when some bad news came of the war with France. She, standing there, might have been anyone, or no one; sick with terror, she had been unable to move or speak, watching only with a kind of frozen fear that cold old lion, with his blue eyes hard as ice and his very beard seeming blanched with rage. He was never hot with anger, Edward of England; only cold, cold, always the lawyer. "Justice will be measured out to the last iota." She could hear him say it with regard to France, to the besiegers of Stirling, to William Wallace. She could see him devising the details of Wallace's death; castration, hanging alive, evisceration, quartering, beheading. Each sounded clear and separate, like the measured steps of the old man up and down his room. Justice . . . and for Robert of Carrick and all his possessions, an eye for an eye, a tooth for a tooth, humiliation heaped upon insult for having been made a fool of all these years by the man who rode by his side when hawking.

He would catch Robert in the end. How could he fail, with half Scotland hostile over the death of Comyn and the other half in the power of England? He would hunt him to death through valleys and over hills, past burning walls and choked rivers piled with the bodies of the slain. He would trap him like a rat, and drag him prone at last on a hurdle through London. "And I?" Elizabeth thought. "And I?"

She reached for a fresh thread to put through her needle and found to her annoyance that her hand was shaking. She had always prided herself on her outward reserve. She looked for some diversion now from the fact of her own unease, and her eyes fell on the child, Robert's daughter, kneeling by the assorted threads among the straw. How she disliked that child, always awkward and silent—sly, very likely, with her sullen grey eyes! It had been difficult enough coming north to a step-daughter when she herself had been so young; if it had been a pretty, affectionate child the task would have been easier. But gentle words made no impression on Marjorie, and she, Elizabeth, felt as a rule too indolent to employ force even if Robert had countenanced it, which he did not.

"What are you doing with those threads, in the name of heaven?" she cried. "Do you suppose they are easy to come by, in these days? Let me see your hands, they're sticky and filthy from the stables, you groom's brat."

Suddenly she raised her hand and slapped the child swiftly, once across either ear. "Go and wash yourself and don't come back into my presence until you're clean. How am I to bring you forward as a nobleman's daughter when you'd disgrace a peasant?"

"My father's the King."

Marjorie kept her glance down; she had known worse hurts than the slap. "By God, I'll have you beaten civil," said the Lady Elizabeth. "Get out of my sight."

She turned back, with a high colour, to her embroidery when the child had gone. The brush of words had hardened her mood and steadied her. Within herself she felt a small voice raised, of the person she had used to be. That girl who had once been herself had been made for soft things, rich gowns and pleasant cultured talk; not this. . . . It was doing something to her, making her hard and angry and unwomanly. She must not let her voice get out of control so, or her face set and deepen in angry lines. What if she should awaken one morning and find herself old?

"Riders, my lady," said one of the women, and the

silence eased and altered. Who would it be this time? thought Elizabeth. God knew every beggar in the land had cause to ride in at Robert's gate now, calling himself a man-at-arms for the sake of food and shelter. If this went on they would have little enough to feed themselves, let alone the rag-tag and bobtail that had followed William Wallace and his dead ally, Andrew Moray; bishops soon to be in trouble with their Church, nobles without silver, a grudge or a crazy notion being all their riches. All of them came here, now. She, Elizabeth, would not go down. The only way to save anything at all of what had been was to preserve, while one could, the old standards, the old dignity. Robert could do as he would, paying no heed to her; only, men were so selfish that they never realized their belongings were embroiled in everything they might do, and liable to share in whatever might befall them.

The Queen stitched miserably, tightening her narrow mouth.

Isobel of Buchan had ridden night and day to be in time to crown the King. The news that his great step had been taken filtered slowly, in the course of things, to her husband's estates in the south; she would not have heard, normally, for two months. But nine days since, a Buchan rider had come in, hot and weary, and flung himself at her feet, mouthing the Gaelic that she had never forgotten in all those years in the south. It was her mother-tongue, that she and, above all, her brother Duncan should have guarded jealously; but Duncan, Earl of Fife, dined now at Edward's table, knelt at Edward's knee. Duncan cared for nothing any more that was not English, ever since as a little boy of nine he had been taken south, after their father's murder, and brought up side by side with Edward's sons at Court, and married at last to Edward's young kinswoman. So the message had reached him in vain.

"They only laughed at the English Court when it was told, laughed and spoke of King Hob and how he might be let rule for a season."

King Hob! Reflected in the wet dark eyes that were upturned to her as the man knelt, Isobel saw another face; golden, with the hair like an aureole and the eyes the colour of the grey skies, the grey sea, that she remembered from childhood. Ah, she recalled enough to resent still the clipped English tongue, the brisk English kindness! Duncan might have sold his birthright, but not she.

"Saddle my lord's horses," she had told her man. "I ride north."

Buchan was from home, and when he returned he would be furious at the loss of his horses, "more," she thought wryly, "than at the loss of his wife." The future was nothing to her now, and the past much. Not her own past, not her own life, dragged out year after year childless, unloved, half-scorned, alone at her lord's alien estates which she stewarded, but further back; into the old mist, older than men's memories, as old and as young as bards' songs. For the bards still sang of the crownings of Scottish Kings of old, when the Thane of Fife would set the crown on the monarch's head, for without that touch no luck would attend the reign. It should have been Duncan who rode north, not she; and Edward, no doubt, would smile to himself in the knowledge that the blood of Fife was tamed now, never thinking of her scorned self as other than at home with her greyhounds, her herbs and her apple-trees, sitting while her women curled her pale hair or brought her lint for spinning. Buchan would not follow, or miss her till his return.

So she had ridden north in wind and rain. With every mile something of her late self fell away from her, and much of her child's self returned. Now, so weary as to feel no fatigue, she was no one; only a woman, with a task which must be done, and once it was done she could die. She rode into Gasconhall, the King's place, which would have news of him; no one on the road seemed certain, or being so would say. They told her nothing, but gazed after her, a young girl in the twenties, almost without escort, light hair flying uncurled; a shining in her eyes as though the moon lay behind them, and lips that smiled always. Fey, they said, she looked, like those who have been told that they must die to-morrow, but for to-day may have anything in earth or heaven that they ask.

So she rode into the courtyard, and knew at once that the King had gone. There was hardly anyone there save the grooms, polishing girth-leather; an old man, mending a spear; and a child. No one came to take the horses, but the child turned from watching the grooms and stared up at Isobel, and, coming closer revealed itself as Marjorie of Carrick, with a grubby tear-stained face and mud and straw on her gown.

Isobel stared down at the grey-eyed child. She felt her senses swim for weariness, and reeled in the saddle; she had had no rest for nights, and now that the goal was so near she recalled that, but above all saw through the mist those eyes clearly; Robert of Carrick's eyes, that she remembered so well that although all other memory should be taken from her, those would remain. Robert, who had been kind to her in little things, in the old days at Edward's Court, as her own lord had not been; stringing a lute for her, leashing her hounds; partnering her in the dance when otherwise, shy and foreign as she was, she would have been left aside. Grey eyes. . . .

She opened her own, pulling her senses together. "The crowning?" she said. Robert's child was unkempt, she thought. What must they be thinking each of the other? She herself, after the cruel ride, had no longer the appearance of a fine lady.

"Madame de Buchan," said Marjorie politely. She could not keep her eyes from staring a little in wonder that the Countess, whom she remembered as so soft and pampered, should be here now dishevelled and hatless, with her hair streaming back from her fallen hood like a maiden's. But Lady Buchan would no doubt explain why she was in such haste when Marjorie had answered her first question, and she replied that the crowning was ended, in fact it had been to-day.

The Countess gave a little cry, and the glow she had had faded, as though a light which burned within her had gone out.

"I'm late, then, I'm late; though God knows I made all speed." Suddenly she looked about her, wild-eyed.

"No matter how late I come, there *shall* be one of us crown him—if he wishes it so! Where can I find him? Will you take me there?" She stared at Marjorie like one child at another. It was a demand so simply put, with a child's simplicity, that Marjorie became for an instant adult and cautious; remembering the roads, the

Comyns, the danger; remembering, too, that the King would ride home in due course.

But she could not persist in her withdrawal in face of this most spirited lady, this elf now freed from spellbind, who had ridden so far.

"My father's at Scone," she told Isobel. Suddenly grinning, she ran to the grooms.

"Saddle Fleet for me, and tell Will to come. I'm riding out for a little with Lady Buchan. Oh, not far!"

She laid her grubby hand on Isobel's bridle as though fearful that she would escape.

Later, when Marjorie had time to assemble her thoughts, it occurred to her to wonder at how little stir there had been over the matter of her riding beyond the walls. With Lady Buchan, true, she was officially guarded; word reaching Elizabeth would conjure up visions of a posse of men-at-arms, and her step-mother was so annoyed with her she would be glad to let her out of her sight on such an excuse. Haste, excusing Lady Buchan from presenting her compliments to the new Queen (*did* Elizabeth secretly relish her title, for all she pretended it would not be hers for long and that this was a mere venture, a flowering of the May?)—the lack of servants to raise an outcry, for most had gone with the King; all these things had helped. But Marjorie did not think of the matter in that way as, skirting the town of Perth where the English garrison lay dangerously close, she, the heir of Carrick and of Scotland, rode with one servant only, and the Countess with her weary three, into Scone.

She would see a crowning. All things had shaped to achieve that end, ever since Isobel had ridden out on

her lord's stolen horses to accomplish it. The visions
Marjorie had had of Palm Sunday, the savage longing
herself to have been there, would be appeased. She
lifted her head as Isobel had done, and smelled the
clean air of freedom. A presage of long-awaited things
was in the young pale leaves, the sticky buds of willow
that soon would burst open, the sun itself, warming the
silent roads where no one knew where the King had
gone. It gilded the towers of Scone, and Isobel's hair,
and the harness; it shone through the rayed clouds like
the crown they would soon see. They spoke little as
they rode, she and Lady Buchan; there was nothing
to say.

They found King Robert in the Abbot's house, not
by direction, for his whereabouts was secret, but by
sense. In the great Abbey the candles were douted,
everything soaked, still, with the burnt-out smell of
incense, left from the crowning. It clung to the King's
robes, which he wore with armour beneath. He sat by
the Abbot and the Bishop of Glasgow on the high dais,
after meat; but when he saw the woman and child at
the door he rose, and came down to them.

Marjorie watched him, forgetting Lady Buchan,
who had dropped to her knees on the straw, laying her
cheek against the King's robe. The little gold circlet
that he wore on his head did not look unfamiliar; not so
grand, so awesome as the stolen crown of Scotland had
been; a goldsmith's hasty work, a fighter's diadem. It
might have been made for Robert, or he for it. It bore
little trefoils, beaten out in the gold.

He bent, and, almost the same moment that Isobel
knelt, raised her. "You must not kneel!" Marjorie

heard his voice, very deep and touched with tenderness; an instant's envy, the last, pricked her. Who was she to complain at Isobel's reward after such sacrifice? Would the Earl of Buchan be very angry? What would old Edward say?

Isobel was crying, she saw; suddenly small and drooping, hands clutching at the King's surcoat. "I rode north . . . for this; to come to you, to crown you . . . if a woman may serve. . . ."

His arm was about her. Watching, Marjorie felt the tie strengthen between them, not the mere body's bond. Love, as it was elsewhere called, had no place now. In another time, another land, they might have been lord and mistress, lover and beloved, those two. But not now.

"Serve?" His voice lightened with joyous laughter. "For this service, my arm and my life, always, as long as I can fight; you'll not leave me again, Isobel, my dear. . . ."

"Dear." His voice lingered over the beloved word. She might have been a saint to him, or his mother. Half supporting, almost carrying her, he bore her to the Abbot's dais. Marjorie followed, silently; the King had not spoken to her yet, but she felt no chagrin at this time.

"To-morrow. Or the day after. You're tired now." They spoke of the crowning. She heard Bishop Wishart's guttural tones greeting the Countess; saw his dark eyes, with the thousand wrinkles about them, smile at herself. She insinuated herself beside him; she remembered the Bishop, although they had not met since her confirmation.

"No! No! To-day!"

Isobel's voice rose frantically. "I'd not keep you here

longer in danger. I'd not have you lose time for me.
You've not heard, as I have, of the vengeance they're
preparing. You've not seen the forces muster on the
way north. I tell you he's a serpent, and will strike when
you are least aware. Don't linger on here, dear sir,
where there are no walls."

Robert laughed. "We can be serpents also, and rely
as little on walls as that beast need do. No, my dear,
you'll rest here, while all is again made ready." He
turned to Wishart, who began conferring with him in
a low voice. Over the Bishop's mailed shoulder the
King's eyes met Marjorie's, and smiled.

"You ride the roads too?" he said. "Well, there must
be an escort granted you."

"I had Will," said Marjorie. Her glance sought and
found Will's, standing tall and languid among the
other servants in the lower hall. Will always obeyed her
commands without questioning.

"Ah, but he's no soldier," said Robert, and frowned.
He turned to Wishart again and she heard them con-
clude the arrangements for the second crowning ceremony, two days hence to allow for certain ones who
were absent to return.

So Marjorie saw her crowning, with the age-old rite
of the Fife touch and blessing, as she watched the
slender hands of Isobel place the circlet once more on
the King's head. About her the colour of furred robes
mingled and merged together in the incensed air; in
her ears was singing, and about her were faces she
knew; Walter's, Andrew Stewart's—thin and flushed,
as ever; he looked ill—Nigel, fair as an angel in his
green robe trimmed with vair; Ned, with hair flaming,

and by him a young man with a dark wry face, who lisped when he spoke. His name was James Douglas, and he was a kinsman, but there were so many kinsmen in the Abbey she scarcely troubled to recall him later when they met again.

It was soon over, even the singing by the old bard of all the King's fathers. Robert, son of Robert, son of Robert, son of David, son of Henry, son of David, son of Duncan, and so back; into the mists, back to Fergus, back to Scota. Then when she had kissed her father's hand he placed her himself on her mount beside Isobel's, and bade them ride back to the Queen's charge.

"Whatever befalls now, we stay together," he told them, and lifted the young Countess to the saddle with his own hands. They rode off, and Marjorie could hear, above the sound of hoofbeats and the rattle of girths and mail, a low continuous murmur of voices, speculating, talking.

"Edward. The Comyns. Valence." Who was the last? These three names seemed to enter into all the talk which rose and fell about them.

Edward she knew. That was the wolf, who was not yet dead in spite of the time that had passed. When would he die? She would pray for his death, so that the English might soon be without a strong leader. The Comyns she knew. They were her father's hereditary foes, made bitter by murder, a worse danger than Edward. They were everywhere, knowing their way in the land, ambushing roads, murdering servants. It was the mercy of God that they had not caught herself and Isobel, but surely God's hand had been laid on them both during that ride and kept them from harm till the task was done. And Valence, the third; who was he?

"Sir Aymar de Valence, Edward's lieutenant in the West, who will meet the King, he knows, soon now," said Isobel. She stared straight ahead of her with lips compressed; Marjorie thought she sounded like Aunt Mary, who made flat statements in a voice like a man. What had altered Isobel? She was harder, older; the light had gone out behind her eyes, like a candle when morning comes.

Marjorie heard a little breath, a whisper from her, as they rode again towards Gasconhall. "If I were a man, to lend my arm to them! If I were a man!"

"You've lent your hands," said Marjorie. Hearing, she was astonished with herself. It was seldom that she thought of the clever thing, the right answer. Perhaps this day had changed everyone. How often she too had wished she were a man, so that she could tilt and fight! Would the fight be soon now, and fierce? Would many die? Would Nigel, would her father?

"God would not have let him be crowned only to die at once in battle," thought Marjorie fiercely. She rode on with her eyes fixed ahead like Isobel, whose task was done.

VII

Marjorie was able to stand at her window a great deal in those days without being rebuked. The Queen seemed to have given over chiding; she sat quietly watching everything and everyone, with unreadable pale eyes and smile fixed like a cat's. Sometimes the King would come and she would greet him with formal courtesy, which he returned; they were like polite strangers rather than man and wife. Robert would stay for an hour or so in the women's place, watching their

needles ply while he talked to them or to Nigel or young
Randolph, a kinsman of the Stewart's, who had lately
joined him. It was not altar-cloths or finery they
fashioned in these days, but surcoats; plain solid stitch-
ery, weaving of wool and flax thread to cloth, cutting
and sewing together. Already there were banners sewn
and linen made and folded ready for wound dressings.
No one mentioned Sir Aymar de Valence, or Edward,
in the women's hearing. Everyone waited, and among
the bent busy heads was still that of the Countess of
Buchan. She had fitted into the ways of the household
quietly and unobtrusively, shrinking again into her
place as though she were a maiden. News had come out
of England of the Court's laughter, as had been foretold. King Hob had a mistress . . . so hot that she had
ridden north, through mud and fords, in the spring
gales, to find him. The Earl of Buchan was furious, they
said, at the loss of his horses. And Edward had drawn
his lips back, once, at mention of Isobel's name. Oh,
there was a reckoning coming, after the manner of
lawyers.

Summer. Daily below the window rode fresh troops,
horsemen from the Campbell country and from Athole's
forests. Athole himself rode down; a gentle tall man,
slow of speech, constantly by the King's side, silent
unless consulted on some matter. Marjorie had heard
him once tell of the manner in which the King's word
had come to the north, one man running with lighted
crossed sticks through the night, while the flames
streamed above him. At an appointed place another
runner would take the fiery cross, then another, and
another, spreading the word.

So they waited while the dark round-skulled men

came down out of the hills, armed with black daggers. They fought best on foot; they were swift as cats, the soles of their feet hard as leather. She watched them, marvelling at their difference from the Borderers, the little stocky men whom James Douglas had sent up on their ponies. For a Borderer's horse was a part of his body, and he would sooner die than be without it in a battle. These men had a sign-talk all their own; in their country, James Douglas said, they had meaningful carved stones standing, which strangers would not understand. Liking and hate were strong in them, but they laughed more than the Highlanders ever did; they did not kneel to Marjorie and kiss blades like many of the glen men, but one of them gave her a little pair of green pebble beads, with a medal of St John in silver, saying it would bring luck. The Queen said it had most likely been stolen.

Then there were Norman-speaking knights with Sir Gilbert de la Haye; their voices sounded odd and clipped among the soft Gaelic and the salty east-coast tongue and the Border drawl. They wore chain armour, some of it rusty with long use. Often their helms were of the old style, straight-sided with a cone top, and a nose-piece and slit for the eyes. Once Marjorie would have laughed, and her father too, at such old-fashioned contraptions. But no one laughed at anyone now.

Yet there was still laughter, gay and carefree as if there were no war. It mocked nobody, except maybe England. It would be heard at nights when the torches were lit, and the motley army sprawled about tables, or on the floor if there was no other room, by the dogs who lay there. The fires blazed high although it was summer, for with so many to feed the meat hung roasting always;

four or five great carcases browning and basting, with the smell making everyone's mouth water even while almost fainting with heat. Then, after they had all eaten, there would be singing and telling of tales. The King often, with his lute, played as he had used to do at the court of Edward, his voice clear and true as then. "It must have been like David and Saul," Marjorie thought. A little pang went through her; she would never love music as the King did; she had no ear. She liked it best when he told tales, particularly the ones of far lands; France, where twelve knights had ridden out in search of adventures; Spain, where the infidel built golden spires and where, the King said, men must soon fight again for Christ, as in Jerusalem. And Norway, where there were mountains all of ice, and the snow lay thickly in winter about the palace where Aunt Isobel was Queen, and the trees pointed to the sky and were green all the year round. How many things the King could tell of! What was it that made him able to hold men so, silent and rapt so that there was no sound in the hall except that of his clear voice, and behind it the little snap and flicker of the flames on the hearth?

She would watch and listen, always withdrawn as she was among the women of the house or, rarely, on the high dais near the King; close enough to touch his sleeve and feel beneath it the hardness of mail, reminding one that this very night there might be word sent that Valence had marched. Waiting was like that, she thought; pleasure and laughter and ease on the surface, hardness of iron beneath.

Yet even now it was hard to think of the King as of iron and not of gold. His hair shone, as it had done that night by Egidia's fire; with the warm light upon him, he seemed larger and more splendid than any man there. A giant, she thought, a great shining warrior like the heroes in his French tales, the kings who slept beneath mountains. Was it because of the consecration of Isobel's hands, of Wishart's blessing, that he had grown so in stature?

"They say King Alexander was a big man, long-limbed, large-boned." The spirit of that dead King was upon her father now; she felt a little thrill, and shivered. There was no spectre here as there had been at Fernie-hirst; no bones would dance in masque at Gasconhall.

"You're cold, Princess. Have you an ague?" She knew without turning that the speaker was Will, the lute player. He was a big man, too; but not as her father was—the bigness was all in white fat and over-shot bones. They said geldings were often thus, no manhood ever having come to harden them. For the first time she thought without shyness of that fate of Will's in Spain. Had the lore of herbs that he had learned of the infidel been worth more than the loss of his manhood to him?

She turned and smiled at Will and he bowed and grovelled; his manner to her was always servile and loving, like a great cat's. All his thoughts ran on herbs and healing, every least thing being diverted through those channels; he was convinced that she had an ague now because he had seen her shiver. She laughed, and because she was not afraid of Will she told him what her thoughts had been, to explain it.

He did not laugh or scoff at her fancies; his plump white face grew considering in the firelight, and he raised a hand and caressed his beardless chin.

"King Alexander's spirit? Ay, and Wallace's too.

For any man to bear *that* load must break or fashion him. Has he broken, and will he? I say not. They'll think less of that old skeleton at Ferniehirst by the time all's done; forget it, Princess."

Marjorie closed her eyes. How long since anyone had spoken to her of Wallace? Again she saw the head, with sun-bleached hair blowing lightly in the wind from a southern river, and dead eyes staring. The noise in the hall faded; she felt very cold.

"Ay, you have an ague," said Will. He began to issue fussy instructions to her women.

She had never been pampered; always she had been as strong as a pony. Rain had not chilled her, running in it as she had always done and shaking it out of her hair and eyes. She had accepted her health as one does who has never known illness; the Queen's nurturing of her own body aroused in Marjorie a faint scorn. She herself cared nothing for what she had heard of the southern women, the way they would bathe their limbs in goat's milk and rosewater, and paint their faces with red and white lead and pluck their brows. When she found Will compounding pig's fat with sorrel leaves and an infusion of the bark of hazel, for the Queen's use, she shrugged, and did not ask to sample it. So it was less hard for her than for the other women that summer, being as she was, still a child; when word came of what had befallen it meant the less to her.

It came two months after the crowning at Scone. Ned Bruce, whose Isobel still remained with them, rode in one day white about the mouth. They saw him come, and remembering the Comyn killing crowded to hear what he should say now. Had he been set on? Had the English come? But it was neither of these things.

There was a silence, in which Isobel of Ross sidled up to her lover and laid her head against his shoulder. She was not made for solemn ill news, only for love; her red lips pouted up at him as if ready for kisses, and her hand caressed his surcoat. Ned stared ahead as if he did not see her; his brows were drawn together.

"What is it?" said Isobel. "Tell us why you are so grim." Her creamy lids flickered and a glance passed over the other passive women; in an instant it mocked them all—the Buchan girl who had not the sense to take Robert from the wife who had lost him; the child who knew nothing yet of men; Mary Bruce, who did but cared little for it; Christian, a hen with her one chick. Women! What was a woman without a man? She curled up against Ned closely, a cat ready for cream. She scarcely listened to what he was saying, as it did not concern only herself. Outlaws? Who were outlaws? Themselves? She laughed a little; the word meant nothing.

Ned took her by the shoulders suddenly and spun her round. Facing him, she thought he looked stern; what was troubling him? Agape, she had to listen; the unaccustomed thought made the words impinge on her brain, like little hard pebbles. She gave a gasp of fright.

"Don't laugh, you little fool, till you know what outlawry means. Do you even begin to understand? Edward's declared you beyond law, to revenge himself on us."

"On me," said Isobel of Buchan. Her voice was low, and Ned might not have heard her. He blustered on; a little vein had swelled up in his temple, as it did with both

107

him and the King when either was angry. He blurted
out the news now without leisure for tact; his grasp hurt
Isobel's shoulders, as though she had been an enemy.
He ignored her writhing; he no longer saw her.

"That means there's no redress in law for you—for
anything," he said. "Any thief can rob, any murderer
ravish and slay you; there's no appeal. Hear that, Rob?"
He turned to his brother, who with Nigel Bruce and
Athole stood in the doorway; they had just heard. "By
the blood of Christ, I can stand honest war, but *this*!
Ah, the Angevin's true to race, devil-bred, damn his
eyes for a lawyer—to war on women!"

The King came in silent, slowly, almost precisely
pacing the floor. His face was expressionless; one finger
smoothed a targe he held. Marjorie saw clearly the
light caught on the little separate knobs of patterned
bronze, beaten in the taut leather.

"The flower of chivalry has great precision of detail."

"Ay, in the manner of his executions," growled
Nigel. No one else said anything. Presently, a small
frightened sobbing showed that Isobel of Ross now
understood that she could be dragged from her horse
on the high roads and ravished without recourse to law.
The other women were silent. Marjorie stared at Ned's
mistress, watching the helpless clenching of her small
waxen hands. She had never before seen anyone so—
frightened. The cause of it still escaped her, as being
too adult for her full understanding. Somewhere in the
background came the Queen's cool voice. Edward
would not deny her redress, she said. Her father would
speak for her.

Mary Campbell's grey eyes met Christian's dark
ones. Neither of them thought it necessary to speak.

"This is my cause," said Isobel of Buchan suddenly. "If you all come to harm through me. . . ."

"And you?" The King strode over to her. Taking her hands, he laughed. "We stand or fall now—together. Give me your prayers when I ride against Valence, that I may not fail."

It was not to be spoken of that he should fail, thought Marjorie. Not with that host, and that cause.

She watched the army with the King at its head ride towards Methven, a place beyond Perth. Word had been brought that Valence was advancing eastwards; the smooth plain would be a suitable place to choose for battle.

When they had all gone and the last sound of riders had died, she followed the other women into the chapel and took out the Borderer's gift of little coloured beads. All that remained to do now was pray, as the sewing was all done. Even the linen for the wounds was finished, taken and stowed away with the baggage train. There was nothing to do but wait till word came, and say the Rosary over and over.

A new prayer, she thought. As she repeated the Aves and Paters and Glorias the light shone on the silver figure of St John. St John had been the great friend of Christ who sat beside Him at the Last Supper. It was so much easier to remember that than to think of the vision of Our Lady a century ago to a priest in Provence, and the instructions she gave for this very prayer, to be said the world over with the help of little beads. So much easier . . . and to see the figures of the kneeling women, and to forget to pray; to be so full of the thought of what might even now be the fight, with men wounded and horses hacked to death, and bodies on the field all slippery with blood, and a horseman riding, riding through the dust to tell them all to mount in haste and hurry away from Gasconhall, because the King had been defeated and his army slain, and there was nowhere to go in all the world for outlaws, who had no recourse to justice. But that had not happened, could never happen, to think of it was to make it so, it must not be, and the only thing was to pray. . . . Pater, Ave, Gloria.

"Quickly, Quickly. Never mind the hangings. Bundle together what you can—here, no, not that. How do we know how far it is to ride? Hurry, it will be light in three hours."

Dark shapes, changing and huddling together in the light of a lantern. Haste, without time for crying or bewailing evil news. That was what had come in the night, and was now. She was here now, ready and dressed in her warm garments, with a heavy cloak although it was summer, and an extra pair of shoes and hose in a bundle that was her shift. Everyone was like that, queerly dressed and shapeless, carrying bundles. So many things would have to be left, and there was no time to think about them. Soon the English would be here, were on the way here now, after plundering the dead on the field of battle. Everyone must be got out of Gasconhall before the English came. There would be only dead things left here too; hangings, beds, furniture, cosmetics, wheels and looms.

"And food," growled Mary. It had not been possible to take all the provisions. If there had been time she would have fired them, poured oil over and set a light

to it. That was what Ned had said should be done, with
an enemy in a fertile country. "All our corn and salted •
meat and fish left lying for pigs to eat!"

She glanced at Marjorie and shepherded her to the
courtyard, where horses were waiting. "You'll ride
with me, child; they're short mounted." Her thin
mouth curled in scorn at the sight of Elizabeth, who
had been got, pale-lipped, on to a horse, and sat there
moaning for her jewels. "Spare yourself!" Mary called.
"They'll not load their slings with your rubies, or melt
your golden gear for the tips of arrows; it's safe to
leave such." The nearness of danger seemed to fill her
with a terrible mocking joy; her eyes burned like coals,
and Marjorie shrank a little from contact with her in
the saddle. She was so thin and intense, like a witch;
different from the flabby shape that was the Queen.
How danger altered people! Before it had always been
Elizabeth who was in command, and Mary had been
an untidy queer person who made jerky statements
sometimes and was silent for the rest.

Mary shook the reins and the horses moved off.
Clinging hard, shaken with the speed as she would not
have been in her own saddle, Marjorie heard the shreds
of talk blown towards her on the night wind. Everyone
was making pretence to be as usual, except the Queen.
Above the swift thudding of hooves and the pull of the
wind, Marjorie heard certain things clearly. Some she
had heard before; that they were sparsely mounted she
knew; that the King had skimped his own supplies to
mount them at all, she did not. Where were they going?
No one knew. Someone said that they had had orders
to make for the north-east. The impassive faces of the
men-at-arms showed for an instant as a cloud scudded

away from the stars. They were all old men who had not been at the battle. If the party of riders was set upon, they might fare ill.

"Once we are away from these parts, they'll recognize us less easily," said Christian Seton, pressing her mount close up to her sister's. Her placid eyes held no hint of what she felt concerning Seton, who was with the King. Were any of their men alive? There had been no time for any word. . . . Behind her, the Earl of Mar's querulous young voice could be heard, complaining because he was put up at the back of a servant, crying out at the jolting speed.

"I know well enough where we're going," said Mary. She jerked her chin in the darkness, thinking how the Flemings of Aberdeen had told the King long since that they would shelter him and his, if ever there came such a day that they would need shelter. It was not safe to breathe their destination now, even in the swift darkness. Better for some not to know . . . and ride, hard, away from the pursuers, who could not be far behind.

"We'll get there, God willing," thought Mary grimly. She tightened her woollen hood with one hand and dug her knees into the horse's sides. "Marjorie, child, cling on. You're silent, aren't you? Not like the Earl of Mar." She grimaced and grinned. "God be thanked I've no bairns," she murmured. The thought of Neil crossed her mind and she wondered how he fared. Neil and she understood one another. If she heard he had fallen in battle, she would waste no tears, but fight on.

"Women fight now." Had it been shaping so ever since the day their mother, the King's mother and hers, had won herself a lord by force? That had been one beginning of the recognition of woman as a rightful being, more than a cipher to bide at home and weep and spin. The Countess of Carrick would have approved the Countess of Buchan, who had ridden over conventions to come and crown her son.

"But, dear God, is his crowned head safe?" Mary knew that she would rather by ten times that Neil had fallen, provided the King was unhurt. "For without *him*, where would any of us be?" She glanced down at Marjorie, the heir to the kingdom; all the trouble had started when a girl-child was to be Queen, it would not do again. No, there were things that women might not accomplish yet . . . "but in time it may come," thought Mary.

They had no rest during that first terrible ride. Later, they would sleep in the open, wrapped in cloaks, with fires lit against the prowling wild beasts of the night. But now they dared not stay, and every hour meant further danger, until they should overtake the remnants of the King's party, making its own way north. The country was etched with brown rivers and scarred with forests; there were no roads. Any rock and tree might hold enemies; less likely English yet than Comyn men, who would know the district blindfold. They hurried along the guides' tracks, not taking leisure to grow fearful over a shadow by a stone, a movement behind a tree.

The King was safe. So much word had reached them by the messenger who came at last, one evening after sundown. He was that queer eunuch from Spain who had attached himself to the service of the Princess Marjorie. He had not fought, his white arms which were no stronger than a woman's having no force to grasp a sword. But he had made his way back through the English camp, unhurt, and had come to them. He rode by them now, his unwieldy bulk slopped over the sides of his mount like flour-sacks. In spite of their mockery of him the women felt safer now that he was here.

"How long will this last?" wailed Elizabeth, on the third day. Compared to what was to come, that first ride of many was easy; but to them, still flabby from indoor living, it was becoming a matter of chafed flesh and raw palms, too soft yet to be calloused with riding. Valence's guards were posted along the coast paths, so they could not go there. Often it rained, and the smell of soaked woollen garments added to their discomfort, with the wet running down into their eyes beneath their tied hoods, and chilling them.

This would be what they must become, nomads, like the wild tribes who lived in the deserts in the Holy Land. "Only there they have sunshine," thought Marjorie, "and not enough water." She shook her head free of the wet like a puppy, and watched the road ahead. The Queen, she knew, thought always of Norway as the end of their road. Would that indeed be the end of it, and all this endurance to no more purpose than that they should live as strangers in a land over the sea?

Her eyes narrowed. The summer trees were bowed with rain, and a grey mist hung over the skyline. It was difficult to see where ground ended, and sky began. The trunks of birches rose out of nothing, like fairy trees, and their boughs were of lace.

"I do not want to go," she thought. No, even with the wet and discomfort, and having no roof over one's head, and not knowing what would happen next. This was how Wallace had lived for many years. Would they indeed ride the roads for so long till she herself should be grown? She would be as happy so as she had never been at Gasconhall, with the alien laughter of the fine folk in her ears.

A long low sound, like an owl's call, came from the trees. She could hear it clearly above the tramping hooves; raising her head, she listened.

"Will." She saw him near by, head lifted, sharp fat profile alert, with the water streaming down his face in little runnels. Suddenly he spurred his horse and galloped ahead. With a wild uprush of hope in her heart, she followed. Behind her, the plodding hooves grew fainter. They had heard nothing, or if they had were afraid. She forgot them, all of them, in this moment, as though the past days and nights had never been.

A man rose out of the mist, then another, and another. As they neared she could make out the space between the trees clearly; it was full of waiting men. Later she would laugh at herself and Will, careering ahead so boldly; it might have been Valence with all his force, waiting there to take them. But she knew from the instant's sight of a red head that it was not, and in a moment she was out of the saddle and clutched tightly in Uncle Ned's arms, while his bearded face grinned down at her.

"Ned! Nigel! Father—where is he?" Her hands grasped Ned and shook him, in sheer joy. Laughing together, they each had sight of the other—what a brigand Ned looked, with his unshaven stubble, and his mail all dinted, and his sleeve torn! "And you're no better, you with your elf-tangles, and wet as a puddock, and caring naught," he told her. Then she saw his eyes wander and heard the others come on, with little cries of surprise and thankfulness, and knew that he had seen Isobel as soon as anyone. Standing alone again amongst the sounds of joy and the hugging and kissing on all sides, she sought the King. Where was he? Was he well? And did he wear a strip of linen about his arm or head, like so many of these? She glanced up at Nigel, who like herself stood lonely, not having any woman to kiss, and caring nothing for it. She saw the little lines about his mouth that had come there in the past few days; suddenly, it came to her notice how much older they all looked, beneath the laughter.

"The King's safe." He responded to her unspoken question, while his eyes searched the skyline as if for enemies. "No, he'll not come to you here. . . . Do you think it would be a safe thing for all to meet together, with none to fight a rearguard action if need be?" And he told her how the King, with her other uncles Thomas and Alexander and the Douglas and Sir Gilbert, guarded the ways, keeping them clear of ambush.

"Once we win to the north, we're safe—for a time." Nigel's mouth set, and the thought crossed his mind of how the English might, again, march north as far as Tain, as they had done at the time of the Berwick massacre. He opened his mouth as if to speak of it, and then the small figure of the dark-haired child who stood before him came, suddenly, like a shock, into his clear vision; he had found himself, he realized, about to confide in little Marjorie as if she were a grown woman. "Or a man," muttered Nigel, who had no great opinion of women. He smiled at his brother's child, reassuring her as to how, if all went well, the King would meet with them in Aberdeen.

They rode at last into the northern town, and for a while at least it seemed as if there were no war. The great-boned folk, who were nearer Viking than Norman, welcomed them in their rapid broad speech; but their truest allies were the Flemings, who ruled here a kingdom of their own within the township, as the doomed merchants had done in Berwick long ago.

Gathered in coast and trading towns from the Baltic to Sicily they were found, these Easterlings, who kept their own speech and their own ways but mingled so well with the places of their adoption that they brought wealth to the towns as well as to themselves. Marjorie had heard of them and of their honesty in trade, which was such that even now in England the word "sterling" applied to money meant "honest" or "fair value." But she had not before set eyes on them, and almost more than the meeting again with the King she was to remember her first sight of the round-bodied, jolly burghers, clad in bright fine wools and furs, and their wives whose head-linen was white as snow against faces high-coloured with good living. They were so clean, the Flemings, that the streets in front of their houses were swept and scoured daily to free them from dirt and rubble—a change from elsewhere, for pigs roved free in the town, and fed themselves from the garbage that lay heaped in the centre of the roads, impeding horse-passage. The Flemings would mince placidly on their high wooden pattens over such muck, lifting their bright skirts aside from it.

Marjorie and her father and step-mother were lodged with the Guildmaster and his wife, whose house was in the vicinity of the fishmarket and faced the sea. Although it was still summer the air was snell here in the north, and Marjorie was glad of the comfort of the warm new clothes the merchant's wife provided from those of her own family. "They are only a little worn, but clean, and they will do till better come," said the good woman, frowning. Marjorie could see very little wrong with the snowy shifts, warm mantle and new scarlet hose and shoes. The children of the house were all dressed so, and had stared at her when she first came among them in her own clothes, shrunk and shabby from the long days' riding. She had felt shy at first sight of them, so plump and comfortably clad and fed, chattering to one another in their North German tongue, which they still kept up when amongst themselves. "But we must all learn French and Lothian also," said Johan, the eldest, to her, "and later Italian and perhaps even Russian, for if we are sent to the far north without knowing the tongue they speak there, what use will we be to trade?"

All Johan's thoughts ran on trade, and to her it was strange to hear him, for always hitherto she had been brought up to understand that boys were bred to love war. But Johan would scarcely know what to do with a lance if he were given one, and when Marjorie boasted about Walter and his exploits at the tilt she found the merchant's son regarding her, gravely, with one thumb in his mouth.

"All that is very fine, no doubt, but there are other things besides fighting," he said. "Where would the towns be if all our men thought only of how to kill each other? Everyone would then live in caves, like the barbarians, and eat raw flesh."

He began to shake with laughter at his own fancy and she found herself growing angry with him. "Where would your towns be if there were no fighting men to defend them?" she said hotly. "What use would you be in a war?"

"Oh, I would defend myself, as my Uncle Gerhard and his four sons did, in their guildhall at Berwick. But all were burned alive."

She flushed, and begged his pardon. She had forgotten the tale of the Red Hall. But Johan bore no rancour, and had gone on almost at once to think of something else. They walked together along the road that led out of the town, watching the grey breakers roll in from the North Sea. On its surface tossed little ships, some of them native boats, others herring-fishers of the Hansa.

"That little fish is our fortune," chuckled Johan. "Should he change his course and breed in other seas, we would all be ruined, my father and I, and my uncles in Gothland, and my cousins in Lübeck, and the rest."

"But you trade also in hides and wool and linen and spices and silks," said Marjorie. She felt as if her mind had been opened up and scoured in the last few days. How strange it was to hear Johan and the others tell of kin in far cities as though they were but a few miles distant, and as though different countries did not matter in the least, or different tongues! Was it true that kings in Norway and Denmark would ask the permission of the Easterling merchants before they passed certain of their laws? Yes, said Johan, because if the merchants were offended they could retaliate by refusing to sell their goods at low prices.

"But surely then the kings could buy their goods elsewhere."

"No, we control all trade in certain northern towns and coasts. It is not worth while to make enemies of us," said Johan, and began to wave his hands and talk about blockades and monopolies. Marjorie stared at the sea, dimly understanding a new kind of war, without bloodshed; a siege, but lacking walls or engines like old Edward's Loup de Guerre. "But the other side would starve just the same."

She looked at Johan with interest, thinking for the first time how they had all been sheltered by this clan without, it appeared, arousing any fear of reprisals from Edward. "He would not dare attack us again after the Berwick incident," said Johan. "Too much trouble was called down on his head by everyone in the League who heard of it, and he had to pretend that it was an accident that the Red Hall was burned, whether it was or no."

He suddenly turned his large face towards her; his eyes looked mournful. "It is not possible for you to stay with us longer," he said, and jerked his head towards the sea. "You cannot go to Norway now, even if you would; out *there* there are the English ships lying. I have heard my father talk of it with yours; believe me, I know. I do not know what will happen, or where you will go; or whether we shall meet again." He sighed, in a way that almost aroused her laughter, even while she felt sad at his words. Johan could cry very easily over a thought or a song, like all his kin; the other night, when her father had played and sung,

they had all sat in a circle listening with great vacant
faces, and the tears running down their plump cheeks.
But it would be a pity, she admitted, if they were not
to meet again; and she tried to make herself feel melancholy, looking out to where beyond the grey heaving
horizon Edward of England's sails lay. Yet all the time
her heart sang a little song of joy. They would not be
going to Norway, then; they would all be staying
together. Whatever happened now could not be un-
endurable, if only because of that.

It was true that Aberdeen dared no longer harbour
them. With the encroaching of alien forces from south,
west and seaboard; without reinforcements to make a
second stand, or powerful allies nearer than the Isles,
there was a choice of two things for the King of
May. His wife carped at him to fly with them abroad;
to risk capture by Edward's ships, leave everything,
take refuge with the Norwegian Queen.

He looked at her, seated there in her new Flemish
clothes, her face sullen and pale without cosmetics—
where were they to be obtained in this burgher's town?
—and turned away. They had so little in common in
these days that there was nothing to be said, nothing
that had not been gone over a thousand times before.
He watched the squat grey houses and the ever-
changing sea. Down in the street were two children,
striding and laughing; the merchant's son Johan and a
girl in a scarlet cloak. He smiled a little to see them.
How Marjorie had grown in the last weeks! She was
brown with sea air, and stouter for the Flemings' good
feeding. God knew they would all need what health
they could muster for the months that were coming. He

thrust the thought of it from his mind; what use to blame himself for the trial that must be endured by the women? He had risked that when he risked all, and now there was nowhere that was safe for them.

He spun round. "There is nowhere you can go, Bess, now. Surely you see that?—and the weapon it would be against me if they captured you, as they might well do, either by land or on the seas between here and there."

"That's all you care for," she said bitterly. In her own heart she was frightened. If she were captured, now, what treatment would she receive? It was no longer so certain that her father the Red Earl held any power. "And if I leave him now the Buchan girl will not," she thought. How many things had come between them, while her own mind no longer seemed able to hold any matter but what was small and mean! At times, such as now, she was still able to catch a glimpse of herself.

She went to him suddenly. "I will stay with you," she told him. "What other choice is there?" She smiled wryly. "Once, I would have stayed for choice only."

He stared at her, still seeming not to see who she was. "Ay, we've both changed," he said.

"Where are we now?" said Marjorie.

Behind them, in the encroaching night, little points of light showed. That cluster, like distant star-figures, was the town; they had ridden out in silence, trusting to darkness to cover their direction. It must have done so, because on the far hills little separate flares still lingered, unchanging; the enemy camp-fires.

They were as close as that. All through this open country they would be close, Nigel told her. "Once we win to the woods of Athole, we'll be safer. There's cover there among the trees." But now it was a matter of silent hard riding, without lights to guide their way. By day they must remain hidden, in any cover they could find, sometimes under a roof if any dared shelter them, sometimes not.

There were not many supporters. Had the King won his first action at Methven, it would have been different. Many then would have flocked to his standard, as they had done for Wallace after his victory of Stirling Bridge. "But now, although they are not all of them hostile, they'll wait to see which way the tide will run; trusting meantime not to drown themselves, while the sands are shifting."

That was Will's voice; he always talked like that. He rode in the column now, behind with such baggage as they had been able to bring. The less they need carry the better, the King had said. Food was the most important item, and shoe-leather; other things did not matter so much, and he had laughed at the ladies' wish for some finery. "If you are covered at all we may think ourselves lucky," he said, and made Marjorie leave behind her scarlet cloak in exchange for a darker one, because the bright colour would show up too clearly if they were to lie hidden. She had been sorry to part with the cloak, but saw the reason for it; and soon forgot her regret in the queer sharp excitement of riding thus by night, as they had come. But now the King was here and all his brothers, and James Douglas, who rode near by. She glanced over at his dark, erect figure, noticing how every now and then he would spur ahead into the

darkness to make certain that all was safe. He had eyes
like a cat, and could see many yards ahead; "and a nose
that can smell an Englishman a mile away, or so he
says," thought Marjorie. She smiled at that saying, so
like James, hearing it again in his curious lisping voice.
He was an odd person; if she had not heard of how
terrible he was in battle, she would have thought him
womanish, with his smooth dark face that was almost
the colour of lead, and his long straight hair. But Nigel
had thrown back his head and laughed when she told
him that, and said that James was so bonny a fighter
that the English had heard of him even now and called
him the Black Douglas and used his name to frighten
their children with. "Wait you, if it falls out that we
tarry long in Athole, it will be James that catches the
fattest hare, and brings down the finest stag, and has
every woman on a string but cares for none," he said.
"I'd sooner have him with us than the wing of an army,"
and then bit his lip, thinking of the army that had come
to them once and been slain at Methven, that lost
battle of which no one spoke.

They rode on for many days, over mountain tracks
and little-known roads. Once they encountered reinforcements from England, making for Perth. It was
while they were in a dip in the hills and could avoid
being seen, and everyone must light down from the
saddle and crouch, holding meanwhile a hand over the
mounts' mouths. Marjorie felt her fingers tighten and
tremble over the horse's velvet muzzle, and heard the
drawing to a standstill of the whole train, the shuffling
and clinking as the women alighted to the ground, the
sidling forward of her father and Douglas and his men.

They stood with swords ready, and she could see the look in their eyes; no man wore full armour now, only plain helmets and coats of buff, with a shield and sword and short dagger and an axe. She watched James Douglas, seeing how he almost grinned at the prospect of a fight. They said he always rode into battle laughing, like a lover to his mistress.

The sound of riders came, and their raised voices, dimly heard and faint. "They aren't afraid to let themselves be heard," thought Marjorie, knowing that they must be well armed and many in number to ride openly so. The waiting men's bodies grew taut; almost, she could sense the desire they had to fling themselves swiftly on the horsemen as they rode, bring them to earth with a sword-stab and the ready swing of an axe. "But they cannot, because we are here."

The thought stayed with her, spoiling her relief at their return, after the horsemen had passed, and the ability to move again her cramped fingers and rise and stretch her limbs. There was no sign of anyone now among the dark mounds of moor. They must all wait for a while till it was quite safe, and then ride on. . . .

She heard the curt orders and some jesting pass between her father and his men. Behind her, the relief from strain was showing itself in some of the women, who were sobbing quietly. Presently they all mounted and rode on.

James Douglas dropped back again into line, whistling a little French tune between his teeth. His ugly grey face was quite expressionless. He did not turn to look at Marjorie as she drew by him.

"You find women a burden, don't you?" she said. His black peaked eyebrows shot up quizzically, and he looked down with something of the air of an eagle who surveys an ant. "Do they say so of me?" he enquired. Marjorie felt herself flushing.

"No one has said anything, but I know you wanted to fight, and you could not because we were there, and it might have meant danger for us. How stupid women are!"

The Black Douglas looked down on the child who was not afraid of him. "They are not all stupid, nor all a burden," he assured her. Suddenly he smiled, and the whole of his face was lit by it. "If you were disappointed, Princess, that there was no blow struck, I myself will endeavour to recompense you on some other occasion. Meantime, may I acknowledge myself your very humble knight?"

She scowled; he was talking like the English folk at Gasconhall, which was absurd when one considered how they all looked now, bedraggled and unkempt, with freckled skins, and the men each one of them with two weeks' stubble. Then she caught the Lord James's eye, and he looked so comical that she had to laugh, and they were friends from that moment.

Danger was never absent that summer, but it was the happiest of her life.

Always she had wanted to do the things that boys did. Now it was made possible for her, because no one, not even Elizabeth, could be a lady now, in this open-air life that they all lived, first of all in Athole and then, when the country there grew unsafe, far in the west, in Lorn. Marjorie took no account of the weary rides, the rising at night and hurrying off, to a new hiding-place miles distant, through a country surrounded by enemies. All that she remembered or cared for was that she could run wild as any boy, could learn to fish and to shoot arrows, and cook over her own fire made of sticks and bracken.

James Douglas taught her to fish, showing her how to bait a line of sheep's guts and leave it fastened to a branch over a running stream. Or sometimes, when the young brown trout were thick (and James always knew when they were) he would teach her how to guddle for them under the stones. Standing barefoot in the cool water, she would feel the slippery pebbles slide and then settle under her toes; then with sure balance, and two hands swiftly dug beneath a stone, the wriggling fish would be brought up, hooked by the gills so that it did not slither back again. And how delicious the fresh trout tasted when they were rolled in clay, as James showed her, and baked in the red ashes of a fire! It was difficult not to burn one's fingers in the impatience to eat. She liked fishing better than shooting down pigeons with arrows, or catching wild hares with a snare set for them; they always looked so pitiful with their great eyes glazing, and the fur and feathers streaked with blood. It was harder to be sorry for a fish.

As for being sorry for themselves, that thought occurred to few of the women that summer. Danger there was, constantly; hidden behind trees, waiting in ambush by a curve of a hill, a dip in the road, the wall of a ruin. Yet in the manner of Robin of Sherwood's ladies a century before, there was laughter among them still. The winter would come, no doubt, and when it did their bones would ache on the hard ground, with the cold. Often, waking in the early dawn, they would do so even now, with the damp that rose before the sun, whether or not it had rained. But no one spoke of winter, or of what would happen once it was here. Perhaps the King would have a turn of fortune. Perhaps the old wolf would die.

So they feasted, on the wild meat and venison that the Black Douglas and others killed; and slept, those who had lovers, in their lovers' arms, as though the world were young and this the Garden of Eden. But all the time they knew in their hearts that the serpent lurked near, and might strike while they were least aware of it; and that every kiss might be that of farewell, and every song sung the last.

For they would sing, softly, still, and tell tales, at night about the kindled fire, where a carcase roasted. Only now there was no high dais, and every least servant was as good as his lord. The King sat among them, taking his turn at the spit, or stood back in the shadows of the forest, keeping the watch. This must never flag, lest they be taken unawares while they lay and slept, or dozed after eating. So hungry were they after days and nights in the open that often they would drop asleep after the meal, heads nodding and drooping in the glow of the fire. Everyone looked sated and content at these times of much meat, even Queen Elizabeth, who until night fell was miserable with gnat-bites which swelled her fair skin. "She is forever moaning and wanting oil from Will to rub on it," muttered Marjorie. Her young scorn of the Queen was heightened now by the appearance Elizabeth presented; crimson with the sun, where the rest of them were brown and freckled, her features were almost obliterated with the swelling from that and the insect-bites. "If my father took Lady Buchan now as his mistress, nobody would blame him," Marjorie thought, her mind turning over the adult talk she had heard among the women. But the King grew gentler to Elizabeth as her beauty vanished; it was as though pity were an easier emotion than the love he could no longer feel.

Turning her head to where Isobel of Buchan sat, bearing her share of the constant mending tasks that befell, Marjorie was struck by her resemblance to a young nun. Her eyes were downcast over the jack-coat she was mending; her hair hung limply, like a veil. Like them all by now, she had hands roughened with work, weather and hard riding.

For they were seldom long in one place. Twice now Marjorie had seen men killed; once on the road, when they were set upon, and once when she and James Douglas were alone, and two men who had been concealed by the river's bank leapt from their place into the water upon them. But James had been ready with his sword and killed one man, and seeing the river water all red with his blood the other took fright, and made off.

That the King had many such encounters she knew. Once she saw how he had to be helped from his saddle after an all-night ride; he staggered, and when they took his mail off him she saw blood on his shirt. Another time he had been wounded in the arm; she saw the dark stain spreading through the linen with which they had bound it, but no one spoke of what had occurred. Only, a man of the Campbells who was a bard sang later of how King Robert had been attacked on a hillside by five men at once, and had beaten them all off, killing three. So had the songs grown about the deeds of Wallace, Marjorie remembered.

But how long could they, with their small numbers, hold the attackers at bay? Day by day they seemed more and more like the beasts that prowled beyond the fire's circle, these enemies, who were never seen. Gradually it began to seem to Marjorie that every least sound, the passing of wind through trees, the fall of a leaf, was a man's step, and that man a foe; like John of Lorn, who was against her father for the Comyns.

When the leaves began to fall in earnest there would be less cover from the trees. Then the days would shorten, and the heavy dews of early morning grow thick and chill. "You'll be in a palace of snow and ice then, with frost-flowers in your hair," James told her. But she knew behind his laughter he was thinking the thought that must soon come to them all; this queer nomad-life, with its laughter and suffering, its danger and delight, could not outlast the latest leaf. For they were not peasants, bred to the cold earth, but gently nurtured women who already were beginning to show signs of ill-health in the constant open; sore throats, sore bones, a cough; and sometimes, as with Ned's pretty Isobel, a bite from one of the dogs, very slow to heal. Ah, they must have a roof over their heads before the winter. . . . But where? Norway was so far away, with a sea to cross as well as a country bristling with hostile spears.

Marjorie could feel the change take place in herself while the summer still lingered. In a time when girls were wives at eleven, she had been slow to mature; but long before the body's change came the mind's sharpened awareness. Scents, sounds, movements, all had an increased significance; small, inconsidered things made her want to cry or laugh. She withdrew into herself a good deal, saying nothing often for hours together. She had never been a talkative child.

Often at night she would lie awake, even her weariness not sending slumber. The darkness bore changed sounds, beyond the turning sighing women about the fire. She could see their sleeping shapes, mounded and faceless; the muffled cloaks giving anonymity, the hair hidden. At times terror would seize her with its fancy that, in the light of dawn, they would all be stiffly mounded dead, heaped in grave-clothes. A tiny movement would arouse gratitude in her, in a world where everyone slept.

Yet the forest was alive. She felt its creeping nearness, and often fancied she heard sounds there; beyond the watchers, the constantly armed men, who stood by in turns till light came, and again always by day.

Once she rose, stepping carefully over the sleeping women to make her way to the outer circle of darkness. The dogs lifted their heads and subsided again; they knew her. She saw Nigel, sitting broad awake a little way back from the fire. His profile was towards her; he did not turn. "He thinks it's one of the women gone to relieve themselves, and will not look," she thought. She felt swift, nervous laughter rise in her throat, and choked it. The darkness pressed in heavily, like a blanket on her shoulders.

Outside the fire's circle the trees rose up, dark and serried, their branches netted together near the ground so that she had to clamber across them. An enemy would have that barrier to contend with, coming secretly; would fall, may be, before he met the King's spears. But the men of Lorn, who knew their own forests well enough, would come stealthily as the beasts, making no sound or blunder.

Once she was in a place where she could remain unseen Marjorie stopped, leaning her back against a tree and feeling the rough bark caress her cheek where she turned it. The sleeping circle about the fire were still visible, helpless as they must appear to all heaven, if heaven were looking now. Did God remember them? The child considered it solemnly, weighing the things she had been taught against the things that had been. If God looked now, what would He see? Isobel of Buchan had turned in her sleep, a straggle of fair hair across her face, and her lips parted. She looked like a child, innocent and serene; one hand, palm upwards, lay outspread on the ground. Was her lord still angry? What would become of her? God knew, but He would not tell.

Near her the Queen slept in darkness. Her breast rose and fell evenly and she made no sound. "She has quieter nights now," Marjorie thought, recalling how the poor woman had been tormented by itching and troubled with dreams, so that she had tossed and whimpered and kept those about her awake. Did dreams mean anything? Were they the message of God? The Queen had dreamed of a red river, and James had laughed and said it was the spate, the autumn rains. But *she* had seen a little stream darkened with a man's blood; perhaps that was what the dream meant. If only that were all. . . . Her grandmother, the old Countess of Mar, could have told. Marjorie had never seen her, but they said the past and future were as one in her mind because of her blood, which was that of the dead princes of Gwynedd.

Was it because of that same blood in her own veins that her mind ran so darkly? Here, now, there was nothing to make her afraid. Yet she could feel an increasing dread, compassing about each one of the sleepers in the circle, and leaving her out. Athole lay with his fine face relaxed and calm; his dog was across his knees, awake and staring at the fire. Young Nigel, with his delicate profile between her and the flames, was still; the thought of harm to Nigel came to her, and she realized how she loved him. Father, Nigel, then James. The others, even Ned, were nothing. How strange things were! She could see Ned now, a little way off; he slept noisily, his red head lying on the breast of his Isobel. She smiled in her sleep, as though her dreams were pleasant.

A wreathing mist had arisen, just visible in the greenish dark. Beyond it, she could see little Mar lying by his mother, the querulous pout of his lips softened in sleep. Donald was forever complaining about the hardships of their life, and did not care to come fishing with herself and James in the pools. "A spoilt brat," James would say, "best leave him be." But it was difficult to be curt with Mar, as he deserved, because Christian would be so hurt if any word of it came to her; and as Christian hurt nobody of her own free will it was surely worth putting up with a spoilt little boy to avoid that. She slept now, her gentle face peaceful and calm; Seton, her husband, was near her, his wound from Methven almost healed. No one had heard them complain of the lands they had lost; it was sufficient to them to be near one another. Not so Mary Campbell, who lay quietly now with her strange eyes closed; her lord was on the watch, and she was alone to-night. It suited Mary to be alone, Marjorie thought; she had never fitted into the role of spouse at all. Easier to imagine Mary brandishing a sword in a fight, or inciting an army to battle with brave words. She should have been a man.

"Like me." But Marjorie could not feel herself as belonging anywhere on this night, or being anyone. Physically outside their circle as she was, she felt the curtain of events descend between them and her. Who was she except a child who had come amongst them? If she were to die to-morrow, fall prey to a wild beast or a foe's sword, they would be no better off and no worse.

Loneliness overwhelmed her. If she had only been needed by someone! Whatever happened now she would be always just beyond the light of the fire; different, solitary. "If I had been a boy," she thought. The King's son, fighting with him! There was nothing they would not have dared and won together. Yet now. . . .

Someone moved in the undergrowth. Marjorie stiffened; she had been seen. There was no time to cry out or move before the hands were upon her. Then a voice came out of the darkness, lowered and warm, speaking her name.

"Marjorie." It was the King. She slid her hand in his without speaking. His solid presence banished the night, the mist and her fears; she felt them recede.

"Were you taking your turn at the watch?" he asked her. Always he seemed to tease her, a little, when they spoke together; as if afraid to take either himself or her more seriously than need be, in case things were spoken of that should be left silent. She felt laughter and tears rise, knowing how little she could say of the things which troubled her.

"Nigel's awake, and I was watching him." Stupid, trite words. She leaned against her father, glad of the strength of his encircling arm. How like iron it felt, with the hardness of the sword-muscles with which he had slain the three men! She had forgotten that he was one of the watch; she had forgotten him altogether. How strange things were!

"You love Nigel, do you not?" he said. There was no longer any teasing in his voice, only a kind of reflection. She wondered what lay in his mind. It was often the way with the King, she thought, that his thoughts ran ahead of other people's, so that he often knew what someone would do before they had done it. "That was why he felt so bitter about Methven, because his own knowledge betrayed him," she thought. She watched the King through her lashes.

"Yes," she answered his question about Nigel. Why did she love Nigel so much? "It is not that I know him very well." Was it because Nigel should have been a girl, while she should have been a boy? Were there reasons at all in such things? "Better than most," she said, in answer. She was cautious when speaking to the King of persons. She hesitated, brusquely.

"Better than your father?"

He was laughing, but sad; reproaching himself, as he had done ever since she was born, because he could spend so little time with her. "No," she said gravely, "everyone loves you best."

She moved a little, comfortably, in the warmth of his cloak. If only they need never go from here! If the fairy, who cast spells on folk so that they slept seven years, would come now. . . . She spoke of it.

Robert laughed. "There's more will happen in seven years than sleep, can I move matters so."

"Then you'll be a king, in a palace, with a crown on your hair." She was beginning to be drowsy, and remembering James's words.

"Please God . . . the first part, at any rate."

"Will it take so long?"

She glanced up at him; the stern face in the glimmering light seemed carved of rock. Did he know, then, how long it would be? A sense of desolation overwhelmed her. To fight on; without hope of reward, as yet; without peace, or any justice; harried, persecuted, slaughtered. Was it worth all the toil, in the end? She watched him, and knew the answer.

His voice when he spoke again was light. He talked about old Edward, who was ill with the flux. "So common a thing overtakes the best of us," said Robert dryly. "Perhaps, with so old a man, it will be the finish of him; and yet, there's fight in his body yet! That was a month ago. . . . And while he lives he will hunt us; and the winter comes."

She knew what he would say, hearing of winter. "And we?" she said. "Ever since that first ride over to the westward, when James and you could not fight, I've known we were a burden to you. That's true, isn't it? If we had not been here. . . ."

He glanced down, with tenderness in his face. "If you had not been here your uncle Ned and I would have led ourselves into ambush, most likely, with having nothing but our own skins to care for. Yet, as you understand me—and God knows many grown women

136

would not!—then you'll know how little peace of mind
there is for me, until I've met with them in force again,
and harried them" He raised his head, and she saw the
eyes keen as a hawk's; he talked on, as though to a child
no longer, and she heard the great names pass his lips;
Angus of the Isles, who would shelter him; the men of
Ireland of the glens, who would aid him; the Campbells, who would help him to destroy John of Lorn and
win at least this part of the country for his own. "But
to do that I must have nothing to hinder me! *You* see,
as others do not—were you once safe, and the Queen
so, I could fight with greater heart. This life's not for
women; there's one at any rate far spent now, used as
she is to softness and furs against her skin." His voice
held no contempt, only a flat quality of weariness, as
he said, "Marjorie, I would have one promise from
you, lest we should not speak alone together again.
Will you, for my sake, show kindness to the Queen?
For she has lost as much as any of us, and has neither
the promise that we have, nor the joy."

Very soon now dawn would come, between the trees.
She watched the growing light, by some means knowing, even when he used words beyond her experience,
what he would say. She had never heard him speak at
such length to her; she would remember every word,
long after the night was over and other matters had
come between. "There may be suffering," he was saying to her, "no, *will* be; what Wallace endured in his
body must be atoned for by every one of us, whether
in the spirit or in the flesh. For we killed Wallace as
surely as ever did Edward so; we were deaf, blind and
craven, and Wallace spoke to us in vain. But his death
was like Christ's death in that he now lives for ever;

and he has changed us, I fancy, so that we are like men born again. Did you think when you saw your father in his coloured samite, with his hounds by him and his lute between his fingers, that one day we would stand here, vagabond, outlawed, with not so much as the trunk of this tree against which we both lean *ours*, without our swords? It's all to be won again, this Scotland; every inch of bog and mountain, every fertile valley and grey town and little isle. And before the issue is fought out, there will be that endured which will make this summer's space, with its meagre hardships, seem like a day's feasting. I look to suffer, in my flesh and in my heart. I do not think that any here will come out unscarred. Yet we will fight, and not only because death waits for us if we lose. I would rather my body were in a thousand pieces than that my soul lay in chains."

She knew he thought of Wallace still, whose body had been torn in fragments to hang above the gates of four towns. She closed her eyes; when they opened she found her father looking down at her again, speaking no longer strangely and high, but gently, as though he remembered that she was a child.

"You, little Marjorie, because you are my blood, will be made to pay also. In a manner, you have made part payment already. You have not been happy always, or near to me, as my only child should have been. That may be only the beginning of it; but if you suffer any evil, remember—if I should not be with you—that every ill done to you will weigh the balance of wrong, and strengthen the vengeance of our arms with swords, when the time comes. That is the only comfort I can offer you, because I have traded my right to be a parent for my desire to be a king."

"I am glad that you are a king," she said. Suddenly, and not only to break the silence that had fallen between them, she told him at last of that meeting of herself and Walter with Wallace, so many summers before. It was true what the King had said; they had had so little time together that she had never had the leisure, or the facility, to tell him until now.

He was silent until she had finished, staring at the whitening sky. Then "So you saw him," he said, when the tale was done. "I am glad."

He said one more thing to her before they made their way back to the fire, when the watch changed; it was almost time. She felt his awareness of her, as a person, at last; surely things would from hence-forth be as they should have been, long since, between them.

"As long as one of us remains alive," said the King, "we are not defeated."

The long days shortened imperceptibly and the colour of the sunlight deepened. No one could cling to the summer, to make it stay; soon, with the turning leaves, frost would come, and the branches would be bare. Then there would be no concealment in cave or brake against the eyes of those who watched, watched always, the men of Lorn, the men of Comyn.

They would be like the red deer then, who fled before slaughter. Only a deer could hide itself, when autumn came, against the colours of the changing hills, the bracken that had kindled like fire, the purple shadows of sunset. How much better, in some things, to be a beast, who did not mind the cold, and had horned feet that knew no crying need for leather, and could run for miles lightly, without growing weary! And in a way they were almost becoming beasts now, with the long danger; the men's faces had grown altered and wolfish, with eyes that glistened at each sound. Even James's laugh was heard seldom now, his lisping talk scarcer and his jests few. His face had narrowed, like a starving dog's, and the colour of it was like lead.

One day the King came to where Marjorie knelt with the other women patching at the attire that was all they had left to wear. They were mending it with the hoarded needles that Christian had thought to bring with her out of Aberdeen, and their threads were thongs of split dried leather. The days were long past for linen and fine things; Marjorie's fingers had been raw to start with over the rough work, and then had grown hard at the task. She mended cheerfully, no longer minding the Queen's carping voice; she would always remember the words her father had spoken regarding that. There were some for whom it mattered more than anything in the world that the props they had always known were swept away, and they had nothing left.

"But she still does not like me," thought Marjorie. She stole a glance at the petulant face, released by cooler weather from the torment of gnat-bites it had known in the summer. They were all of them, even Elizabeth, like nomads now; skins fissured and dark with the weather, hair bleached and lifeless as straw. And thin, also, now, when food was growing scarcer. Marjorie caught sight of her own forearm, extended above the needle; how like a piece of brown stick it was! She stared at it curiously, thinking at the same time, in spite of herself, of the empty ache in her stomach that was often there now. But everyone else was feeling exactly the same, and she would not be first to speak of it. Perhaps if she could find some ripened sloes the bitter taste would take her hunger away. James had told her that, and how to bite on the stone to keep from yearning, always, for meat. He had stolen little young pigs, the other day, from some farm; and brought them, clustered and squealing, back to kill and roast them on his sword-point. He must not do things like that often, it was not safe, and the farmers would not blame foxes always. . . .

The light darkened as her father's shadow crossed it, and looking up, Marjorie smiled at him. He stood there silent for an instant, watching them all, and she remembered how he had used to come on them all at Gasconhall, sewing. "We look very different now," she thought, "and so does he." His eyes seemed tired, she thought. She waited, with one hand poised over the needle, for what he should say.

Mary Campbell had risen. She of them all was first to know when some untoward thing was in the wind. She said nothing, however, and only stood with her eyes fixed on her brother's face, and her hands idle. It was left for Elizabeth to break the silence; the little, querulous word crossed the space between them.

"Well?"

"Not so," said Robert. He moved to where his wife and the women sat, and dropped, rather heavily, to the ground by them. His face had lines of fatigue upon it and the bright hair and beard had traces of grey; little beads of sweat lay about the rim of his casque. "The Prince's army comes north," he said. "Lochmaben fell three weeks since. Word has just reached us by a man of Gilbert's."

A little, sobbing breath came; a woman in fear. Lochmaben was only a name now, Marjorie thought; only a faraway place, somewhere on the Borders; a place where she had once watched feathery snow fall from the trees, and heard the sounds of horsemen riding in by night with news of murder. Now Edward of Caernarvon sat there and the courtyard would be trampled with his mounted men's horse, and he would lounge in the hall where word of Comyn's death had come to them, and drink red wine. "And then he will march north," she thought. Was that why Elizabeth was so afraid? How long would they tarry in Lorn now? What would the next move be?

She heard a name mentioned, catching it idly amongst other names. Kildrummie, Mar's castle in the north, which he had left to come south to them all at Lochmaben. It would be a refuge, where they would be safe from the rigours of winter . . . safe from Edward. "He'll not reach so far, well-nigh into Ross's country. If it were his old father . . . but *he'll* bide in winter quarters till the better weather comes, and by then we'll have other shelter. You'll be under protection there—all of you—till the spring."

Robert talked on, his mouth and voice cajoling while his eyes brooded. He answered their questions patiently. "You'll give us escort," quavered Elizabeth, "and horse?" Yes, he promised, Nigel should escort them (poor Nigel, who hated women) and they should have all the horse he could spare. Later they heard that this arrangement left the King with none; but his mind was easier, he said, if it was so. "We'll take to the heather in truth, and fight as the glen men do, on foot, and none the worse for it," he said. "There's many a tract of country where a man's tread is safe but a mount's cannot go." He grew, as the arrangements were perfected, almost gay, she saw; it was as if, with the prospect of true action before him, the weary cloak of waiting was cast off, and he was transfigured. Already he was talking as if they were gone, and with a winter's campaign ahead he looked to the spring, and the meeting with young Edward.

A little chill took her. What promise would there be for any of them by the spring? With the whole force of two countries arrayed against them, spread out fanwise to south and east; and harsh frosts, blood and treachery waiting for the King of May?

Then she made herself smile, as if she believed in him against all odds. If their faith failed, who was there to succour him against black despair? Another Methven might mean the end of all of them.

"He must not believe that he can fail," she thought. She met his eyes bravely. Not a tear, not a question of any doubt must he see in hers. For an instant their glances held, and her smile was returned; she saw his tension relax, as if a finger had smoothed it, and a moment later he was laughing again and describing Edward, that spoilt prince who liked not war, lolling by his fire at Lochmaben till the cold was past. "He's been put to much endeavour to gratify his sire. Will you, then, ride north to gratify me?"

He reached over and laid a hand on hers; the warm vitality renewed in its touch heartened her. As long as he needed her to cheer him, she could brace her mind against the sinking of dismay that had come.

"When . . ." she heard herself say, but Elizabeth forestalled her. She had moved slightly against the stones whereon she sat; her pale eyes blinked against the sunlight, and in them was renewed hope and fear. "But you'll accompany us also?" she said. "You've seen that what I said is true, and that we were wrong to come south? What good do you do here, with no men? If we can reach the Ross country we're near enough the coast. . . ."

He frowned; the light went out behind his eyes. "As soon as may be I'll rejoin you, madame," he said shortly.

Would they ever meet again? Would this time, with its dread chance and odd happiness, and that one hour when they had spoken together without barriers between them, be all she would ever have of him? She would remember that, she thought, whenever bad times befell; and the days in the burn with James, fishing for trout. Danger, fear, separation, loneliness; worse might come. But while her mind remained, they could not destroy memory or take away that picture of the dawn lightening in the long misted glades. Perhaps soon, for all of them, true dawn would come.

"Ah, take care of yourself. Take care of yourself." So many of them were saying that, all about her, now, while she felt the strength of those strong arms about her, and the roughness of his beard against her cheek. Lover's farewell to mistress, husband's to wife; women riding off into danger, leaving the men to uncertain fate. A kiss, an embrace; words sought, never found; her name. "Marjorie," the King was saying. "Marjorie."

There was nothing else to say. She could see his lips still forming the word, turning back in her saddle to see the last of him, standing bareheaded and watching, with his casque in his hand, until the horses carried them on and out of sight.

VIII

They made their way north by forest paths and the black detours over bog and torrent that were known only to the natives of those parts, who guided them. By day they lay mostly hid, fearing the word spread of their coming by Lorn's men or, even so far into the mountain country as this, by those in the pay of Edward. With summer's dying, the weather broke, and day and night they were drenched with rain-storms, which swelled the streams till they grew to giant cataracts over which the horses could cross only by sinking their riders to the shoulder. Sodden, cold and chafed by turns, as the leather of girths and saddles rotted and made sores against their flanks, the women would sink by day into a sleep of exhaustion, only to be wakened by a chance sound, or an alarm called by the watchers. They dared show no fire lest enemies guess at their presence; they huddled together for the warmth from one another's bodies. Often the night would come and find them still wakeful, torn between the fatigue of endurance and the intolerable aching of throats or limbs. They were never in comfort, and never free of fear.

During all that time Marjorie kept close to Nigel, obeying him as though he had been the King. The young man was indefatigable; he rode at the head of their little escort of horse, sounding every track, questioning every guide to make certain of his fidelity. Adversity brought out the jesting humour in him that it had done in James Douglas; only whereas James was compared to the devil by his enemies, surely no one, Marjorie was certain, could compare Nigel with anyone but the angels or the saints. "But it is not a thing to tell him of," she thought, "or he will dislike it in the way that boys dislike curled hair, or too long eyelashes." Living in the company of her father's men had given her an insight into the workings of their minds; she was wiser in more than years since the days of Walter and Dundonald, when she had resented his ordering of her. Few men minded being called wicked, she had found, or breakers of hearts, or lions in war; but to tell a man he was as bonny as an angel would be to make him a life's foe. Yet Nigel still reminded her of someone not of this earth at all, riding with the pale hair backblown from his chiselled young face, beardless as any boy's. Ned had freckled with their open-air life, and her father had bronzed; but Nigel's skin was fair as lilies still, so that any woman might have been proud to own it. He was upright and slim as a tree, riding; the hardships and dangers they had all lived through seemed to have set no mark on him at all. He was always sweet-tempered, never losing patience or complaining at the task that had fallen to his lot—"and well enough we all know how much he would sooner have stayed with the King, keeping by his side whatever befell, instead of being packed off with a party of women as if he were one of them." Yet Nigel was no woman, as she knew when he had to use his sword. In his company it was not possible to give way entirely to despondency, to

believe, as they might otherwise have done, that all was
lost. To live from day to day was all that was yet
possible, but at least the thought of their final goal
became real, and the great round tower of Kildrummie,
as Nigel described it to her, was clear in Marjorie's
mind long before her eyes saw it, one chill dawn, with
the land between half-hidden in little swathes of autumn
mist.

For the first time in many weeks they sat by a fire.
Marjorie heard the crackle of logs drowsily; the steam
from her drying clothing, the warmth and the hot
spiced wine which old Lady Mar's servitors had given
them to drink made her sleepy. Somewhere she could
hear Nigel's voice issuing orders; he had put a guard
on the great tower and archers on each of the five
smaller ones. How like her father he sounded, she
thought; perhaps leadership made people similar.
Nigel had always been so quiet and retiring among all
the rest, no one would have known that he would make
so fine a commander. But the King must have known,
which is why he had sent him.

She awoke to the sound of wrangling, and the light
of a lamp held high above Nigel's head. "Sacrilege?"
he was saying. "Fortunate to have leisure for such
excuse! No, you'll store the forage where I say; it's
safer. There's the ditch and well behind. . . ."

"God'll take no objection to honest food." That was
Mary. Someone was objecting, if God was not; to make
a larder of the chapel! "My lady would never hear of it,
were she here and not in town." A Welsh voice, reminding one with its sing-song that grandmother, the
old Countess, held this castle as her abode, although she

was not here at present to welcome them. Marjorie opened her eyes again, blinking. The lamp swayed and flickered, showing her Kildrummie's spacious hall with the little runnels of damp, from the ditch outside, forming tracks among the hewn stone; and the faces, like her own drowsy with wine and sleep, of the women who had come with them; and among them a new face, that of the Sheriff of Elgin's wife, Lady Wiseman, who had lately joined them because her husband was out for the King.

Nigel strode about directing the disposal of the stores and weapons, and impelled by curiosity Marjorie got to her feet and crept after him. Following him into the chapel, she could see the growing piles of neatly stacked provender, disposed behind the altar below a tall narrow window whose three panels were framed with stone. The coloured figures in the glass looked down at the preparations, it was uncertain whether in disapproval or not. The Welsh servant was muttering about those under the ban of God, and Marjorie heard Nigel give a quick sharp command, then the man was silent. She heard it queerly; there had not been time for the fact of the King's excommunication after Comyn's murder to be brought home to her. But it was true they were all under the ban of God, if God and the Pope were one; "and as we obtain no benefit from the common use of altars, we may put them to uncommon use," said Mary flippantly. She was like a man striding about, carrying bundles with her own hands, supervising disposal; she seemed tireless. Afterwards she took Marjorie down to the inner wall, where, half hidden behind malt-sacks, a doorway showed in the stone.

"That's our exit, if so be we should have to make our
way out unseen. Don't tell any of it, you secret child."
Listening against the closed door, Marjorie heard,
seeming far away, the sound of running water.

"Pray that we'll not need to douse their flames so,"
said Mary harshly, and Marjorie realized that, perhaps
for the first time, her aunt was afraid. In the open it had
been different, they would at least not be caught like
rats in a drain, with the way of escape cut off. Here,
they were walled in by silence, more oppressive than
the muffling mist outside.

"How long will it be before we have word?" said
Mary, and struck her hands together. Marjorie leaned
with her back against the cold wall, and said nothing.
She was not certain whether Mary meant word of the
menfolk or word of the English. It was doubtful which
would come first.

Word of the English came first. The Sheriff's wife
of Elgin, who had brought a handful of men with her,
received messages now and again by a man of her lord's.
She would retail them placidly to the Queen and the
women as they sat on warm days in the little walled
garden which the old Countess had tended; with her
absence, weeds had shot up quickly, and nothing but
an occasional bright-headed marigold thrust up now
among the dockens and couch-grass. Nothing ever
seemed to disturb the Sheriff's wife; she had brought
a seam with her, and sat calmly sewing at it, while relating news of life and death in an even voice. The seam
was a shift; when it was finished she would parcel it and
despatch it by the Sheriff's man to him. Marjorie
pictured the Sheriff as always suitably clad, with his

linen white and his hose darned, among the bracken as he might be and fighting for his life.

"Word came of young Edward's movements before we left," said Lady Wiseman, and threaded her needle. "No, they say he has not gone into winter quarters as expected. He is bold enough, in his own way, when his sire is absent; and being in great discomfort over this campaign at all will no doubt be anxious to complete it as soon as he may conveniently do so."

She began to stitch. "Then he will march north?" said Elizabeth. She had the air of one to whom all things have happened, like a bare tree stripped of its leaves. She sat with her long hands idly in her lap, and no longer showed great interest in anything. "North, or west," replied Lady Wiseman, "no doubt." She plucked at a small knot in her thread, clucked with annoyance, then righted it again. "Linen is not what it was before the war. I doubt if my lord has more than three shifts left to his back that were made in the days of truce; then there was still the Irish flax available. But with all the upset, maids are lazy at their wheels, and weavers at their looms; no man has anything in his mind but to fight, and how can we say where it will all end? If they hold siege here, or if we are driven out, there is sanctuary in the girth of Tain; I can think of nowhere nearer."

"That will be the girth of Saint Duthac," said Christian Seton, leaning forward. "I know the Prior well; in the year my son was born we made pilgrimage, his father and I, in gratitude to the saint for him."

She sighed a little, while Lady Wiseman sewed without pause. To Christian, the dead were as near and as dear as the living; it was doubtful which of them all she loved best, her son Mar, her dead first lord his father, or the absent Seton, who had accompanied them to Kildrummie but rode out frequently, as now, into the surrounding country for news of movements.

"It is a different Prior now," yawned Isobel of Ross. She was always sleepy these days, thought Marjorie; perhaps it was because she was going to have child. She lowered her eyes so as not to stare at Isobel, who had put on so much white flesh that she looked like a great cat, and who no longer troubled to comb her hair or wash herself now that Ned had gone. The Countess of Buchan, beside her, looked like a nun still. How greatly their differences had all emerged, since the life in the forest, and later the journey north, had taken all pretence from them!

"Christian is the same," the child thought, "but no one else." And she herself? Had she changed? But she had never pretended anything.

The siege began before winter. One day Nigel came to her, very white in the face; an army had been sighted, he said, whether or not the English main body no one yet could tell. Marjorie watched him, hearing his words and instructions which she knew were as much to give reassurance to himself as courage to her. She was to keep close, not to go up on the towers, even now when the enemy was too far for an arrow-shot to strike a target at such distance; even though there was no sign yet but, every now and again, a gleam of sun on metal, a helm or a spear-head miles off, drawing nearer.

"We're well stocked with provisions," Nigel kept

saying. "Even if no reinforcements come before spring, we can hold out with what we have." He went on relating details of arms and provisions to her, while she strove to keep down the rising excitement that might be fear, or relief maybe; all the time a voice kept saying inside of her, "They have come. There will be no more waiting, with nothing to watch but the mist." Then she remembered the siege of Stirling Castle, which had gone on for three months, at last giving in just before King Edward loosed his Wolf of War on it. Would there be a wolf-engine brought up here?

Nigel gave a little short laugh, as if he read her thoughts. "Pray God there is no heavy attack," he said. "This tower was not built against modern warfare. If it falls out so, then you'll have to be got out, all of you, while the men stay." Then seeing her white face of terror, he hastened to comfort her, saying what a brute he was to frighten her when there was no need. "I tell you, as long as we need not starve we're safe from them!" he boasted. His young face was flushed and eager with the prospect of action, like a boy's.

The army came and encircled Kildrummie, and from the narrow peep-hole between the stones of the outer wall, she could watch, before she was sent back, and see the pattern of moving casques and spears, flash in and out of thickets and behind little mounds, like a trail of ants in armour. That night they battered at the walls with slings and stones; she could hear and feel the impact, like giant hail, from where she knelt close by the other women, many of whom had their ears stopped with their fingers and their eyes closed tightly. Then before dawn an attempt was made to break in past the outer wall; she heard the clash of arms and shouting, and later one of their own men was carried in with the blood running from his head. They laid him on the ground and she helped Christian to bandage him, but long before they had finished the blood ceased flowing and grew sluggish and dark, dripping heavily to the floor. Then Christian made the sign of the Cross over him, as they had no priest, and bade the men carry him away, as they must save their linen for those who were still living, in case more was needed than they had.

"They are waiting for reinforcements," Nigel said. "Young Edward's at Perth."

He was gaunt and haggard in these days; he had not slept since the besiegers came. Night after night they had resisted, beating back attacks such as the first had been. By day the surrounding country was quiet, in a silence only now and again broken by sortie, or a volley of arrows. They themselves attacked little, reserving their stores for the defence. "They should not have come till spring," thought Nigel. Someone had sent word south.

His eyes dwelt on the small figure of Marjorie, kneeling sideways at the slit where she watched by the hour. "Someone's moved," he heard her say. "They're sending —oh, Nigel, they've brought fire up to the fosse. They're making as if to fling it."

She moved aside to let him see. All of her movements were calm, as if she had lived all her life under siege. Nigel focused his eyes past the wall's thickness and saw, as she had described, the flares rise orange against the night. He was not greatly perturbed; to fire the castle they would first have to surmount the ditch, with its guards about it; there was no shortage of water. "Get word to the women to have lavers ready, and douse the flames where they take," he told her, and heard her slip quietly past the leather curtain into the women's quarters, beyond the open pentagon that surrounded the great tower. When she had gone Nigel straightened, and rising to his feet gave a curt order to the man-at-arms who waited by him; then he went to the door, and jerked the curtain aside to go out. As he did so a sound of shattered glass reached him, and he swore softly; God knew how much damage would be had to their account by the old lady if she returned, as she must do.

A woman screamed. If they were all like Marjorie, calm and yet resourceful, not puddings like the Wiseman woman, not fools like Ned's trollop that he had been saddled with! God knew, when this coil was done he, Nigel, would never look on a woman again, he would make his way to Spain and fight with the Templars, all other monks being bone-idle. How Robert and he used to talk of the deeds they would do, the crusade they would one day lead, winning back the land of Christ for those who followed Him, chasing the infidel back to his own Black Stone, and beyond! And now here was Rob with a crusade on his own ground, and the Vicar of Christ his sworn foe, and Edward with the blessing of all the legions of heaven out to rid earth of the pair of them, with his shrines of St Christopher and St John and a Mass wherever he halted.

"The stores! The stores! They've fired the chapel!"

Running feet; his own; his voice calling orders. Words were such folly, he had uttered far too many of

them. Someone should have been in that chapel day
and night to prevent this very thing, this one devil-sent
contingency that could only have happened by blind
ill chance, for even an informer could not guide the
enemy's hand. Someone should have been there with
water.

Nigel roared for water. It was far too late. Before his
eyes the carefully stacked bales of wheat and flour, the
casks of oil and wine and the salted dried carcases and
powdered herbs went up in flames. The attack had
begun again on all sides, and the thunder of the pro-
pelled stones nagged at his mind and hearing. The
walls shook; it was as if the besiegers surrounding
Kildrummie knew that the heavens were with them, and
wielded their slings and engines with a greater will.
Water was brought, and brought again, by willing
running feet; there was not enough vessels to hold
even a tenth of what they would need, a deluge of
water as if the river could have been turned to their
use.

The river. A picture of the little door of escape,
downstairs, came to him. Running with sweat, his
hands and face smoke-grimed, flinging the useless jars
with their libations that only seemed to feed the flames,
Nigel thought of it, even then, for the women. Without
stores they could not last for long. Get them out . . . and
then buckle his own belt more tightly, and fight on, if
need be, till the last stone fell. Time . . . time was the
answer. How long could he hold, while the women
rode north on their way to Tain? The longer the better,
until some word could be got to the King, or to Isobel
in Norway. "God aid me now, if I may still pray to
God," thought Nigel grimly.

Once before she had seen the hurrying figures of women, cloaked against the cold. They had been leaving somewhere in haste, going nobody knew where. Now it had happened again, and in a daze she saw their faces, unnaturally pale in the light of flares, and heard the sounds of the attack outside and felt the ground quiver beneath her. No one spoke; it was not like that first time, when danger was new. No one had any bundles now; and the horses which she could see waiting, herded together by the inner wall, had been led there quietly, without fuss.

She felt herself lifted into the saddle and thrust gently ahead into the dark. Everyone was disappearing in the shadow of the great wall; the air was heavy with the reek of horseflesh and leather and the acrid smell of demolished stone. Marjorie felt her lungs fill and her eyes smart with the choking dust; she moved with the rest, conscious always of the terrible sounds above. How soon would they breach the wall? Where was Nigel?

The sudden chill of water met her and she clenched her teeth to keep them from chattering. Someone was guiding her rein; the stream rose high and deep. Other shapes, on foot and mounted, were struggling by. She did not dare speak till they had forded the stream.

"They are all across," breathed someone in thankfulness, and in the darkness she recognized Lady Seton's voice. No one had stopped them, or seen them; soon the beleaguered castle and its fury of attack had been left behind a little, so that the thunder of stones was dulled and the air smelled sweeter. Faintly, at first, among the other noises of the night, the familiar clop-

clop of hooves began to be heard. How many weary nights had she heard that sound on the way to Kildrummie, which had been their haven then!

"Are we going to Tain?" she asked, recognizing the Sheriff's wife, who rode by her. Her head was muffled in a dark hood and her eyes glanced always backwards, with an odd wary glint like those of a fox. She placed a finger against her lips now, although Marjorie had not spoken loudly. Later, when the enveloping darkness of the woods had been reached, she leaned over and whispered, as if the besiegers could still hear. "They'll not violate sanctuary," she said. "It's a long ride, but don't be afraid."

Marjorie wished to say that she was not afraid and to enquire for Nigel. How soon would he be able to escape also, through the river door, and come after them? She tried to look back to where Kildrummie stood. It was no longer visible in the thickness of the surrounding trees, but above where it ought to be the sky had a curious bright tinge, like bronze. In the end she said nothing, pressing her knees into her horse's sides to keep up with the others.

After a week of constant travelling they came to the Firth. The horses, which were those that the King had given them, were blown and exhausted; some had died. Lady Wiseman's husband had arranged for them to be met on the north shore and freshly mounted; they sat huddled together in the boat, cloaks wrapped tightly about them against the numbing wind from the sea. "If he has failed us it will be a good walk to Tain," said Mary grimly, thinking of the beasts they had left behind on the south shore.

But the Sheriff did not fail them, and mounted once again and feeling their destination near it became easier to think more clearly of what lay before them and of whether, as Lady Wiseman suggested, they should stay all winter in Tain, or whether it would not be wiser, after all, to risk the bitter North Sea crossing and take refuge with the Norwegian Queen.

"How much trouble would have been saved if we had done as I said, and gone there in the first place!" interposed Elizabeth; and for the first time in many months Marjorie hated her, thinking of Nigel in his lone defence, and of how they had had no word.

The Prior of the girth of Saint Duthac received them with not too good a grace; for a party of ladies, no matter how noble and hard pressed, must be fed. But he had them conducted courteously enough to their quarters, which although cramped were dry. That night Marjorie lay with the rest on bracken in the stone-built cell, hearing hour by hour the chant of the Office sung in the chapel above. Dead King Alexander's gifts of gold and silver to the girth were stolen away and melted now, but the reliquary containing the saint's bones was still on the high altar. King Edward was particular about never robbing a church of its relics or the lead from its roof. So Saint Duthac, who had been a bishop here in King David's time, was free still to work his miracles, which they said were many. Everyone would be up before dawn to hear Mass and ask the saint to have an eye to their safety.

"And Nigel's," thought Marjorie, "and the King's." She rose and dressed with the other women in the grey half-light, not having slept much even for weariness. She was hungry, and the meal of herbs they had had the previous evening on arrival had not been very filling. Feeling the chill hard stones of the chapel floor strike her knees, she watched the Prior say Mass. Long after it was over and the douted smoking candle-spirals stilled, the women knelt on, telling their beads. Marjorie could not assemble her thoughts to pray in the way that Bishop Wishart had told her, long ago, to do. All she could think of was the empty ache where her stomach ought to be, and how she would dearly love a meal. She stared down at the little Borderer's gift of beads, seeing the markings in the green colour of the stones, and remembering in spite of herself how James had cut her portions of his caught roasted deer, or broiled a hare in a casque together with wild garlic and all manner of flavoured plants; or cooked fish in clay; or even, once, wolf's flesh, when they had nothing else to eat and meat was scarce. It had seemed tough and tasteless at the time, but how much better it would be than nothing! She would never make a nun, she thought, kneeling here thinking of food, when the girth was filled with frightened pious women, praying. They could not believe in safety; they had been fugitives for too long. What was safety? To stay here and starve? At midday they would be issued again with a broth made of herbs, served in wooden bowls which they must rinse afterwards. The stones of the refectory would be as chilly as the chapel floor, turning her feet to ice although it was still only autumn. She had not seen a fire since that reflection in the night sky that might have come from Kildrummie, and she did not want to think of that.

"They have come," said the Sheriff's wife.

Her good placid face, that had the drawn look of hunger in these last days, turned towards the light that came through the high cell window. Above and beyond could be heard trampling of horses, and voices calling in the Gaelic.

"They were bound to find out sooner or later," said Christian Seton. "They can't harm us here."

Deliberately she folded her hands on her lap, and smiled at her son, the little Earl. Mar's eyes glanced nervously towards the window; he had a dryness of the skin these days and his nails were bitten. Sulkily, he avoided the glance of his mother and his cousin Marjorie. If this were really the English, come to take them, he would be glad. He was sick of riding back and forth across bogs and through torrents, dragged up from sleep at all hours and given bad food. It would be better in prison than here, with a lot of priests and women. Surreptitiously, his thumb went into his mouth and he began to gnaw it.

"It's Ross," said Mary Campbell, who had gone to look out. She glanced quickly at Isobel. Ross had been the King's man. Could he have come with word?

No one answered her. Christian Seton still tried to smile. The bones of each one of them had grown so bred now in fear that they could not believe any news was good until they had heard that it was not evil. When they heard would be time enough to make some sign.

After a while someone knocked at the door of the cell. It was a lay brother, his expression a mixture of curiosity and fear.

"My lady—" he addressed the Queen—"there are soldiers outside."

His hands, roughened with day-to-day work, screwed at the rope that bound his gown. Marjorie noted the small curious flicker of his eyes among the company; he seldom saw women. She was filled with a distasteful anger and was, suddenly, proud of Elizabeth, who turned her head where she sat and addressed him as he deserved.

"Soldiers are no concern of ours here," she told him in Gaelic. "This is sanctuary. Be good enough to close the door to behind you; the draught blows cold." And she bent again to the work they all were at, but her hands were trembling. The brother did as he was bid and they heard his footsteps, resentfully shuffling away.

The noise outside had not ceased. They talked resolutely among themselves, resolved to be rid of it. It was not, in any case, an affair of theirs. Marjorie felt the echo of the Queen's words sound in her mind and knew that they did so in that of everyone present, like a talisman. Sanctuary . . . the power of the spirit of God over the strength of armed men! No one would break sanctuary who feared God. Even thieves and criminals were safe on consecrated ground.

Sanctuary. . . .

The sounds outside grew louder and presently there began to be the shouting of commands over the tread of horses, and then suddenly everything ceased and they were quiet. The silence was worse than the noise had been, possessing a power that was terrifying. The Sheriff's wife, who still stood by the window, said in a low voice, "They are coming in."

"Who?"

"I cannot see if it is Ross himself. He wears his vizor. There are others with him."

They waited again while voices sounded above and suddenly a woman started whimpering. The thin, helpless sound continued softly for a while and then ceased.

The door burst open presently and a man stood on the threshold, sword in hand, vizor thrust upwards and a posse of armed men crowding behind him in the shadow of the wall. His white-lidded eyes surveyed the women blankly and without recognition; his mouth smiled.

"Come out of your warren," he said coarsely. One of the men behind him laughed, and Marjorie heard the Queen, with a crimson spot high on either cheek-bone, ask where the Prior was.

"Under guard abovestairs, and in chains soon unless I say otherwise. And there's my flighty Isobel!" His eyes sought out his sister where she sat, and an ugly look, half lechery, half triumph, appeared in them. "Fruitful sport you've had, I see, the harvest's nearly gathered. We'll see when my leather's made you smart, fair sinner, whose touch is remembered longest; mine or Ned Bruce's." Isobel screamed, and he strode over and dragged her roughly to her feet. "Stay you with me," he ordered. "The rest——" he jerked his head in contempt——"get your gear together and come on. We've a long gait to go, you and I; better it's well begun before nightfall."

"What right have you here?" said Mary Campbell. He laughed at her.

"The right of might, madam, which most agree to be a sound possession. No, wildcat——" to Isobel, who had wrenched free, replying with a blow across the face, which left her whimpering—"not you; you'll bide in Tain, though not in sanctuary." He regarded her for an instant with half-shut eyes; his closed lips were smiling. "There'll be the less laughter for you . . . come on, the rest, no more words! I didn't ride sixty miles to hear women's talk. Collect your gear, as I say; if there's one of you left in here by the next quarter-hour I'll burn the girth to ashes, and so I've told our friend above-stairs. Hurry, I say."

"We have not a great deal of gear," said Christian Seton.

Mary suddenly strode forward and spat in the Earl's face. The spittle struck him full on the mouth and he recoiled, for an instant, then wiped it off with a move-ment of his hand. "To add to my reckoning, Mary Bruce," he said smoothly.

"Reckoning? What of ours, you perjurer? Who was the King's man? Who licked Edward's shoes in secret, hoping for profit—ah, never blame my brother Ned for the stain on your own black soul! I pray that all the reward you earn is a roasting-spit in hell, and the prongs of a thousand devils stuck in your flesh!"

"Hush, my darling—hush!" Christian put her arms round Mary and tried to draw her away. "To break sanctuary!" Mary screamed, not heeding her. "Is this a man's war, or one of women and devils?" Her eyes flashed, and she heaped abuse on Ross while they all made ready.

All through the ride south Mary taunted the Earl. Marjorie heard her railing in a kind of dream, and wondered at last why their captor failed to silence her,

as he could have done by force at any time, since he had
the power. She shivered; the Earl of Ross had as much
power, it seemed, as the devil Mary had spoken of. He
had sent poor Isobel away, with a strong guard on
either side of her, to one of his own castles in the north;
Marjorie hoped that the child would be born safely, and
that the Earl would not ill-treat it, or Isobel either, now
that she had been returned to him. How dreadful to
think that he had planned such a vengeance all this
time, ever since Ned had carried Isobel off, and would
kill Ned also if he could find him! But it was by pure
ill chance that Ross had been able to capture all of them
in the girth of Tain.

She felt unreal, but there was no unreality about this
ride south; the wild weather that marked the autumn
tides continued. Tied every one against a man of the
Earl's for greater security, the women's thighs grew
raw with the long, unremitting ride. They had long
given up all attempt at appearance; their hair hung
wildly, and their skins were like leather. Most of them
were sullen now like caught animals; only Mary still
showing any fight. At night, when they were herded
together within a cordon of guards, Marjorie would
hear her voice still carping, railing. The rain beat down
on the roofs of their tents, or the barns where they
would occasionally sleep; the muttering of the guards,
that she was a witch who talked so, came occasionally.
They had grinned at first to hear Mary fly at the Earl,
but gradually they all grew to fear her, that hostile
woman, with arms thin as brown sticks, and eyes of
fire.

"Can no one make her stop?" moaned the Queen.
Her moment's dignity at St Duthac's had long de-

serted her; she was now a pitiful thing, flaccid as meal
and liable to break down into tears at the least thwart-
ing. They would all die, she said, at the hands of young
Edward; why should anyone show mercy to wretches
as powerless as they?

"For God's sake, then, if they show not mercy, let us
show courage!" blazed Isobel of Buchan. She, who had
scarcely opened her lips since parting with the King in
Lorn, rode now thin as cord, hard as flint, still with
those luminous eyes. Every vestige of her soft pretti-
ness was gone; she looked, Marjorie thought, as a saint
might do on the way to martyrdom. It was almost as
though she welcomed the coming of the end, if it
were so.

Would it be the end? Marjorie felt she scarcely
cared. Half drugged with weariness, she was glad of
the support the man-at-arms' solid back gave her. The
rancid smell of his sweaty leather jack-coat had made her
turn away at first, but now she had grown used to it.
The man himself was kindly enough, and saw that she
had water to drink and clean straw to lie on. "Like a
beast," she thought. How like animals driven to a
baiting they had all become! Even the men-at-arms had
been warned to have no speech with them; no one must
let them think that they were, or had once been,
human.

Sometimes they would pass through towns. In a
manner this was welcome, because it meant shelter for
the night, and hot food. But in another way she loathed
the journey through the streets, because of the way the
English garrisons crowded to laugh and jeer, shouting
bawdy jokes and singing snatches of songs about them.
She felt more than ever ashamed of Elizabeth at such

times, knowing that they would point out the blubbered face and slouching figure as those of King Hob's wife. And that the Scots inhabitants of the towns, clustered silently behind the interlopers, should see her too seemed worse, somehow, although they said nothing at all.

They came to Perth at last, and Marjorie saw the high wall as before, rising steeply from its moat, a long way off. She wondered what the English had done by now to Gasconhall, and then left wondering; it did not seem to matter any more. In the forefront of the party ahead of them rode eight men, mounted and bound, with their hands tied behind them and their feet secured beneath their horses' bellies in the way that Wallace's had been. That thought had been with her strongly, ever since these men had been first brought in, joining the Earl's party on its way south. One of them was Nigel, and she could see him now as he rode, light hair fallen forward over his face because he had no hand free to thrust it back. All along the way women had called out to Nigel, blowing kisses or shedding tears for him; calling him their bonny boy, their darling; even English women. He and most of the others wore linen tied over the burns they had sustained in their defence of the castle of Kildrummie, which Marjorie remembered as one other place where she had been. There had been a high narrow window framed in stone, and someone had flung a bar of red-hot iron and shattered the coloured glass with its saints' figures. . . . She could remember more of it, but she was too tired.

Perth opened its gates to receive them, and even in her

stupor of weariness Marjorie noticed the quiet streets, devoid of the elbowing throng of two winters ago. Now in the mud of the long street there echoed only the guards' tread. Everything was swept, precise, and soldierly, as if for the reception of some great personage. There were not even any swine or cattle in the streets; she caught sight of them later, penned and driven away in herds. The prisoners were led past everything towards a grey square building which seemed, from the hum of life within it, to be like a great hive of bees; and taken inside and to an upstairs chamber where a pale young man sat at a table. His short beard and curled fair hair were essenced strongly, and his linen and finger-nails scrupulously clean. As he spoke to the prisoners, Marjorie saw that he had a little ivory pick in his hand, and he would clean his nails with it as he talked, seeming to give more attention to that than to the people before him. One after the other they were brought before the young man, who would survey them once with a quick, shallow flicker of his pale-blue, rather prominent eyes. Now and again he would turn towards a gaily dressed dark man who stood by him; the dark man would bend and whisper in his ear and they would laugh together.

"The Lady Marjorie de Brus."

The voice, in the clipped polite tones of a Frenchman, recited her name flatly, pronouncing it in the older style rather than the one they all used nowadays. He had not called her Princess, but as this was Edward of Caernarvon, whom his old father had made Prince of Wales at birth after slaying the last of the rightful Welsh rulers, perhaps that was too much to be expected.

"How old are you?" said Edward of Caernarvon.

She told him, giving him no title in her answer, as he had given her none. Oddly, she felt pity for the elegant pop-eyed young man, so obviously ill at ease in his surroundings. Someone prodded her, and the guard requested her to address His Highness; she remained obstinately silent.

Edward of Caernarvon turned and said something to the man behind him. Her pity receded and dislike grew as she heard them snigger together.

"Youth and beauty! Doubt if the old man's thought up anything new . . . only one set of organs, after all, in the body. Something special for the ladies. . . ."

He stifled a yawn behind one elegant hand, motioning the guard to lead Marjorie away. "*Mon Dieu*, what a sorry procession!" she heard him say to the gaudy dark man. "Why did we trouble to come north?"

Marjorie heard their laughter again as she was led beyond the door.

IX

She had never before seen Berwick, and when they reached it she saw a wooden bridge and towers, wreathed by a broad band of silver water.

This was the town that in the great dead King's time had been called the modern Alexandria. Here goldsmiths from Italy had petitioned him to be allowed to set up their trade of setting gems in precious metal. Here the Easterlings, Johan's kinsmen, had sold their merchandise of woollen fine stuffs, and here had come the shipmasters from Wisley and Veere, trading spices from the Far East, and silks and sables and wine. They said that long before King Alexander's death, King Edward had envied the prosperous town, which vied too well with English trading ports. Having now done his worst in Berwick, washed the blood from the gutters and put out the ashes of the fires, he had built a new brash town on the ruins of the old, and put Englishmen in it.

She looked at Nigel, wondering what his thoughts were. Although they rode close on that journey south, she had not been given the opportunity to speak to him. Now and again he had smiled at her, turning his head; she could see how in the last weeks his haggard haunted look had fled, so that he seemed a boy again, fair-fleshed and comely. There was hardly a sign now of the strain of the siege, or of the fierce struggle she had heard he had put up on capture.

A ray of sunlight, filtering through cloud, outlined the bridge as they approached. Beyond it was a trellis, seen clearly against the sky; something was impaled upon it. Marjorie saw Nigel's head lift and his eyes behold the impaled object, which was a human limb. It was withered and scarcely recognizable. A murmur, a little breath of a name, went through the train of riders. She could hear it whispered above the din of hooves, as the leaves might whisper with a stirring of wind among them.

"Wallace." They raised their eyes as they passed below the place; it was a wordless salute, an instant's remembrance; for some, dedication to a like immortality. Below and around them, the river glittered brightly as swords.

Nigel was hanged at Berwick a few weeks after their

arrival. There had been time by then for word to have come from Edward; the "old man" had not renewed his ingenuity. The deaths resembled Wallace's in each detail. Seton suffered at Dumfries, his brother at Newcastle; Marjorie's two other uncles, Thomas and Alexander Bruce, who had been captured at Lochryan, were executed also. As with Wallace, the vengeance was spread over to include a number of towns. Athole was dispatched to London, to suffer there. His blood, which was noble, would ensure him a higher gallows than the patriot, who had been a poor knight's son; thirty foot of difference, for that and for the pole on which, later, his severed head would rest over London Bridge. "He's just, the King," said Sir Henry Percy comfortably to the child in his charge. "You'll see, if you watch, how no one will suffer out of proportion to what they deserve—he's strict, the King, for detail. That Lady Buchan, who did mischief of her own will, you'll see he'll punish more severely than your good aunt, whose fault lies chiefly in her being your father's sister and Seton's wife. As for the other, I can't say," said Sir Henry, recalling how Mary Campbell's name had become a byword. Indeed, they were not all as calm, these ladies, as this child now in the room with him; he'd had her brought up here, not thinking it fit that a child like that—whatever the orders might imply —should be left alone for long, as she had had to be while the execution was taking place—with the pity that the boy excited in the crowds who came to watch, they had needed all the extra guards they could get. Himself, he wasn't a vindictive man, and until definite orders came through regarding the women he would employ his own discretion as to Marjorie. A quiet little thing, she was, he decided; sitting hunched there in her corner, saying nothing, except to answer when spoken to; he liked a docile child like that, without fuss or precocious nonsense. "Why, when you were a bit of a baby King Edward sent word to put you in my charge, and bring you south to him," he said jovially. "Looks as if it would happen after all, this time, doesn't it? It's never well, I tell you, to go against the good King."

The door of the room had been stout and nailed in that place below the drawbridge where they had put her that other day. Often, as now, through Sir Henry's chatter, she would see it again, and try and put it from her mind. She had heard the crowds murmuring, high above; heard the murmur swell and grow to a roar as the cart approched, with Nigel in it. She had hammered on the door till her fists bled, screaming to them to let her out to see Nigel, to get to Nigel. But no one heard . . . and presently there had begun to come cries from the crowd, and silly high sobbing gasps from the women . . . then a long pause, and then a sudden loud cry of pity, from a thousand throats, and then stillness. She had seen nothing, nothing, only when it was all over she had knelt there looking at her hands, which were running with blood from the studded nails in the door. They were healing now, her hands.

"Hey, a cat's scratched you," said Sir Henry genially. "Or is it the frost so early? Better to keep 'em wrapped in your cloak when you ride, this sharper weather. We've a long way to go, you and me, young lady; but you won't find me an unkind gaoler, as long as there's no nonsense from your side. Understand?" He talked on, and presently sent out for wine; Marjorie took what he offered her and drank it passively, which he was glad to see, and said so; women's stomachs were prone to turn at such things as had just been, and he would warn her when the time came not to look up at the trellis over the town gate, where the young man's head was impaled beside the piece of the other rebel, whom everyone would have forgotten now in the late excitement. Ah, sooner or later the whole thing would die down . . . if only the old man were not over-vindictive. In spite of what he said, Sir Henry felt a shade of worry cross his mind at what might be the outcome of that. But no word had yet arrived.

Marjorie stared at the wine, seeing in its colour the blood run down the silver Tweed, and the head of Nigel all bloodstained, with a lock of fair hair blowing across its eyes.

x

From then on for a very long time she became as an animal who has been too long caged and lost all appearance of desire to be free. Even her instincts were abated; anger, passion, liking, weariness, sorrow, hunger and thirst. She was given food and she ate it, impartially. She covered long miles in the saddle, hardly seeing as she rode the smug fat land that was England, and the curious, inhostile stares of English folk. There were fruit trees, she noted, in blossom. It must be many months since she had seen others ripen, down the roads from sanctuary at Tain.

Isobel of Buchan did not ride with them out of Berwick. The Countess of Buchan was in a cage.

172

Marjorie had seen her, suspended high outside her tower, as they all rode under the drawbridge of the castle; there was no difficulty about such a sight; everyone was to be free to look up at Isobel, and point her out, whenever they wished. The lattices of which the cage was fashioned crossed between the Countess's body and her face, making her appear like a painted figure which has been in part mended. The eyes seemed bright and calm under her head-cloth; she did not yet seem to be feeling the disgrace of having been "hung up alive and after death, a sight to passers-by and an everlasting scorn." Marjorie remembered the slender girl with lightly curling hair who had ridden into Gasconhall that first day, and of how she herself had scorned her then as a creature of no strength.

Mary was given a cage too, at Roxburgh on the border between north and south. Gradually the party of women was growing smaller, each going separately to her own prison. Lady Wiseman and Christian were imprisoned in the north shires; for the first time Marjorie saw Christian weep at parting with her son Mar, who was to be taken south. "What has he done?" she cried. "Was he of an age to do anything but what he was bid, and where would his place have been if not with me and my husband?" Her tears flowed faster, thinking of the death of Seton and of how she would be quite alone if this befell, and then, remembering Mary, shuddered. How dreadful to thank God that her state was not *that*, to be so craven as to feel grateful that her bed would be under a roof, no matter how dark, and that she could sleep unseen! To be pinioned in the air like a crow, to have neither privacy nor shelter from the wind, scarcely to be able to stand upright to move to the privy that Edward had ordered to be built off at the side. . . . "Does his clemency allow me so much in private?" Mary had mocked, when she was shown it. "I could not mock," Christian thought. "She is of better stuff than I."

Percy was speaking now of the King's orders concerning Mar, in an endeavour to calm her. "Rest assured that no ill-treatment will come to him, for the King is kindly towards young folk," he told her, adding that Edward had given special instructions that young Mar was not to be put in chains in his prison until he had reached man's estate. "What, am I to pray that he may never grow to manhood?" demanded Christian bitterly. She was almost distraught when she left them, riding away to the east with her veil drawn over her face, and her escort by her. Mar saw her go with a few childish tears at first, and then consoled himself; he had soon ingratiated himself with the guards, whose discipline had relaxed a little now that they had crossed into England. Marjorie heard his high laughter resentfully, as though feeling stirred in her again.

Kindly towards young folk. What was in store for *her?* Days passed and nothing was said of that, and always they rode further south. Sometimes Marjorie would catch a glimpse of her step-mother's face; the Queen would not meet her eyes. Elizabeth had so far recovered herself as to feel a little ashamed of the company she was in, as if a subject of England should have no need to be riding with guards; and indeed the captain had taken pity on her, finding her a comb and pins for her hair, wine to drink of the better sort at the halts they made, and some cosmetics. She had lost the look of sagging terror that had been hers in the north;

"soon," thought Marjorie, "she will forget that she is a prisoner at all."

She was slightly ashamed of her relief when she found that the Queen was to be sent to Brustewick, with a separate household. It did not sound as though Elizabeth's imprisonment would be very rigorous; no doubt the Red Earl had had a word to say, as expected. Marjorie sensed the newly perfumed coolness of Elizabeth's cheek, in the instant's parting embrace that custom demanded. "She would no more have kissed me of her own free will than if I had been a monkey," the child told herself.

Now she was alone. They had not told her where she was to be taken, and she would not ask. The green country on either side of them grew richer and more closely wooded day by day. There were no more hills and the lack of their jagged peaks against the skyline left her with a feeling of tameness and loss. This, then, was England; Longshanks' country, that he had governed so reputably for forty-one years. They said he was a model ruler; fair-minded, courteous, able and pious. He had loved both his wives and they him.

Kindly to young folk. "His son is afraid of him." She remembered Edward of Caernarvon's prominent pale eyes. Strong sires often had feeble children, so it was said. Why should that be? Did they overshadow them with too much strength?

"My sire is strong," she thought. Suddenly, a great rush of pride rose, sweeping away the stupor and submission that had been hers since Berwick. Let them do what they would! Let them do their worst with her—cage her, flog her, put her in chains! If they never met again in life, let the King be proud of her; let her never, not for an hour or a moment, give him cause for other than pride. "I have forfeited my right to be a parent in my desire to be a king." Well, then, although they might never again be parent and child together, let them fight side by side in spirit.

"Tilting is not a lady's sport." Strange how Walter's prim young voice should sound down the years again, reminding her of so many things she had forgotten . . . of his brother Andrew, taken prisoner and, they said, coughing his life away in captivity in the north; of Bishop Wishart, whose escort they had passed on the road, bearing him in chains to Nottingham. There would be no more tilting, no more fighting, for any of them in this war.

Where was the King now, and how had he taken the news of all these captures? A great longing rose in her mind at thought of him. How did he fare, in all that great tract of country where every stone, every tree, might hide a betrayer who would strike him down? Strength of a giant, heart of a lion, he would need to fight them all.

Her hand clenched over the little hard beads she carried. She had never been pious or given greatly to prayer, but she would tell her beads, from now on, every day, and ask God to send aid to the excommunicate, her father. It was not possible to credit that God, Who was merciful, would look down on things like the cages Edward had built for women, and the scaffolds of Berwick and London and Newcastle and Dumfries, and be pleased to overlook them because Edward was the Pope's dear son. Yes, she would pray for the King, and for Uncle Ned also, that he might keep his red head out of danger. "And perhaps some day we will all meet again."

Perhaps—perhaps! As they rode further into England it seemed less likely than a dream. She stared ahead of her, thinking rather of the past than of the future, which she could not picture at all.

Part Two

THE PRISONER

I

"I TELL you she must be moved."

Sir Henry Percy's brows drew together in a harassed line, and he stared beyond the window to where the spires of York rose not far distant. Turning, for the view afforded him no satisfaction in his present state of mind, he surveyed the leech-fellow they had brought for Marjorie Bruce, who was sick. He was a queer enough kind, in Sir Henry's reckoning, and there was something not canny about his heavy white face, with its hairless chin, and the plump soft hands like a woman's. Yet there was no doubt that he knew his business, and without the sight of that tall stout figure in its long blue gown, dismounting from a mule at the Priory gates daily, Sir Henry would have been a deal more worried than he now was, and knew it. "You came in a good hour, and we're indebted to you," he went on. No need to load the leech with praise for having saved a life! It was his trade, after all—though not many practised it to any satisfaction but their own. "Not a doubt of that; but two weeks now have we tarried here, and the written order from the King's Grace states explicitly that this prisoner, the Lady Marjorie, is to be brought south to London forthwith, and placed in the Tower."

"Inside a tower or out?" said Will of the Simples. "If she is hung in a cage she will die. Even a woman in health cannot long remain so under those conditions." He thrust his lower lip out, and surveyed Sir Henry from beneath his brows. The Lieutenant restrained a little movement of assent. In his own mind was running the terms of the order that had reached him, long since, in the north, and which he had deliberately kept at the back of his mind till now; the description of the cage, which equalled in savagery both of those occupied by the Countess of Buchan and Mary Campbell, to be hung outside the Tower of London, where every barge passing and every traveller who went by would see the child, the heir of Bruce, confined there like a beast in the open. Sir Henry repressed a feeling of nausea; at times the exigencies of his sovereign would fill his mind, which was not inhuman, with this sensation, which, he reminded himself, must not be encouraged for his own sake. Two female warders had been provided; they would be sitting there now, if he knew Edward; "sober women", by his description, guaranteed to protect the unfortunate child from any access other than that of the public gaze. "Good God!" thought Sir Henry, "even the few wretched Jews in the outer court, half dead in their misery, are better off than that!"

He found himself gazing helplessly at the physician's hands. "I cannot go against my orders," he was saying. Why was he, a soldier, questioning the matter at all? What was a little rebel to him, that he should stand here in speech with—what? With a gelding, a charlatan who, because he chanced to have a lucky skill with herbs, had laid his smooth hands on the body of a child in torment and healed her with potions brewed over a fire?

"Say what you will, we ride to-morrow," he growled. "She is not so ill now."

"If you ride to-morrow, she may live till the next halt, but no longer. How will your King act then, baulked of his due prey?" The man's ingratiating silky voice and manner softened the full impact of his words; Percy listened, incredulously. "It were better that she should remain alive to greet Edward when he rides north," the leech said. "He will do so soon, do they not say that in the town?"

He moved a little nearer to the Lieutenant, using his hands and eyes to give effect to his manner. "Write, if you will be advised by me, to the Queen, Margaret of France," he said, "Does she not rule the King?" He smiled. "Women may do more by gentle means than all the armies in the world together. Say to Madame Margaret that this child is sick, that she has a heady humour of the blood that burns her flesh away, that she cries night and day for water but will take no food. Add to that that by edict of my lord the King this child, who is no higher than his hand, is to be hung in the air above all London for no crime except that she is her father's daughter, and how is that a fault of hers when she had no say in it?—and that, by the clemency of Madame Margaret, it would be better for the child's life in God were she placed in a convent. This being written and sealed from the Priory where we are, it is certain that the Queen, being merciful, or so they say. . . ."

"Peace, then, for you have too much wisdom," muttered Sir Henry. "And hold your tongue concerning it."

"She's fevered still," the voice said. It was a woman's voice, and gentle. So long now she had lain hearing

strange voices, with the blood pounding hard against
the vault of her skull in hot waves. Fever . . . and her
throat was dry, still, as it had been ever since that day
they last rode through a town, its streets heavy and
thick with yellow dust in the dry weather there had
been. But she had not thought to complain of her
throat, knowing it was no worse than those they had
often had, all of them, in the Forest of Lorn.

A forest! Had she ever gone back? The other day it
had seemed certain that she had returned and stood
watching the sunlight slant through green trees. Then
again they had been like thin upright shadows, people
walking. They passed before her eyes now; only to
open them and look was painful. Where was she?

"Where am I?" she said aloud. They did not answer,
only then or later someone came and cupped her again,
they had been doing that often. . . . She could feel the
little, sharp pain of the knife and then weakness, while
the blood drained from her.

Blood. The smell of it in her nostrils made her sick.
What was it she must not remember, something concerning blood that flowed and ran? A river. . . .

"How she cries out still!" said the woman's voice,
and a hand smoothed her forehead. Every now and
again someone would come and comb her hair, passing
a damp cloth over her face and hands and body. The
cloth was dipped in vinegar, she could smell its acrid
scent. It was cool; she wished they would come back
again.

How rough the straw was, chafing her as she lay!
She could hear it rustle as she moved. It was pain to
move, yet she had to turn to ease the weight on her
chest, which crushed her. Everything was pain, even

184

to breathe, to call. How loudly her heart beat! She could hear it, caged tightly in her breast.

"Edward has a cage for me," she thought. At the distance away she now was, she could smile. That old man and his cages . . . and his rages.

"When the wolf's dead." Why could he not die? If she died before the wolf, it would be stupid, because she was young. Perhaps the pain was not as great; there had been a time when she would have preferred to die. How strange that she had heard Will's voice just now, or thought she heard it! Will was far away, they had none of them seen or heard of him since that time in Aberdeen. He knew his limitations, the King said, and he was not a man of war. Physicians took no part in fighting, they could come and go freely between the lines. Will was a minstrel and a physician as well.

Will. How strange he had looked in the saddle, overflowing on either side of it like a great sack of flour! She wished it *had* been Will, speaking to her. What had he said? Princess, Princess . . . no one ever called her that now.

"Princess, you must not die." That had been low in her ear. Well, she was not going to die now. She was very much better. What had he dosed her with? They had put a poultice on her chest once, it smelled of dung. Leeches used foul remedies to drive out foulness. How dry her mouth was! If she called for water, perhaps someone would come.

Shadows, moving between her and the light. Someone brought the water and she drank. Soon she sank back into a drowsy slumber; through it, the voices sounded still, whether in the past or present she could not tell. Now that she was asleep she could remember what Will had said; how strange to know that it was a dream! And yet his voice in speaking to her had seemed so clear, and his touch firm and warm.

"Princess, you must not die." And she heard the name of Scotland. For a while again trouble beset her; what use could she be to Scotland? She was a woman, and women were useless even when they were brave. Nigel had been sent away to guard the women, and lost his life horribly because of it.

Scotland. All the trouble the land had known arose because a woman was to have been queen. What could she do for Scotland? Never reign, to start another war.

"Princess, you must not die, for your son will be king of Scotland." That was what Will had said in her dream. How strange that she should remember it still!

A sound of singing came, very faintly. Women's voices (was she never to be free of women?) coming from outside, from over the way. She turned, and opening her eyes saw the single window, with a trefoil wrought above, and latticed in the lower half between the panes. The walls of the cell were whitewashed, and a crucifix hung by the bed. She put out a hand and touched the wall, hesitantly, still hearing the voices. Vespers, sung at an hour when the sun was newly set. What hour was it, and was it spring or autumn? How had she come here, and how long lain, seeing nothing, knowing nobody? Fancies raced through her brain, heightened with the facility of late fever. Those shadows, the walking trees, had been nuns. Did Edward want to make her a nun also?

Later a lay-sister came in, with gruel in a bowl.

Marjorie took it, for the first time since her illness knowing what she took, and liking it. It was not bodiless, like the herb-broth had been at Tain. Perhaps this religious house was not a strict one. She looked at the lay-sister's garb, but was without strength to question her about herself. One thing she struggled to say; it had nagged in her mind, waiting to be answered.

"Where is Sir Henry Percy?" she asked. "Have they all gone?"

"How do I know?" said the lay-sister. "A great train of men went back north," and grumbling, she removed the bowl, for an invalid made more work to do. Marjorie lay and watched her, seeing her sweep the cell out with a broom of twigs and fill the earthenware jar with water, carrying it back from a well outside. Beyond the window the voices soared and ceased, and she heard steps returning. Soon they would be here, the shadow-women, and see her awake for the first time, and conscious; what would they think of her? Curiously, she turned her head to where an arm, thin as a bone, lay by the covers; it was her own, and she moved it cautiously from side to side, turning the wrist and elbow on the straw. This was her arm, and what was her face like now, and her body? Later, when she had more strength, she might see herself, reflected in the flat surface of the water, when she got up to walk.

Whatever the reason, Edward did not pursue his own edict with regard to Marjorie; possibly, on reflection, he saw that the hysterical joy with which the London populace had greeted the dismemberment of Wallace and Athole might not repeat itself now, at sight of a child in torment. It might be, alas, that he was sated. For either cause, she remained where she was, in the Priory of Walton, for eight years.

It was very cold that first winter. Lying at night in her cell, or kneeling in chapel along with the other women, Marjorie thought almost constantly of her father. There had been no news, except the confirmation, from His Holiness the Pope, that "this Robert Bruce" was excommunicate. Nevertheless, Marjorie prayed for him, telling her green beads with the stiff uncertainty of someone who finds expression difficult. It was all she could do, while she waited; that, and wondering where the King lay hid. Did the harsh rain, that she could hear beating against the convent walls, fall on him as he lay wrapped in a cloak, with a pillow, perhaps, of a stone? Once she had half-dreamed of a little boat, tossing on the grey waves, and the sound of singing. But she took little heed to any dreams that came; God knew, the King might well be in a boat, to Ireland or the Isles, or even, at last, Norway.

In truth her mind, slower to heal than the body, was still half-frozen; she could feel no poignancy for anyone. There were so many dead, and so few still living, that she had loved; one must pray for them all daily, nightly, with the green beads slipping through one's fingers. In this way nuns were made, she thought. Did Edward wish, now that his sharp desire for immediate vengeance had passed, to make one of her?

She accepted the danger and guarded against it, but without any strong revulsion. She was like a bird ice-bound to a branch, its claws lashed solid; all movement long ceased except for the small beating of the heart beneath the feathers. She scarcely felt time pass in her own reckoning, so like one day was to another; a feast of the Church, candles, singing; one or the other of the ladies' birthdays, when gifts were exchanged, but she had no money for gifts. These marked the hours that were like days, until she would remember the things, and people, that had passed as shadows rather than reality. When a storm blew, she would think of Lady Buchan in her cage, drenched and frozen; but with ever less pity, with growing acceptance of a fact that could not be altered, and would be not forgotten but meanwhile thrust aside. So many things lay in the back of her mind that she could not bear to remember them all clearly.

One of the nuns had a little brach which she carried about everywhere. She fed it on milk and bread, sweetened with honey; it never had meat, the Lady Eleanora being, herself, under a vow not to touch this. Marjorie felt sorry for the little dog, and often wished it could have an hour's benefit of a raw bone, such as the least of the hunting dogs had had in the Forest of Lorn. So much here at Walton was like that brach had become, soft and useless; whey-fleshed with lack of sun and air, flabby with lying all day in its mistress's arms, or on her lap while she told her beads. The Lady Eleanora was like several here, under half-vows; she could come and go as she would, and every now and again would disappear for a season—to a lover, the ladies whispered—and then return. That she had powerful relations Marjorie knew from that soft sibilant gossip of women that flowed everywhere here like a river. She herself

was too silent, too awkward and, from the first, too
disinterested to join it; she knew the women regarded
her as they might have done a strange fish, swimming
in clear water and watched by all, without escape or any
place of concealment. Often, therefore, they would talk
as though she were not present, without any intention
of unkindness. Indeed, she preferred that they should
ignore her rather than offer the clinging love they had
for one another, as if they were so many plants whose
roots had become entangled with closeness, till they
could not separate.

Yet the Lady Eleanora was not like these, and when
she came weeping to Marjorie one day with the little
brach in her arms red-eyed, its tongue swollen and pro-
truding blackly, its limbs twitching, she was sorry and
would have helped the foolish woman if she could.

"I think she should have meat," she suggested. The
nun's tears burst out again and she said that indeed,
indeed she would have tried even that, "but I gave
Clairette goat's whey yesterday and she vomited, and
since then has brought everything up, and I am afraid
she will die." Distractedly stroking the animal's brittle
fur, she told Marjorie why she had come; there was a
leech, she said, a learned Scottish leech, who had been
with the party of horse when it came from the north.
"He rescued you, madame, from death, so everyone
said at the time; perhaps he can save Clairette
also."

Marjorie almost smiled at the description of Will.
"But, madame, there is a war in my country, and he
may have gone back there. How do I know where to
find him?" But the Lady Eleanora protested and said
that if anyone at all could be found her kinsman Clifford

could do it, and to give her this man's description and
title and Clifford would find him with all speed.
Marjorie gave it willingly, at the same time fearing that
the little dog would be dead by the time Will was found
in any case. "But, Madame, if you should find him, beg
that I may see him also. I have headaches, and he may
perhaps give me something for them." She was surprised at her own facility in lying, as she had never had
a headache in her life; but the Lady Eleanora nodded
wisely, and said that as this Will was a eunuch there
would be no difficulty about his entering the convent.
Marjorie was aware of a new air of conspiracy about
her; the Lady Eleanora, bored with convent life, might
relish a trifle of rebellion in the bringing of news to a
prisoner.

That night she could not sleep at the thought of a
chance, however remote, of hearing news. At times
terror would beset her; supposing it was evil? No, in
that case she would have heard by now, in the same
smug manner as they had told her of the King's excommunication "because he was a murderer." Anger
rose in her; he had been absolved long ago by Wishart
for Comyn's murder, but Wishart was a prisoner now
at Edward's pleasure, and the Pope was Edward's man.
Any excommunication was for Edward's sake and not
Comyn's.

Will came, when she had long given up all hope of
seeing him. He had been found in a village thirty miles
from York. He seemed more abstracted and fidgety
than usual, bearing with him pastilles in a little bag.
He took the brach from the Lady Eleanora and carried
it over to the window; its head hung limply and its

tongue lolled. Will sponged its tongue with a lotion from a flask he carried, talking in a low voice as he did so. Marjorie hugged her knees in her corner and listened. Although Will was watching the brach he was talking to her, using the Gaelic. The other women stared blankly, but the Lady Eleanora kept her eyes downcast. "She is praying for the soul of the brach, no doubt," said Will.

Other things he said, and Marjorie listened joyfully. The tide was turning in Scotland, slowly, at last. James Douglas, who had taught her to fish, had captured Douglas Castle in Lanark while the English garrison was in church. Later he had heaped all the bodies in the cellar, pouring, oil, wine, honey, grain, and the rest of the stores over them, and set the whole alight. "They are calling it the Douglas Larder in the north," murmured Will, "and they laugh a great deal as they tell of it. But the English are not laughing."

He took a small box out of the bag he carried and opened it to disclose a scarlet ointment, with which he smeared the dog's eyes. "Tell this *bodach*," he said, "that she must feed her dog, first on broth of boiled bones. There has been a great battle won in the north, somewhere in the mountains. I do not hear very much. Feed it later on scraps of cooked offal, of an ox or sheep, and on fresh malt from a brewery. Failure to give the one or the other will render both useless. They fight as an army which is not seen, Princess, and as they withdraw they scorch the earth. The King has been across the water to Angus of the Isles, who has aided him; but he is back again on the mainland. I cannot say more. Later this dog must have meat to eat; if I can I will come again with paste for its eyes."

"These are very long prescriptions," said one of the ladies. "If he gives all this for a dog, what must it be for a woman?"

Marjorie translated the orders. The Lady Eleanora screamed, and others laughed. "Feed it on offal! And who is to cook the offal, prey?" For liver, lights and the rest were considered foul, and flung away, not being eaten even by the poorest of persons. "I think your leech is jesting with you, madame, and I would have him beaten instead of giving him silver," shrilled a haughty old nun called the Lady Hextilda. Everyone silenced her; one could not beat a leech as though he were a barber-surgeon. "He learned his craft from the Saracens," said Marjorie. "If you do as he says, the dog will be cured." But everyone cried out again at the mention of the very name of the infidel, and Will was forced to leave. The Lady Eleanora came later and said that she would give the dog meat, and the bone-broth and perhaps red wine. "But it will be hard for me to smell it, and take no part of it at all," she said plaintively. "He was a strange creature, your leech; I sent silver after him. I regret that he was not permitted leisure to cure your headaches, madame." She pressed a little box of sweetmeats on Marjorie, and took her leave. Marjorie stared down at the lid on the box, feeling in her mind a half-forgotten stirring of joy, like shoots upthrusting from deep in the spring earth.

She suffered less in body than Lady Buchan or even Wishart. She lay in no dungeon and was fettered by no chains. Often, especially in the later days of her imprisonment, she was permitted to ride out, closely guarded on either side by the ladies, or by the Prior of

Walton's men, or the Bishop of York's. Both these dignitaries interested themselves in her, and she knew that the answers she made to them, and the deportment she observed at such interviews, were duly noted down and sent in report to old King Edward, who was lying ill of his dysentery at Carlisle. As the season progressed, she felt a tightening of discipline towards herself; could this be because they had suspected she had news from the north? Later she was convinced that this was so, and that the strict times, when she was brought meals in her cell and not allowed to mingle with the other ladies even at Mass, were by reason of the nearness of the Court, which might come to York.

She did not care very greatly, being occupied with the changes in her own mind and body at that season. Since Will had come she had felt a great lightening of the blackness that had been with her after Nigel's death, and with that new awakening, the hope that was almost certainty, came her own change, the end of childhood. She was not sorry to leave it behind, nor was she glad that she had left it; she accepted this, as everything else, without question, although the sisters fussed round her with advice about the drinking of raspberry leaf infusion to dull pain. The closeness of the earlier life among women in the Forest of Lorn had left her with few illusions, and no curiosity. She was more interested in news of old Edward, whose least move in the direction of the north sent everyone here into a flutter; sometimes he and his first queen, Eleanor of Castile, had visited the shrine at Walton, and now that Eleanor was dead and he had married the young French Margaret (who was said to be pious also) they might visit likewise.

Marjorie felt a little thrill of fear at the thought that Longshanks might see her. Once, in the surface of the Convent's flat well, she had caught sight of her reflection. It was not that of a child any more, and she felt afraid, remembering the instructions about Donald Mar and how he was to be put in chains when he was a man. Would Edward, now, remembering the first white heat of his rage in this new flare from the north, order her to be caged, now that she was a woman?

"If I was brave, like Isobel," she thought, "I would welcome it." She let no one know of her fear. Mingled with it was a great curiosity to see him, this old man, who could inspire such awe by his personality that its decisions were awaited with tremulous obedience by women fifty miles distant.

When he came, however, she was not asked to appear before him. He rode in suddenly, so there were few preparations. It was early morning; Marjorie heard, in the courtyard below her cell, the clatter of horsemen, and when she rose to look out there were the two standards of Saints Christopher and John, left by their bearers while the King was in church; and by them the English leopards, gaudy against the pale sun. "When he is in York Minster they will bear these after him before the high altar when he hears Mass," Marjorie thought, "and everything will be a blaze of bright banners and gilded crosses and painted glass." Then she remembered the gold and silver, the gems and sacred embroidery and the irreplaceable manuscripts of Scotland that Edward had filched and taken south, as well as the crowning regalia and the stone that was said to have been Jacob's pillow, and she felt ashamed of her almost wistful curiosity to see him in his splendour, here in his own kingdom, his rich England that he ruled so well. She was not English; she only sojourned here, and not of her own will. Nevertheless, she knew she would not close her eyes to avoid the sight of Edward should he pass below.

Presently the chapel doors poured soldiery, who lined a way among the nuns. The Prior was there, Marjorie saw; he wore a furred velvet cape against the cold. He came bowing low, with his back to her where she stood at the window; and presently, with some ladies alongside it, a litter came out. It was open, and as it passed with its occupant below, borne by four bearers, Marjorie could see a long old man lying there. His hair was white, which testified as to his age; but his face was smooth and the eyes, which searched the little crowd about him, intensely blue as a youth's. She could see their colour from where she stood; presently, as though he knew her window, Edward looked up and saw her.

Their eyes met, only for an instant as he passed below; she discerned a glint of shrewdness in them. He did not look unkindly, this young-old man, who was a lawyer and devised savage deaths. The memory of Wallace rose in her, and of her father; and Nigel, whose head this old man had posted on a bridge. More would have come crowding, but there was no time. She stood erect, giving Edward glance for glance; the lattices of the window, she knew, would conceal a part of her face from him, but he must see her eyes. "They are grey, like Father's," she thought. Did he remember, did he feel, Edward of England, for an instant, that he was looking again into young Carrick's eyes long ago at

Westminster? Whatever he thought, he made scarcely a sign; only, with one long hand raised, a fraction, from his cushions, sketched the beginnings of an acknowledgment, a recognition.

The litter and the throng passed on; Marjorie found herself trembling. Whether it was with hatred, reproach, wrong, surprise, or fear, she did not know. But she had seen that old man now, and he would die soon. She need not be afraid of him much longer. If he could no longer ride his horse, if he lay passive like a woman in a litter, he would soon die. It had been a sign that she would acknowledge to God, that sight of him.

"When the Wolf's dead. . . ." Ah, let the turning tide gather strength!

III

Will had not come again. Perhaps he felt it was unsafe, both for himself and her. No one came, and she began to sink again into the slough of denial, of acceptance. Captives became so, she knew, when all outer access was denied. She heard of no one and nothing now, saw nothing that was not England. The nuns' black and white made unchanging patterns. Often she would see them in her dreams, the pattern of kneeling, of praying, of asking blessing before meat. Sometimes dreaming became inseparable from reality, so that again, as on that night in the forest, she was behind a curtain, watching the circle of light from where she stood. She did not care for them here, or they for her; they were kind enough, but it would have mattered very little if they had been harsh. They were a strange orthodox, placid yet thorough, stupid though shrewd, patronizing, kindly, alien people, these English; she had nothing in common with them.

Sounds also were part of the routine, prescribed and accepted from hour to hour, and day to day; as prime, terce, nones. Rough voices and jarring notes were not heard; everything was gentle, even the soldiery who came with old Edward had kept their voices correctly low. She had not heard a minstrel, or a man's deep laughter or shouting, since she came south. Gradually she ceased to miss them, taking the sexless plainchant of the choir's song as background, half-heeded, to her thoughts.

Spring came, then summer. She had been at Walton since All Souls' Eve in 1306. The old nun Hextilda had sent for her one day and told her that, by order of the Prior received first from *nostre seigneur le roi*, she was to be allowed threepence a day for expenses and one merk yearly for dress. Marjorie heard the news without interest; she had no experience of money. "It will mean that we cannot provide meat for you every day but one," said the old nun crossly.

She did not starve, being allowed to eat her fill of herbs, eggs, and the rye bread that the nuns baked themselves. Sometimes the Prior or the Sheriff of York would send a gift of fish to the convent, or venison. The ladies were well known for their exquisite embroidery, but Marjorie discovered no talent in herself for this; indeed, she had no talent for anything. She was set a task of spinning, which she now did well enough; it was easy to let one's thoughts run on while the wheel spun, and spun, and the foot rocked as though it were a cradle, and the flax from the Priory field slid smoothly through one's fingers. She wondered what the Lady Egidia did now, and if she still had leisure to spin. "She also tried to teach me to sew, and read, and failed."

One day when she was spinning the sound of the wheel came unnaturally loud, and remembering it later she knew that it must have been by reason of the silence in the house, but she spun on. It had become second nature to her, the foot on the wheel thrusting, the hand feeding the flax. She could feel a little less useless when she was spinning, and so the wheel turned, turned . . . now, in the afternoon silence, while the July sun shone in at the window.

A little knocking came with the wheel, a little sound that was not always there. She heard it, at first, uncertainly, then louder; perhaps the wheel needed oil. Then it came to her that the sound was in fact a tinkling, a faint echo of metal on metal, like the hammer on an anvil, of a bell. It struck when the wheel turned round, there was a place on the spinning-frame that corresponded to the striking of a bell.

Released from her foot's pressure, the wheel whirred and cascaded into silence. The bell chimed on. It was far away, deeper than she had thought. Presently there came another, near at hand. Then the great bell of York Minster took up the chime, and she heard their own chapel bell ringing, ringing. All the world seemed made of bells, tolling and calling their news across the shires. The burden would be taken up from valley to valley, across towns and rivers, faster than a man could ride, until it reached Scotland. But above all she could still hear the deep bell of York, the passing bell.

Marjorie rose and went to the window, flinging the shutter wide to hear the full-voiced bells. Below, there was a pattern of black-and-white figures hurrying towards the chapel. She reached for her cloak and flung it about her, with the hood over her head, and went down. Wide open as the chapel doors always stood, she could see before she entered the dark bowed shapes of women, praying.

In less than an hour the Prior came, having told the news first to the brothers in his own care. Marjorie saw his stout flushed face as he hurried his obeisances before the altar; portentous news, the heat of the day, and his furred robe were too much. He rose and turned to the congregation of kneeling women and spread out his arms in a wide gesture. "Mesdames, our sovereign lord the great good King is dead. He died on his way into Scotland, at Burgh-on-Sands, yesterday, the seventh of July, with the full rites of Holy Church. I await news by letter, which shall be brought to you whensoever it comes. Meantime I ask you all to pray for the repose of soul of our late sovereign lord, Edward."

All night she lay awake, seeing the heat-mist curl in little wreaths above the stone of the floor. When her eyes closed they could still see the bright oblong that the sun had made that morning, barred with darkness where the lattices came. Edward was dead, at whom she had stared with grey eyes above the lattice, and who had saluted her. The wolf was dead, who had savaged Wallace, Nigel, the others, and had mauled her father's land. To-night a messenger from the Prior had come, bearing news which had been hastily sent, no one said from whom; news of how Edward, when he lay dying, had sent for his son (how little she could remember of young Edward of Caernarvon now!) and had bidden him swear on the relics of his saints that when he, the King, was dead, they should boil his body until the flesh left the bones, and tie the bones in ox's hide, and bear them before the English army whenever it crossed into Scottish soil, in order that they might conquer under his banner. Would the old man with sardonic blue eyes have said anything of that kind? How quickly everyone put words into the mouth of the dead!

Eleanora had spoken of it, showing more sense than was her wont. "Be advised that, if it is true, the old King was in a delirium when he uttered it," she said flatly. "And young Edward—the King now—is incapable of any such gruesomeness; mark you me, he will turn and bear the body back to London, in as much state as may be, doubtless, but with false jewels on it.'

And that was, as they heard later, what came to pass; and to the sound of the singing of *De Profundis* from every chapel in his land, Edward the crusader, the lawyer, the oppressor, the wolf; great soldier, hated enemy, husband beloved of two women, King with honour in his own land more marked for the stain on it elsewhere, was brought south again, to Westminster, there to lie in open state, in a red silk tunic, a white silk stole, embellished with coloured glass, and his crown. The living Edward, Edward of Caernarvon of the yellow curled beard, Edward the Second, was king.

IV

One vow the new King had indeed made at his father's deathbed was fulfilled in the year of his accession. He had been betrothed for some time to Isabelle of France, who was the niece of the present widowed Queen, his step-mother. As soon as immediate matters were settled at home he crossed seas, there to wed the little Princess, who was only twelve. Stories of the child-bride's beauty filtered north, and the ladies at Walton had a newer cause for gossip still. Some months after the old King's death an altar-cloth, embroidered with twisting grapes by the Dowager Queen's own hands, reached them. It was a thank-offering from Margaret for the hospitality shown her husband on his last ride north; in her widowhood, she would remember most intensely the shrines which he had last visited, and the rest of her life would be devoted to such remembrance—of his will, of his commands, of his person. "When Edward died," she was described as saying, "all men died for me."

Marjorie, again in her fortress of detachment now that Edward the First was more than a year dead, was inclined to scoff at this. What sort of a young girl of seventeen could have tumbled so headlong in love with an old man of sixty—even that young-old man in the litter—that she could live out her whole life in memory of him? She watched the nuns' preparations and excitement listlessly. What if the altar-cloth meant that Margaret was indeed coming north? A court at York might well be at Samarkand for all she, the prisoner, would know of it. She could scarcely recall having seen

Queen Margaret on the last royal visit, although she had been riding by the litter. "I, too, was ravished by the sight of old Edward and had eyes for no one else," she thought wryly.

Margaret of France came north, and tales of her pious conduct at the shrines of Saints Thomas and John, and of Our Lady at Peterborough, and in the other great cathedrals in the manner of her predecessor, Eleanor, were related at the ladies' table. Ale had been brought in, in case the Queen should wish to refresh herself; a chamber prepared, in case—no plans were ever definite—she might wish to stay a night with them. A pleasant, easy, hospitable place, this convent of Walton; no harsh rule, no forbidding vows restricted its inmates; Margaret would be welcome here as she might be in an inn.

Marjorie watched the preparations in hall and kitchen and chapel. It was summer again and the great rich flowers of the Priory garden were in full bloom; large-headed roses, blush-colour, red and crimson and white, and larkspur and irises and the giant daisies of the Queen's name, whose yellow eyes shone in the light of altar-candles where the flowers had been massed. The scent was heady in her nostrils, reminding her of free summers at Dundonald in the sound of Egidia's bees. How long ago that was, and did they—Egidia and the others—ever think of her at all and picture her, kneeling here because she wanted to stare at the flowers? And yet how foolish to picture on her own account the family at Dundonald as unchanged, when Andrew and Walter must be grown men now and the others almost old enough to leave home; the boys to squiredom, the girls to marry. And Egidia's hair would be all grey and there would be lines about her eyes with crinkling them to see her seam by lamplight. A tremor of fear took Marjorie. Did she want to see Dundonald again, and find it changed?

That evening, after supper, the door of Marjorie's cell opened and there entered a lady in white, which was the French mourning. A young girl was with her, but Marjorie scarcely noticed her at first, although she was the more beautiful. The lady was not so, but the expression of her face was sweet and calm, so that one had an impression of beauty. Her eyes were the colour of speedwells and full of sadness; Marjorie felt as if the statue of a saint had come to life. The lady kissed her, and she could smell the fine herbs with which her linen was scented. She drew forward the girl, who was staring at Marjorie.

"This is my daughter," she said simply.

Marjorie stared at Isabelle of France, feeling brusque and ungracious. She was not used to kisses, and the French girl, who was younger and more self-possessed than she, had exquisite clothes. Marjorie stared in her turn; it had not occurred to her to notice dress before, in the days of the Lady Elizabeth in Scotland she had been too young to heed them. Now she felt acutely conscious of her shabby russet gown and patched shoes, and her woollen hose and plain coarse linen and even— such condemnation for every detail was in Isabelle's gaze—her forefinger, roughened with spinning flax, and a nail that had broken.

Isabelle was enchanting. A riding dress of grass-green camlet clung to her elegant child's figure, flaring out above the hips to a wide skirt slit, in the fashionable manner, from hem to knee, showing the under-skirt, edged like the sleeves with marten fur. Her tiny gloves were of embroidered white kid; one hand grasped a jewelled whip, in the design of a serpent's head on gold. Isabelle smiled mechanically and played with the whip so that the serpent's eye, which was a ruby, glinted balefully; she was very bored, one could see, with the company and her surroundings, and with her pious young aunt, and with England. Watching her, Marjorie felt scraps of unheeded, half-heard gossip rise and float forward in her mind. Isabelle of France . . . Piers Gaveston! The girl whom the King had wedded and ought to love, and the man he loved above all other men, and above all women. Gaveston had taken the little Queen's salt-cellars, even her jewels ("but he left her the serpent") thought Marjorie. Gaveston had got Edward back under his thumb as he had been before the old King in his life time banished him from the realm. But young Edward had lost no time in recalling Gaveston and he had been waiting on the quay for the bridegroom and bride when they landed from France, and Edward in a transport of joy had kissed him passionately, and flung the French King's own bride-gift of a jewelled chain about his neck, taking it from his own, while the new Queen looked on.

"That is hard to understand, because she is very beautiful," thought Marjorie. Yet the French child's oval face, with its red curved smiling mouth, seemed predatory and greedy, like a young wolf's. Edward of Caernarvon had been sired and then wedded by wolves.

"Why does the Scottish prisoner stare so?" asked Isabelle. Her glance travelled over Marjorie idly, as though she found her amusing for a moment, as a dwarf or a monster at a fair might be. She spoke with a precise accent that made the broad Norman French of these parts seem slurred; the tiny consonants hissed like little snakes. Marjorie hid her own hands behind her back, feeling them too large. An exquisite, cruel little animal, this new Queen of England.

Isabelle pouted now, as her stepmother chided her. "If you did not have fine clothes you would also want to stare at those who do," she said in French. "We cannot all be fortunate." Turning to Marjorie with her sweet courteous smile, she asked her if she was happy at Walton. Marjorie, torn between bewilderment at the posturing of Isabelle, who had flung away, and the phenomenon of the Dowager Queen's smile, which left her eyes sad and her mouth merry, stammered in reply.

"I wait, madame, to go home." She felt her colour rise. Isabelle, in the background, grimaced a little, she was certain, at her accent. "I am glad that I amuse her," she thought.

"Poor child, what home have you to go to?" said Margaret gently. "The lands you would have had are forfeit to the Crown."

She began to talk to Marjorie in her friendly, gentle way. The two little girls who had been the daughters of Llewelyn and David, the last Welsh princes, had taken the veil quite lately, she said, in their convent near Glastonbury. "They are happy to do so, because they have been all their lives in that convent, and have their friends there," said the Dowager Queen. Her hands, in the long white widow's cuffs, moved a little in her anxiety to speak with persuasion. "It is a cruel world for such women, who have—and I say this to you, my little one, without disguising it, like a purge wrapped in jam, for you are too old for that—who have nowhere to go, as a result of war."

Marjorie clenched her hands behind her back. "King Edward conquered Wales, it is true. He has not yet conquered Scotland, madame." Despite the gentleness of the Dowager's speech, she felt some fear in thus addressing her. No doubt she had loved the old wolf, her dead lord, so well that even the suggestion that his will might yet fail would seem like impertinence. She felt the colour ebb and recede in her cheeks; behind her back, her hands grasped one another tightly.

"Not yet," said Margaret, and smiled a little. "But he left those behind him who will do his will—and—" her gaze strayed towards the window, where the young Queen was looking down into the courtyard, still toying with her whip—"I know well what I am saying, for it comes from my son the King. What hope can a handful of men have, before the great army that he has raised? He will march north, as my dear husband hoped to do, and when in Scotland he will carry out his father's wishes and never rest till they are accomplished."

Her eyes shone and her voice was hushed as though in prayer. Marjorie remembered that this was the woman who had sat in Stirling town and watched, for a diversion, her husband's shooting of the Wolf of War at the surrendered castle, so that the stones shattered the window-glass in the house where she was. A sudden revulsion rose in her. Let this praying widow kneel at her dead shrine! Old Edward had been God to her, anything he did being perfect in her sight. "If she'd been given Berwick to watch as ploy, either the sack in my father's youth or the massacre in mine, she might have thought less of his godhead." But Margaret must have ridden over London Bridge many times.

Memory of that made Marjorie close her eyes for an instant; she heard her own voice speaking a long way off. "And if this army, that King Edward will take north, should be defeated, madame, what then? Will not my father send for me?"

Isabelle of France was laughing, over by the window. The light shone on her gleaming hair; everything about her was sleek and gleaming, like the coat of a young animal. She laughed on, shrilly, showing white pointed teeth. The sound cut through what Marjorie was saying.

"*Tais-toi, Isabelle,*" said the Dowager Queen. Placidly, she turned to Marjorie again. "You are very young, and you love your father," she said, "and so I will say no more now. The King will not force you to take the veil. But if at a later time you should find that perhaps the world will be cruel, remember what I have said to-day; there is a place here." She rose from the bench where she had been sitting, and extended her hand in a gracious gesture. Marjorie shook her head; she would not kiss the hand. Strength, unexpected after her late fear, rose in her.

"The world is a cruel place, madame, I have no doubt. That is the fault of those who were put into it. There are some for whom the veil would be welcome, but I am not so minded. One day I am certain that the King, my father, will send for me. If I use your chapels at all, it is to pray for his victory, and if they make me take the veil I will pray even more."

She scowled, seeing with fierce exultation the gentle widow's astonishment, and a gleam in Isabelle's eyes.

Whether the gleam was one of amusement or surprise she did not know; the little wolf—why had she so quickly fastened on the description of a wolf?—lowered her gaze as she preceded the Dowager Queen out of the cell. Margaret lingered for a moment, as if hesitant about what next to say; she was as unsophisticated as a very young girl, having been ruled in all things by her husband.

"I cannot join you in your prayers," she said gently. "May there come a day when we can all pray as one!"

She raised her hand in farewell, and went out. Marjorie stood staring at the closed door, not saying a word when the lay-sister came, in a little while, to make all ready for night. How swiftly one could love and hate, and how she would remember the two Queens in such love and hate for the rest of her life, even though she never saw them again!

She never did see them again. The rest of the time passed in waiting. But once in the night came news that brought a trickle of fear to the conquerors, a shaken complacency.

"Edward Bruce is at Durham. They say the town may not hold."

Marjorie heard of it incredulously, wondering if she dreamed still. Uncle Ned at *Durham*? Uncle Ned, the fugitive, due soon, if things went as they had done, to join Nigel, Thomas and Alexander, in a grim reason for coming south? But now everyone spoke as if he were a commander, not a fugitive, and leading ordered men, not savages mad from hunger and undisciplined from fear. Uncle Ned at Durham with an army, and his red head still on his shoulders! What other things had happened in the north? Was it indeed true that what Will had hinted to her, four or five years ago now, was coming true, and that a handful of men without a fortress or a yard of land to call their own had indeed won back a country from the enemy?

"If they were not sure of themselves in the north, they would never attack here," she thought. It was not that Uncle Ned would be afraid, but her father would never let him do so unless . . . unless they were on the way to victory! She began to turn over in her mind little things she had heard, scraps of information from Will and, sometimes years old, from the pedlars that came. It was so hard to be certain, buried here, listening to women's talk.

"The Scots have burned Chester-le-Street, they say. It was pitiable to see the burning roofs and hear the women screaming. Savages! Surely God will not suffer the sight of a peaceful country invaded long. . . ."

"How dreadful the war is!" sighed the Lady Eleanora. Everyone began to speculate on what gear to take away with them when—if—would the Scots march as far as York? If that, the capital of the north country, fell, matters would be bad indeed. Marjorie thought of another night, seven years ago now, and of a handful of frightened women bundled out under the cold stars, to ride no one knew whither. Had it indeed come to the reckoning now, with the hunters hunted, and herself a prize to be gained, not a fugitive to be hidden? Would Uncle Ned come and rescue her? For nights she dreamed of it, lived through the days in hope of it, hearing of the ravaged country, seeing the poor folk who had lost their homes flock in to the safer walls of Walton Priory, further away from the place of war.

But he did not come, and after a while hope died when she heard that the Scots had withdrawn after doing much damage and made their way again north. She felt her heart go with them, and it was hard not to rebel against the continued confinement, the slow return to the calm days. So much must be afoot now in her father's country, and she could do nothing but wait and wait. But it was good to know that the time of waiting would not be for ever . . . could not be, with that brave banner still flourishing beneath the sun!

Interlude

BANNOCKBURN, 1314

ON the twenty-fourth of June, two armies met in the north. One was of the chivalry of England, three thousand strong, with its King at their head and twenty thousand of infantry following with stores and equipment. They had marched north to put an end to a guerrilla band which had been making a constant nuisance of itself for the past eight years. They were in no doubt of the outcome. By all the laws which govern the dominion of man over man, and of mounted troops over foot troops, they should win.

The weather was very hot. Among the wooded parts of a district near Stirling, in sight of the Castle which, occupied by its English garrison, rose steeply from the plain, was the other army. Chief among its numbers was James Douglas, of daring remembrance in Lorn and often since; and Randolph, who had been for England but returned now, to fight for the King of Scots. (Already he had surprised Edinburgh Castle by scaling its Rock by night, breaching the wall with a man's body, and taking the place with a few followers. To him was due in a great measure what followed now.) Then there was Walter Stewart, who as a young man had no very famous exploit to his name, but he could fight bravely: and Edward Bruce, the King's brother, who commanded the other division. Leader of all was the King, who rode a small grey horse; there were so many tales told of him by then that no one stood out more than another, but perhaps the best remembered

was his taking of the fortress of Perth, leading the
foray by night himself, neck-deep in the moat's icy
water. But no man on this day would be remembered
for any single deed, as all were to fight as one.

The King sighted the invading army himself where
he sat on his horse by an eminence; a clear shining, seen
between trees. That first day there was an action, and
Randolph's Scots on foot defeated Edward's knights
on horseback; this in itself was an unheard-of thing.
All night the two armies lay and waited, the English
already in fear, the Scots ready; during the hours of
darkness the King himself went round the divisions,
rallying the men and speaking to them; his orders were
clear and, when the fight came, remembered by them.

At dawn the Scots attacked. They advanced steadily
across the intervening plain, and when they were in
clear view every man knelt on the field. "They are
asking mercy," said Edward of England. "They are,"
replied Umfraville, his knight, "but not from you. I
tell you certainly, those men will win or perish."

The Scots said a Paternoster and then rose to
advance. They met the fire of the English archers;
presently the cavalry, sent in by the King on the right
hand, charged and scattered these. Gloucester, the
nephew of the English King, rode into the battle and
was killed instantly; the Scots formations were unbroken and remained so, and the English van under
Hereford was mown down.

The Scots archers fired then from their slope above
the field. Out of the wood came the King, leading his
division. Under the pressure of the steady Scots
advance the English horsemen, driven over a steep gorge,
fell; men and horses were pinned helplessly, crushed

by their armour and by the men above. Out of the wood
now came a little medley of folk, bearing banners of
blankets; it was the untrained infantry, the cooks and
scullions, those who had joined King Robert without
arms and scarcely knew how to fight. The banners
waved, and the English saw another division, and fled.
Among the fugitives was King Edward, borne along
forcibly by his two knights, Pembroke and Argentine.
He was almost taken, the Scots clinging to his horse.
There were many other prisoners. Among them was
the Earl of Hereford, the Constable of England. Later,
after the spoils had been divided and King Edward's
missing seal returned, and Gloucester's body prepared
for an honourable journey back home, terms were
discussed for an exchange of prisoners. The wife of
Hereford was given fifteen Scots to offer for the release
of her husband. They included the wife of King Robert
and his daughter Marjorie.

Part Three

A SEASON OF SUMMER

I

QUEEN ELIZABETH heard the order for her release with uncertain feelings. After so many years in England it was to be expected, she told herself, that her outlook should have altered; acceptance, perhaps, of one's state was inevitable, and who would have expected this news of a victory of the Scots, which had cast into confusion even those more acquainted with the progress of events than she? "I declare to you all, that if our lord the King and his army of near thirty thousand were taken so by surprise at this place called Bannockburn, what should I be?" she said plaintively to Eleanor Edgar, her waiting-woman, as they hurried to collect the gear for her ride north. To Eleanor's smiled reply she felt a sudden, half-remembered jerk of guilt; "our lord the King" had, from long habit, been the young King Edward, but should *she*, now that the positions were so reversed, not have recalled in time that her own husband Robert was, by his personal exertions, ruler of Scotland, and hesitated so to lay emphasis on English overlordship?

"Our sovereign lord"—that was what she had to write to Edward's old father, years ago in the days back at Brustewick when she had had to beg for clothing, a bed even, and money to pay her servants, who were blowing resentfully on their chilblained fingers that first winter, when she was unable to provide them with a fire. Ah, that had been misery . . . but *nostre seigneur le roi* dying just then, it was allowable that young

221

Edward had seen to her comfort immediately, and Barking Abbey and later Rochester, to which she had been transferred, had been quite delightful, with every comfort she could desire, and amusing company. So now . . .

The blue eyes sought out the pleasant English countryside beyond the window. For a moment, unbidden, a shadow of fear crossed the Queen's mind for change, which had come to them all, even to herself, safe here; and how much more, God knew, in the north? What would he be like now, that strange man whom she had married? "If I ever knew him, that was long ago, and he had altered even before we parted company," she thought. Memories of the young, golden Robert stirred her, idly, as a glimpsed portrait of one long dead might do. Would they know one another when they met? If not . . . and even if so . . .

The child Marjorie was his heir. For the first time thanking God for the existence of Marjorie, Elizabeth remembered that she must be no longer a child. How old would Marjorie be now? Nineteen, twenty?

"They can marry her to a man of their own, if all that time in Walton Priory has not made a nun of her," she thought. Remembering the instructions that had come by way of Sir John de Bentley, who had charge of her household, Elizabeth reflected that she would be able to see what change, if any, had taken place in the other captives when they all met at Berwick. How many were left now? Mary Campbell, she had heard, had been released early on, in exchange for an English knight, Sir Richard de Mowbray. The Countess of Buchan had died in Berwick, after four years in the cage on that tower. Young Mar would have grown beyond all recognition; she had heard that he was in much demand with King Edward and his favourite, Piers Gaveston, and was seen everywhere with them. Elizabeth grimaced; no doubt Mar would be as unwilling to return as she, to that chilly bleak land that Robert had fought nine years to win. Her mind still turned over and digested the unexpected, incredible news of the victory, in the manner of one who has heard what is too stupendous for immediate belief, upsetting every standard previously known.

Riding into Berwick as night fell, she beheld a little group of men and women waiting on horseback in the orange light of torches that flared high against the dusk. They watched Elizabeth ride in, and she felt, suddenly, that the tinkle of her bridle-bells was too loud; a tinny, frivolous jangling, out of tune with this meeting "as I," she thought, "am out of tune." She composed her face to smile as her company drew to a standstill, making a circle about the little group which waited, stiffly, with faces turned towards her seeming pale in the dusk.

Cheeks were kissed, courteously; greetings exchanged. They would lodge for the night in the Governor's Castle, where a supper would be given in their honour and in that of the Earl of Hereford, for whom they were to be traded. The Queen looked among the company for Hereford, whom she knew; he was older, paler, she thought, and his mouth was set. What manner of battle had this been with so much slaughter? They said the Earl of Gloucester's body was to be brought south with all honour.

Others she knew, often after a moment's striving. That youth, stouter now and richly dressed, must be

Mar; his mouth had the sullen pout it used to have when some matter did not please him. He was complaining loudly to the tall young man beside him about the fleas in the inn-beds he had had to sleep in on the way. "And worse to come, most like," he chafed. The tall young man, whose hair beneath the casque he wore showed squarely in a gleam of dark gold, did not answer. His eyes were fixed on one of the other riders, a young girl who sat apart, saying nothing. She wore a blue riding-gown; Elizabeth scanned her profile, seeing in it some matter vaguely familiar. The girl turned her head, and a pair of grey eyes met the Queen's squarely. She did not smile, and Elizabeth dropped her own.

Marjorie had altered so little, she thought, with a little flicker of spite . . . and yet so much! She had grown, of course, although she would never be very tall. The dark hair still sat on her shoulders in the stubborn short curls that grew unruly without a hood to cover them. She appeared remote from everything, even the young man's gaze—who *was* the young man, thought Elizabeth?—and yet there was an unnamable, almost tense quality about her, as though she saw all. She was . . . yes, impossible still! "To have to present such a one as one's step-daughter will serve no purpose except to give away one's own age." Elizabeth felt her old frivolous thoughts arise to the surface, released, like bubbles on the turning of a stone beneath water.

She turned to her escort and asked to be informed who the tall young man was. Later, when they were all in the Governor's hall, he was led forward and presented to her as Walter, the High Steward of Scotland. Elizabeth smiled down at his bent head, allowing him her hand to kiss as he knelt to her; behind the smile her brain raced. High Steward of Scotland!—so grand a title for one who was, after all, only a boy . . . how absurd! She enquired for his father, James, the High Steward; he must, if the title had devolved, be dead.

"That is so, my sire's death befell five years since, and my mother's. And my elder brother Andrew died in prison, so I am now the head of our house."

He spoke with a becoming gravity, she thought. "But I wager he is not always so grave." She essayed a jest with him, and the sudden gaiety of his smile flashed out, showing white teeth, as he answered readily. This was too fair a falcon for Marjorie to fly! Without turning her head, Elizabeth knew that the girl sat further down the table, silent, picking at her meat. Did she not rejoice to be free? "Is there any one of us desires to leave England?" Elizabeth thought, her success with young Walter and the warmth brought to her blood by the ale which had been ordered, in its barrel, especially for her delectation, making her laughter rise; banishing for a while the fear she had of that meeting which was to come.

But then they led an old man into the hall. With a sense of sudden terror Elizabeth saw that he was blind. They led him with a guide on either hand, taking his arms and assisting him to the place on the dais where he was to sit. He raised his white head towards the rafters as he came, as if they were the sky and he sought light there. His eyes were filmed over like milk. This was Wishart, the Bishop of Glasgow, freed after many years' imprisonment in Nottingham Castle. His wrists still showed the scars of the chains.

But he spoke cheerfully and blessed them. Elizabeth

heard his voice asking for one and another, out of his darkness that could not tell who was here and who was not. Where was Lady Buchan, he asked? And the Lady Mary, where was she?

Sudden anger took Elizabeth. It should have been *she* who had been sent for at the first exchange, not Mary Campbell who was nothing but the sister of the —of the King, as she must accustom herself to hear Robert called! Why, it was an open insult to herself, an admission that she and he were no longer man and wife, that she was nothing to him. . . .

"A brave lady," said the old blind man quietly, and made the sign of the cross.

Marjorie heard the talk of young Mar and the Earl of Hereford, beside her at the board. They did not include her in the talk, and she cared nothing for that; it was strange to be out in the open again, after so many years not to feel walls closing one in.

How loud the voices seemed! Presently, when they were full of wine, they would laugh loudly. She had not heard loud laughter, man's laughter, since she was a child. Since then it had been all soft murmurings, the dry sound of rosary beads slipping, slipping; talk, low and decorous, at meals; talk about small things. And the meals themselves had been frugal; particularly for one who, like herself, had been on that allowance of threepence a day, the waste at this board seemed prodigious, it was so long now since she had touched so much meat that she had to leave it on the platter half-tasted.

"They say it was as much grief to your leader as to ours, the death of young Gloucester," the Earl of

Hereford was saying. Marjorie noticed that he did not, even yet, give Robert the title of king. "He knew him well in the old days, before the war; he was a boy then, younger than you, sir, and the Earl of Carrick and he would ride close by old King Edward always, for he liked their talk. It's a wearisome business, this war; though it has not been to our advantage, I hope the late battle will bring the end nearer."

Mar was stuffing meat in his mouth. "I hear the King wanted to fight on by himself, but Pembroke and Sir Giles dragged him away," he said. "I wish I'd been there with him. It was the dispute among the English command, they say, that lost the battle."

His eyes gleamed with admiration of Edward, on whom he doted, and he missed the answering gleam of anger in Hereford's own; it had indeed been the dispute between Gloucester and Hereford that had delayed the charge of the English van. Marjorie watched her cousin Mar without surprise; remembering the spoilt little boy at Lochmaben, she did not take it unaccountable that confinement near Edward, with all the silken amenities of the English Court, had left Mar, like Lady Buchan's brother the Earl of Fife, preferring the country of his imprisonment to that of his birth. "And, as they say of Edward, he too has little tact," she thought.

Hereford, however, had more; catching her glance, he bowed to her. "As a soldier, even one who has been defeated in an engagement, I can admire fine leadership," he said, "and your father, Lady Marjorie, is such a leader. Have you heard how he answered single-handed the challenge of my nephew De Bohun?" He smiled, a little wryly; De Bohun was dead. "I saw that charge made with the lance, by a man on a great war-horse in full accoutrement. Your father was on a little horse, unarmed save for his axe, riding about to see to his divisions. Harry rode out—he was a hot-tempered fellow, and he knew Bruce by the crown above his vizor—and, by God, if his lance had found rest there would have been no battle, nor any need for one. But your father swerved his mount aside and brought his axe down, whirling it above his head, and cleft Henry's skull through his helmet, in the sight of both armies."

She was still, watching him. It was pleasant to hear an Englishman warm in his praise of her father. Mar would not understand; she saw him watching Hereford curiously. The Constable was still talking, relating the recent dispositions of the battle, and maintaining that in his view the tactics Bruce had used would be made a model for many another battle, both on this and foreign soil.

"That unbroken wall of men! and a giant leading it!"

Mar crushed a yawn with his hand; he was drowsy with food and wine. Idly, his glance shifted from Hereford, whom he found a bore, and stayed on his cousin Marjorie. How little she had altered, really, since the days at Lochmaben! Provincial, dully dressed, and silent—not like the brilliant women at Edward's Court, although neither he, nor Edward for that matter, had time for women. Dear Edward, with his silky essenced hair, and curled beard the colour of saffron, made to flee in disorder from the barbarity of a battle Hereford spoke of, having to leave behind all his gear and his jewelled cups and silk tents, and even his royal seal! Let these Scots, in God's name, have their barbarous kingdom again, so that only he, and Edward,

and Piers Gaveston, might sit one day again in Westminster and eat sugared fruits and hear music among
the laughter that they loved. . . .

Walter, the High Steward, ate his meat with the
detached enjoyment of one to whom food has for some
time been secondary to other things while at the same
time welcome to the healthy appetite of any young man
of twenty-two. He washed it down with red wine, and
reflected on the curiosity of fate, which enabled him to
sit in Berwick feasting with an Englishman on the
other side of the table.

Berwick! How long since the name of any walled
town had infected him with that prickle in the bones,
that stirring of heart's blood that meant warfare, and
the taking—by stealth or sinews—of the town? So had
he followed the King and James Douglas to Roxburgh,
Edinburgh, across the borders, ravaging Tynedale, and
back again to the taking of Perth and the hundred
encounters that ended with the greatest battle of all, in
which he, although so young still, had been given a
division to command. Walter's eyes shone and his
cheeks flushed as he remembered that, and how he had
knelt before the King to receive his spurs as the dawn
broke that would see their death or victory. There had
been no half-measures about that situation, it would
have been the one or the other, for Scotland, for
themselves.

But now he sat in Berwick on a mission to bring the
King's daughter home.

Princess. . . . The haughty, unfamiliar title awed
Walter a little, seeing in it as he did a sword's division
between the days when he and she had ridden by

Dundonald and now. He had been stiff with shyness when he first met her again, having had little enough time, God knew, in the days past, to cultivate women. Those he had seen had been alike, shadows; thin of body, with starved dark eyes, after the lean harvests and the short rations of the war years; he knew nothing of fashion, as did Mar. When the King had sent for him to tell him of his mission he had been struck with awkward silence; and raising his eyes at last to meet those well-known grey ones of the King's, found laughter at the back of them for the fact that he had nothing to say.

"Sir, I'd rather you gave me Perth moat to swim again, in the blackness and God knew what ahead of us. What am I to say to her? She'll have been taught to read and embroider and dance."

He thought wistfully of the things his mother had used to do, half-remembered in those other days before the fighting. Egidia was dead now, had died within a year of his father, and Andrew had coughed his lungs away in prison and never been set free. He, Walter, was at times appalled at the responsibility that lay on him, now, as the head of the family, knowing little enough of them as he did after all these years. They had grown up rough from the needs of war, even little Egidia had learned to do with one meal a day and mix hot pitch to pour on the besiegers' heads if they came, and she swore like a man and wore breeches and could shoe a mount quickly. Women had had to learn to do such things if they were to survive at all, and in a way he was glad that Marjorie had been protected from it, as long as they had not ill-treated her. He remembered his still anger on hearing that she was to be put, like

Lady Buchan, in a cage in the Tower, and then his
surge of great relief on hearing that she had not been.

Marjorie. . . . Would she be stiff as a nun, and keep
her eyes lowered at sight of him? Would she be a
mincing Englishwoman now, and look down her nose
at the way he talked? Would she. . . . He had no means
of knowing, until he saw her, and how in all the years
of change and trouble and heartbreak she had altered
so little.

The serving-man brought him a knuckle of dressed
veal, following the fish in butter and the ortolans they
had had. It was good to sit down at table again and to
see the men serving neatly at the board, as he remembered. Would there ever come a day when everything
was in its place again, and a man's castle his own for the
things of peace, not sleight from hand to hand accord-
ing to who won it, English or Scots, and razed for
better safety, and built again in a hurry when the new
owner came? He, Walter, would like a house graciously
built with glass windows, the way they had them in
France and England and Norway that King Robert
had told him of. And he would like a lady for his castle,
not a starved hag with fight in her eyes, but a soft girl
graciously clothed, and the servants would come and
kneel before them both and bring them wine, and a
ewer to wash their hands and linen to dry them.

Walter munched at the veal knuckle, absently;
reached out his hand, and drank more wine. As he did
so he caught her glance—the Princess's, raised directly
to his face, as it had been when they first met yesterday
and she had been handed over to his care by her stiff
English escort of priors and nuns. Grey eyes, clear and
sullen as the water of Trool, where the King had won

his first victory years ago in the West. She hadn't smiled at him, the Princess, and he was glad; simpering women, like that faded failure of a Queen, he could never abide. He would like to make Marjorie laugh, he thought; soften the closed determined line of her small mouth and see her eyes sparkle, like the sunlight on Trool. Gracious saints, was he growing to be a poet, he who had never strung lines together in his life, although he had had enough pleasure hearing the King do it, and tell French tales? *She*, watching him now, would see nothing of that, only that he was a gross common gormandizing soldier, rinsing down his third platter of veal. But he would make her see it . . . as well as making her laugh, later, when they all got back to where King Robert waited for them.

"I could have asked him about Father," Marjorie thought.

She fixed her eyes on the young Steward's straight back, seen riding ahead of her in the escort of the Queen of Scots, who had beckoned him to her. Queen Elizabeth seemed to like Walter's company, Marjorie reflected. Well, it would no doubt suit him better than her own, as she had not been able to think of anything to say to him. It seemed stupid, after so many years in which so much had happened, that she should not have been able to think of something to ask him.

But Father? Would he have changed very greatly? She had been half afraid to ask Walter, that was the truth.

The King was to meet them at Roxburgh and as they rode up to the gate of the castle she could hear, a little way behind her, one of the Steward's men talking to

Eleanor, the Queen's woman, of it, and of how James Douglas had taken it quite silently, surprising the garrison in the way he always managed to do. And inside the castle, when they had all won in, there had been a woman (it was at night) seated rocking her baby to sleep. She sang the lullaby that so many of the English garrison wives, and the English everywhere, were singing now—

> "*Hush ye, hush ye, little pet ye,*
> *The Black Douglas shall not get ye,*"

—and suddenly there had been a hand laid on her shoulder and a voice said, "I am not so sure of that!" and there was the Douglas himself, standing by her. How they must have laughed together, her father and James, at some of the tales there were to tell!

The thought of seeing James here now, as well as the King, heartened her. James could not change, or if he did it would not be so terrible a thing as if her father did so, and if she should not remember him after so many years. And he, what would he have to say to her? Would the barrier have raised itself again between them, in spite of all her endeavour, the stiff and constant prayer, the going over and over in her mind of things she recalled concerning him, as though to do so would keep him from death in her heart? And he had lived; had fought gloriously, had been preserved until they met again.

They dismounted in the courtyard and went into the hall. Under the high rafters she saw figures standing, grouped together in twos and threes. Foremost of all the Queen of Scots made her way forward, was greeted by one of the figures, the tallest; he stooped to kiss her cheek, then they parted and she stepped back. "Now it is my turn," thought Marjorie. She felt her heartbeats clearly as she went forward, seeming the only things alive in that place where all others were turned to stone; silent as stones, watching. They were small and regular, the beats of her heart.

A tall man waiting, in blue; the gilt on his narrow crown shone brightly against his hair, which was grey. She saw that first, remembering how in old days he had seemed to her to be made all of light, of fire, of gold. Now he was of iron, she thought; an iron man. What things the years had done to him! A scar furrowed his cheek, making a little, puckered pallid line among the brown skin. He smiled, and she saw the gap where he had teeth missing, from the stroke of a sword. All this she saw before he even touched her, before they embraced, formally. He must kiss her as he had kissed Elizabeth, for whom he cared nothing, whom he might even hate. Did he hate Elizabeth, who had lolled in comfort when everyone else was in want, starvation, danger? Did he hate anyone? Did he even love anyone now, in a different manner from the love he must have for the men about him, who had borne with him every danger, fought with him through all his wars? Had he any— any—love, feeling, wish left for her? Had he forgotten her, in all that time?

"Father."

His eyes, she thought, were lonely. Did he feel their strangeness? Was this meeting an ordeal for him because, being a King now, he must receive her with state? Would it not have been so much simpler, kinder, to have let them meet alone, not like an escort of envoys he must receive, under the gaze of all the eyes in the hall?

King. Did he feel any gladness now that he was so? Had it been worth all endeavour, for *him*, as a man, now that the task was all but accomplished? Yet there was still so much to do. His Holiness the Pope denied recognition; he must be made to change his mind. Foreign courts must be informed. The kingdom's borders must be protected from invasion, by treaty and by strength. All that had been tumbled down must be built anew, all that had been lost regained. When that had been done he would be ready to die. But now, now . . .

"Father." She cast her arms about his neck. What did etiquette matter when they were both crying?

II

They rode westward, and it was strange to see again the familiar country of her childhood, so little changed in spite of everything that had passed. Nothing that men could do would alter the shapes of the blue hills greatly, or prevent the heather from springing, or the bracken from turning in the sun. Among all the other changes, her heart cried out to these, and welcomed them. She would always be more at home in the west.

The other changes had come to her knowledge subtly, felt in the Queen's silence before she saw them for herself, by chance or by design. One was her father's bastard son, little Robin, now seven years old. His mother had been a lady of Kyle and now that she was dead the King kept Robin by him, treating the child kindly enough but without the special bond that there was between him and her. She could not have borne that, she thought, but now there was no cause for envy of the dead woman. What Elizabeth felt, no one knew. It was common knowledge that she and the King did not live together as man and wife, but went their separate ways. Now that the interest of the homecoming was dying down there were other things to talk of, notably the rebuilding of the King's place of Cardross, on the heights above the Clyde beyond Glasgow. "Father means to have glass windows in it when it is finished, but that will not be for a long while," thought Marjorie dreamily.

She found a need in herself to ride out alone often, not allowing even Will to accompany her closely, although she knew he often followed behind. The constant solicitude of Will irked her at times; she wanted to revel in her freedom, in the knowledge that no one at all was watching her. It became a matter with her of urging the horse she rode faster and faster, knowing with the tearing of the wind through her hair that she was outriding Will and had left him behind, had left them all behind . . . for an hour.

"I am not fitted for Courts," she thought. Although there was so little ritual even in the King's presence, she felt clumsy in company, tongue-tied and heavy-footed. Here alone, on a horse, by herself, she could be at ease. She did not care what they said about her.

One day in the forest of tall trees that spread far over the hill-slopes like a flung plaid, so that there were few roads among the patches of moss and bog, she came on a man kneeling by a horse. At the sound of her own mount's hooves he turned and straightened, getting to his feet, and she saw that it was Walter the Steward. He stood in her way, so that she was forced to stop and

speak to him; this was against her will, and she heard
the gruffness of her own voice, greeting him. She could
not tell why she had been disinclined to seek him out
since Berwick. Since then he had been much about the
Queen, escorting her when she rode out and partnering
her in the new French dances that she was endeavour-
ing to bring into fashion at Court, having learned them
from the ladies at Barking Abbey. He was very light of
foot, as big men often were, or so they said, and everyone wanted him for a partner in matters such as that.
Well, she had nothing to do with it. Yet, looking down
now from where she sat in the saddle, she was aware of
both strangeness and familiarity at the sight of him;
how tall and muscular he had grown, and yet his dark-
gold hair still hung as it had always done, and his eyes
were as blue and level as ever, regarding her.

She flushed for no reason, and dropped her gaze.
"Do you always shoe your own horses?" she said, for
something to say. He replied gravely that in the late
wars they had all of them to turn their hands to anything, "as you know very well, Princess, having mended
shoes with a leather thong in the Forest of Lorn. But
this shoe was loose in one nail only, and I would not
trouble a smith to fix it. Come down and feel if I have
not hammered it firmly enough, and without any
anvil, or anything at all but the handle of my knife."
But she would not dismount, and shook her head
stubbornly.

"I must go back." Shaking the reins again, she
waited for him to step aside and let her pass; he did not,
and to her astonishment laid a hand on her horse's bridle.

"Stay by me a little while, Princess, as we're old
friends." At the back of his voice she could hear

laughter. Why was he laughing at her? Angry, she tried to free herself.

"Why should I stay," she said, "when I don't want to?"

His hand held firm. "Why should you not want to?" he asked her; his eyes were grave.

Marjorie felt the blood rise in her face. "Because I'm not one of your dancing-women!" Suddenly wrenching the reins away, she spurred the horse, which shot forward among the trees. She heard Walter's voice calling after her, but did not turn her head. "I hope Bay kicked him," she thought viciously.

She felt remorse later for her treatment of Walter, but her anger flared again when she found him with the King. For a moment she thought that he had complained of her, and felt quick scorn for any grown man who could behave so; the great cry-baby, standing there crimson-faced in his leather surcoat that he had been riding in, and sulky because she had not wanted to get down and look at his horse-shoeing! But when the King spoke he made no mention of that, only said that he would rather she did not ride out alone.

"It is not a quiet country yet, and you may be set upon. I would prefer that you had escort, and here is a knight who will convey you wherever you will."

As he said it, Marjorie saw the hint of laughter behind his eyes. For some reason this caused her to colour more furiously than Walter was doing, so that they both stood, scarlet, in the King's presence until he released them with a parting word about the horses.

Queen Elizabeth required diversions to cheer her through her lonely days, and of them all she liked best to dance. At night, therefore, after the trestles were cleared away, there would be fiddlers and tambour players bidden to strike up in the King's hall, and those who were not too heavy with eating and drinking would line up in pairs. The older folk did not do it, and the King seldom joined the dancers, being of habit in his upper chamber at that season, for there was much work to be done with regard to letters to Edward, the Pope and the Isles, where Angus of Isla had helped him at one time. The strains of the fiddles would come to him faintly above the scratching of the secretary's quill, and at times he would stop in his dictating and remember other times at old Edward's Court, when some of these measures had been played and he, young then, had sometimes partnered a shy pale child with soft curls. Recalling his savage grief at the news of Isobel of Buchan's death, he did not think that he would ever dance again. Had she lived to hear the fiddles play in Cardross, he could have listened with lighter heart; had she even known that the tide would turn, he could have forgiven himself in part for what she had endured for him.

But she had known nothing at the end, only cold, mockery and pain. At times anger for the careless sounds below would come to him, and he would grasp his chair in an endeavour to fight down the urge to smash the curving wood, to break the strings. . . .

There were new dances such as were in use in the courts of York and Westminster. There were French dances called branle, carole, passacaille. All of these showed to advantage the turn of a brightly lined sleeve or skirt, the elegance of a leg in scarlet hose and pointed shoes of cloth.

There was little fashion of any kind here yet, no one having the money to buy costly stuffs from Italy and France. Isabelle, the young English Queen now at York, would have tittered at the makeshift finery, Marjorie thought, watching the girls in their freshly furred surcoats made in Toom Tabard's time, and their hair bravely looped and plaited as they had been told the French ladies did now (English fashions, like English saints, were out of favour). Queen Elizabeth pranced with the brightest, clapping her hands and weaving her slender figure into the patterns of the dance. Her mouth smiled always, red with the paint she had brought with her from England; her plucked brows beckoned archly. She seemed harder and shallower since her return; she had begun to form a set about her of young men, younger than she was. "She is grasping desperately at her youth, lest it slip by and leave her lonely," Will had said. Will always spoke of what he thought, from his own lonely eminence of being neither man nor woman. Marjorie heard him and the feeling that had risen in her, almost one of hate for the useless woman, left her. What must it be like to be growing old? She did not think that she would mind it greatly, but she had never had beauty to lose, as Elizabeth had.

This night Walter the Steward was the Queen's partner in a baladine. The fashion for this had lately come from Picardy, where it was said to have been copied from the religious dances of peasants on feast-days. Marjorie stared at Walter without realizing she was doing so; he was talking and laughing with the

Queen, she saw, and Elizabeth's painted face, which just reached his shoulder, would lean back in the figure called a rondelle and glance archly up at his height. The light from the wall-torches flickered on Walter's hair, reflecting themselves in its smoothness. "It wasn't so smooth when I'd led him a chase, yesterday; he was very hot and worried, my lord High Steward, after what the King said, in case I'd got lost." How angry Walter had been when he found her! It was just like old days, only now he had to be careful what he said because she was a Princess. In any case she very seldom troubled to speak to him at all, so it must be a relief to him to laugh now with the Queen. Marjorie felt a lump rise in her throat, and downed it fiercely. Let Walter Stewart forget he was supposed to be a soldier, pirouetting about in a ring with a woman nearly old enough to be his mother!

She had almost forgotten to think of Egidia now, it was so long since she had died. . . .

The ill mood remained with her, and after the fiddles stopped she stayed half hidden in her place, trusting to the shadows to conceal her. She did not want to dance; the King was not here, and she would rather have been with him, busied as he might be with urgent matters, sitting upstairs by his fire. "He has no more liking for empty frivolous manners than I," she told herself. Let them laugh at her for an old maid, a nun! She knew what she wanted.

"Will the Lady Marjorie dance the tordion?"

The music had struck up again. Walter stood before her, his broad shoulders blotting out the light of the torches behind him. "If that is the one where we go round and round and never leave go I don't want to dance it, or with you at all." To her annoyance, tears stood in her eyes; she hoped that the shadow he threw would keep him from seeing them.

"Why will you never dance?" he said; he might not have heard her rebuff. To the renewed rhythm of the fiddles, and twisting and turning of the dancers, she remembered the terms on which they had last parted. He had been angry then. What right had he to stand here now, when she had told him to go away? If they danced together she would not come up to his shoulder.

"Oh, Walter, I can't dance, no one has ever taught me."

"Come," he said, and grasped her two hands before she could pull them away. Under his guidance they made two turns of the room; at the far end, she stumbled.

"I'm not light enough of foot," she said sullenly. "Let me go."

For answer he guided her out through the door. The cool silence of the night outside met them; far away, challenging the sound of the dance, came the murmur of the King's cattlemen, singing.

"Come on," said Walter. "I've something you must see."

"What is it?" she said listlessly. In the hall, with the dancing, her cheeks had flamed with the heat; she could not keep back the tears upon them. She picked her way beside Walter over the muck in the yard, holding her skirts aside. Inside the stable door a faint light from a hanging lantern beckoned. Walter took the lantern down from its nail, holding it before her so that she could see.

"Look," he said. In the corner against the wall a grey bitch lay; she recognized it as Walter's wolf-hound, which followed him most days. The bitch had littered and her whelps lay close under, suckling peacefully. Their eyes were still unopened and their coats were the colour of peat. There were five of them.

Walter began to talk in a low voice to the bitch. Marjorie sank down on her knees in the straw and watched the puppies. The yellow light picked out the rough texture of their coats which were beginning to dry out with the warmth. The bitch lay and watched her, with dark uncertain eyes. Under Walter's hand she grew quiet.

"I wouldn't have come myself until she fetched me," he said shyly. "She came to-night—" he grinned— "when I was dressed in my finery for the dancing. So I had to leave her again, but all night I have wanted to come back, and bring you."

"Why did you want to show me?" she said. Like a flood, her happiness had risen at sight of the puppies, and at Walter's words. Without waiting, she talked on; it was easier to talk now that she knew he had not really wanted to dance that dance with the Queen, that he had wanted to be here with his dog . . . and with her.

She raised her eyes suddenly. Walter was leaning back among the straw, watching her. His eyes looked dark and heavy lidded, and tender. She felt queer trembling happiness rise. They said nothing.

Presently Walter reached out and drew her to him. She felt no strangeness at the touch of his hands, as though she had known it always. She let herself lie up against him, easily, like an animal; he was speaking to her, softly, continuous words without sense, small loving things, "as though," she thought drowsily, "I had been the dog." The thought of that made her smile, and she turned her face and hid it against his tunic. He must not ask her what she was smiling at, because she could not tell him. How smooth the tunic was against her face, and how warm Walter was! She could feel his heartbeats beneath her cheek, slow and even. She brought up a hand and stroked the tunic, thoughtfully, over where the heart was.

"Why are you laughing?" said Walter. His arms held her tightly, but she did not answer.

Suddenly, he was afraid of her laughter. They sat there for a while, no longer speaking, his chin resting on her hair, her hands in his. Neither of them knew what to say; the moment, so strangely come, had ended, and they were here in the straw, with a bitch and her puppies, and nothing at all to say. He let Marjorie go gently; seen in this light, he looked uncertain and much younger than he had done in the hall. A lock of the dark-gold hair had fallen forward across his brow, destroying its tidiness. A sudden wish came to her to smooth the lock, but she was shyer now than she had been a moment ago, and could not. She knelt, where she was, looking at the puppies. One had come adrift from the bitch's flank and scrabbled about aimlessly.

"Would you like one?" said Walter.

"That one." She stroked the wandering puppy with one finger, then lifted it gently, back to its mother. "It's like me, lost." The phrase hung awkwardly in the air, and he smiled. "Lost?" he said. "With running away from me on your Bay? That's the second dance you've led me."

A SEASON OF SUMMER

He fell silent and they both remembered that earlier ride, and Wallace. The pace of their minds was so similar that he knew of whom she spoke when she said again, in a strange little voice, looking down at her hands, "You know, I've always loved *him*, Father, Nigel— and now you. But not in the same way, Walter. You know that, don't you?"

"You have changed after all," he said. Something, a kind of hurt, was in his mind at her words; he puzzled over it for a while and then let it go. He might never understand her. "Marjorie, the King said that if you liked it we might marry. I would not have told you before he did so, but . . ." He paused, watching her in the light of the lantern. She was silent for a moment, thrusting with one hand at the straw.

"They keep it very clean and new," she said. "Everything Father does must be of the best, even— even stable-straw." They began to laugh then, and soon, between laughter and crying, she found herself again in his arms. She felt safe there; curled up against him, she hardly listened to what he was saying, not nonsense-talk now, but plans as to how the King would give her Methven, which was so near the site of that first lost battle, "but we'll not have leisure to live there, much, because I'm the Seneschal, as you know, and that means we will have to be mostly on this side, at my Renfrew, when the King's at Cardross, and only go to Methven when he goes there to visit Angus next autumn. Oh, it'll all work out, don't you fear. Have you heard anything at all that I've been saying? Oh, you little wretch, what a time you gave me when you ran away. . . ."

He looked down at her, seeing the dark stubby lashes

245

against her cheek. Short lashes and short hair, she had, Marjorie. . . . Princess Marjorie. He laughed, and kissed her, savouring the pleasurable sensation it gave him. What was she saying? "Oh, you mustn't talk when I kiss you; wait till the end!"

He felt her mouth yield to his, taking time over his kisses, surer with every moment that passed of his mastery over her now that she had ceased to evade him. Presently they would come and search, he knew; he must take her back before that happened. What a stroke of fortune it had been that Seâna had littered to-day! He had begun to despair of ever making her hear him, his wild little wife that the King had promised him, "but only if," the King had said, "it is her will also." Certainly now she seemed willing.

"Nobody will make us dance any more," he murmured. What was she saying? Something about a horse. Walter smiled.

"You were born in the saddle, very likely, and will die in it. What are you talking of now?" His brows drew together. "By yourself? But why should you have to be by yourself, Marjorie, now that I can be with you? That's foolishness, my own dear."

He was to remember her eyes, regarding him unreadably, and her sudden clinging to him. It must have irked her, all that time in prison. He would never let her know any grief or loneliness again.

III

Now that she was to marry Walter the Steward, Marjorie found a subtle change in the manner of the Court towards her. Some, like Elizabeth, hid their envy under a show of spleen; naturally the marriage had been arranged by the King!

"With the dowry that he will give her, of course, the pill's gilded!" That was the way the women took it, in particular the young unmarried women who had perhaps hoped to wed the Steward themselves. Walter was so handsome, and his conduct at Bannockburn had been so gallant, that he was much sought after for these reasons alone, and not because, as the Grand Seneschal of Scotland, he owned more land than anyone except the King. Already he was engaged in helping to rebuild the great Abbey of Paisley, which his ancestor Walter Fitzalan had founded, and which had been burned to the ground by the English in the year of Marjorie's capture. "I should have liked us to be married there, but there is nothing to see yet but a heap of planks and charred stones," he said ruefully.

It was still uncertain where and when the marriage would take place, and Marjorie listened to the discussions between Walter and her father and the Queen, taking no part in them; it might have been someone else's wedding they planned. As Walter had said, she was to have Methven; the list of castles and lands that the King would settle on her in dowry was read out, and she listened and then forgot which ones they were.

Walter and James Douglas teased her regarding it. "Give Marjorie a saddle for a bride-gift, not shifts and damask to wear or make into bed-curtains. Do you know that she will scarcely thread a needle? You'll go naked, Steward, for nobody will mend your gear."

"She can spin," said Walter.

"And she can fish," added James. "It would be

better, perhaps, if you had no roof over your heads instead of ten or twelve; then you would see the worth of her."

"I can see it now," said Walter. He would never allow anyone to bait Marjorie for long. In ways, she was still almost like a sister, he felt; a small unruly sister who had not grown up yet. It was partly because she had altered so little from the Dundonald days, in spite of all that she had come through, that he loved her. At times the strength of his own love would surprise Walter. There were so many fairer women about Court, whom he could have had for the asking, he knew, yet he wanted none of them.

A stab of anger took him at the Queen's talk, which mocked a little, delicately, always, at the notion that he had had any choice in the matter of his marriage. Those plucked brows, which gave the eyes beneath them an air at once shallow and calculating in the painted face, had raised themselves; really, said Elizabeth, she had been surprised that he had found it necessary to spend time in the outhouses before he could declare his betrothal.

"You're man enough, I don't doubt," she said, with a sidelong glance. "But *she*'s green fare! Not that I do not wish you well, Steward. I can recall your dear mother—who was my own aunt, as you know—telling me that this betrothal had been arranged, oh, many years back, I cannot recall whether it was to yourself or your brother Andrew. In any case it is as well that the Stewardship should be thirled to the Crown." She left them smiling, and Walter felt his fists clench in impotent rage. If Marjorie had been distressed by that, as she might well have been! He glanced at her quickly;

she had not turned her head, and seemed to be watching with interest the perching of a bird on the stones of the window. She might not have heard what Elizabeth had said, and Walter ground his teeth over an aside about lying bitches; there was little more one could say in her own palace about the Queen of Scots.

"Father wants to see me," said Marjorie.

He watched her go, seeing the way her hair curled finely on the nape of her neck; the sun discovered little glints of gold among it. He must kiss the nape of her neck, when he had her alone; if only they could soon be alone, out of this prying palace full of eyes. Thirled to the Crown! Damnation take the impudence of that ageing vixen, who was no better than an Englishwoman for all she was his mother's niece! He would take Marjorie east to Methven as soon as might be, away from the very air the woman breathed, and have her to himself for a while before he must leave for the Isles with the King.

He kicked resentfully at the floor-straw, seeing the tiny dried herbs scattered among it. Mincing English habits the Queen had brought back with her from Rochester Castle! Let her perfume her own mind with the strongest herbs she could get, for it stank like a midden. Illogically, Walter remembered a conversation he had had with the Abbot of Paisley yesterday about the re-erecting of a shrine in the Abbey to St Milburga, who had been a princess of Mercia. "Such a saint might not be at all popular, my dear lord, considering that it was that same nation which came and burnt the building down," the Abbot had hesitated, "but after all, if we are to be impelled by considerations that are momentary in the commencing of a task whose results

will we hope be fairly permanent . . ." He had left it to
Walter to decide, for although the High Stewards were
no longer the owners of the ground they had donated
to the Abbey, it was customary to include them in
debating matters such as this.

Overcome by momentary spleen towards all English-
women, Walter decided there and then that they would
not re-erect the shrine to St Milburga. Let her take her
miracle-working where it would benefit those of her
own marauding nation! He would get the Abbot to
have the shrine consecrated in honour of some more
neighbourly saint instead.

Marjorie found the King seated in the room above
the hall, in his long furred gown, with his dog at his
feet. He was alone, and a shaft of spring sunlight had
entered from the window; it lighted on his hair, and
she saw again with compunction how grey it was now;
he was an ageing man. He turned and smiled as she
came in, and pointed to the faldstool by him. Marjorie
sank down upon it, remembering that other day when
she had sat at his feet by a fire, with a dog lying there.
Did he remember Dundonald at all? Small wonder if
not, when so many things had come between.

"I sent for you," said Robert. Idly, his hand with
the ring on it moved a little, sketching an embrace of
her hair. They were seldom demonstrative one with the
other, Marjorie moved closer to him, so that the faint
scent of the lined dressed furs of his gown came to her.
Why was he wearing furs at this season? Had he an
ague? She glanced up anxiously.

He shook his head, answering her spoken question.
"No, only an ill humour of the bones I've had since

Lorn days. It took me so badly in the north one year that I nearly lost an action by it . . . but did not, praise God. It will go away after a time, until it chooses to return again. It knows no season." He leaned over, grunting, and stirred the fire, which leaped. "Not long before I'm an old man—I hope, a grandfather. That brings me to what I would say to you. Has Walter spoken of it?"

"Spoken of what, Father?" As always at implication of the facts of marriage, she felt awkward and ignorant. If only the Lady Egidia had not died! So many years in the convent, and no one except that mocking, envious woman to ask now regarding the things she was uncertain of. She would rather keep silent than ask the Queen.

"Of the succession."

"No. . . ." It had been the Queen who spoke of that. As well that the Stewardship should be thirled to the Crown. . . . Suddenly, on an impulse, she told him of it.

He did not change expression at mention of his wife; the fingers of the idle hand closed and loosened again. "Stewardship to Crown, or Crown to Stewardship?" Quizzically, in the old way, he raised his eyebrow at her. "Walter's my loyal man . . . and you, who have fought a soldier's war, I would not have sold, as cattle are. That is why I would have your full agreement on this, before you marry; for if it is not your will to deprive yourself of the greater part of your dowry, men may well blame the Steward for his thirling."

She stared. "What is the greater part, sir? I'm stupid."

"Scotland," he smiled. "See, Marjorie, what trouble

has come to us all because a woman was to have been queen."

Briefly, he reminded her of what had befallen since the little Maid of Norway had fallen heir to Scotland on the death of her grandfather, King Alexander. "There is another instance, of the civil wars in England, two centuries since, when Henry I's daughter, Maud, was left heir to the throne. In a land rent by greedy barons, there's little strength, Marjorie. Even with Walter's arm to protect you, you'd not find such a sceptre easy to wield. As you know, there are those over the south border with long memories for a weakness; what would hinder Edward, or his sons, from marching north again if so it pleased them, were a woman on the throne?"

"What do you want me to do?" she said. "You have no son."

"None but Robin," he answered flippantly. "My good mother, for whom you are named, had five sons. Three are slain, but two live."

"But would Uncle Ned. . . ." She fell silent, pondering it.

"Uncle Ned would make a king," said Robert, "since all that is most needed now is strength, and bravery in danger."

He lay back in the chair and looked at her. That she would yield he knew; she had no notion of herself as the possessor of anything, let alone a kingdom. He smiled, remembering the trouble he had been at to dower her, and how little she had cared for it. Matters for which other women would lay down their lives were nothing to Marjorie. What sort of a queen would she have made?

"In Elfland, maybe, she would have ridden the green paths nightly, on a white horse with her train behind her," he thought. Regret, queerly, was with him because she must never reign.

And so in early summer, a few weeks before her marriage, Marjorie stood with Walter before the Parliament at Ayr and renounced her right as her father's heir to Scotland.

As she heard the words read, she was conscious of a faint, illogical regret. The loyal men, the known and trusted faces of her father's followers, surrounded her; Walter's, young Randolph's, who had led the unyielding division of foot before Bannockburn against which the English chivalry had dashed itself to pieces; James, with his sardonic face leaden and impassive, watching her. All these and more were there, who had fought and suffered, denied themselves and known prison, faced death many times, cold and hunger and thirst, insult and torment, for a goal. And now it was in sight and the land was one again, and she was giving away her right to it as surely as Esau had sold his birthright, long ago.

But she was a woman and Scotland would not lie quiet under queens. Perhaps in a little while her son would reign, if Uncle Ned had no sons. There had been a provision in the ruling to allow for that.

She raised her hand and took the oath as she was instructed, seeing the May sunlight strike the walls and the scarlet colour of my lords' finery on the benches, and the blue sea beyond the window, and the little islands beyond the sea. Then her eyes came round again to Walter, who stood beside her, and she felt a new

253

security in his presence and in the warm clasp of his hand. Walter might, she knew, have wanted her to be queen so that the Crown would be thirled to the Stewardship, and so that he might have power as her consort. He had not wanted that; all he had done when he heard of her decision was to growl how glad he was that they would be able to go in peace to Methven this summer and trouble about nobody but themselves. But later they must return to be near the King, who would be at Cardross as much as possible, and life would gradually shape itself into something the pattern that it might have done if there had never been any wars.

She smiled at Uncle Ned, whose red head was conspicuous in that assembly of greying men. Let things be as they might, she could not picture Uncle Ned as an old man, or as King! "And may it be long indeed before he need be so," she thought. She took the quill the clerk held out to her, and signed at the place he indicated.

Walter and she would be married as soon as the ending of Lent made preparation possible. Marjorie had not taken any active interest in the making of her wedding-garments; the Queen, who had better taste than she had and who cared for such things, had the matter under her care, and directed her sewing-women. Stuffs were of poor quality and hard to come by since the war; Marjorie had one brown riding-dress, furred sparely at hem and sleeves with marten, not vair; and a green dress of state, for when she rode to the Palace. "It is not the same as the last royal wedding, when the King's sister married Eirik of Norway and had a mantle of scarlet woven with gold, with the cape of it made out of five hundred tiny skins of vair, and fur even on her shoes, which were crimson," said Elizabeth. The Queen had become almost friendly at this time, so occupied was she with the bride-clothes. Marjorie was grateful to her, for she herself had no notion of how to contrive any effect with clothes. Remembrance of James Douglas's gibe to Walter would sometimes come to her, and she would try to accustom herself to the thought of mending neatly—"not with a leather thong to patch shoes!"—but knew very well that she would never be a success at it.

"I'm stupid," she said to Walter. "You'll have to go naked, as James said." Walter only laughed and said he preferred himself naked. "We'll find a sewing-woman to cobble for you, never fear," he said. "What are you going to have on at the wedding?"

"I don't know," said Marjorie. "The Queen will see to it."

But one day she was summoned to meet a great-boned young man with a face like a smiling full moon, and laid out over his two arms was a length of white samite, exquisitely embroidered with pearls. The Queen gasped; nothing like it had been seen, she cried, since dead King Alexander's time. Was it from France?

"From Genoa," said the young man. And when he spoke, in his broad Fleming's Scots, Marjorie knew who he was; Johan the Easterling, from Aberdeen. He had come all the way to the West with this samite as a bride-gift for her—"if the ships had been delayed by storm, I should never have forgiven myself, Princess. Do you remember how you used to have a scarlet cloak, in the days when you stayed in my father's house in Aberdeen?"

She was scarcely allowed to touch the pearly samite, lest she soil it. "I know just how it should be made up," said Elizabeth. She eyed Marjorie's figure shrewdly; a simple cut for the overgown, long tight sleeves; something to display the richness of the white material, without at the same time taking away from the youth of the bride. "If she had been my own daughter, could I have taken more trouble?" thought the Queen. She was, for perhaps the first time since her return, happy in her self-appointed task.

On the wedding-day she helped to dress the bride, herself wreathing flowers in the short dark hair and disposing the gown. At the end, when all was ready, Marjorie saw herself, for one instant, in the Queen's polished mirror, as she had seen her child's face in the Lady Egidia's all those years ago. If Egidia had been here to-day, how happy she would have been! This marriage was what she had always wanted.

But there was one other there from the old days besides Walter and her father, the latter splendid and almost young again in his crimson long-gown, with the narrow golden circlet of Scotland on his head. That was blind Wishart, whose hands stretched in blessing over herself and Walter when at last, and scarcely yet believing it themselves, they were man and wife. And somehow all the feeling which had remained pent up and half-fearful of expression—a legacy of those days when to feel had been to suffer and, too often, to die— had welled up at sight of those transparent scarred hands, and at the sound of that clear old voice.

Many in the church had tears in their eyes, or were

unashamedly weeping, therefore, at his words, "And
may you and your children be blessed." Yet there was
every reason why blessing should attend a pair so brave,
loving and young. The people lined the way to watch
them as they rode back from the ceremony; it was
Marjorie's crowning, as James Douglas had once foretold; and with no frosty diadem, but with flowers.

The feasting was not quite over, but below in the
hall the dancers circled on, calling the figures. She
heard the voices and music and the feet shaking the
floor, and remembered how a little while back she and
Walter had led them, round and round the room in
that dance in which she was still so clumsy. Yet it had
not mattered because they had all drunk wine, herself
and Walter too; toasting one another out of the same
cup. The flavour of it still made her heady, so that she
knew her cheeks were flushed and her eyes sparkled.
"You look beautiful," Walter had whispered, but it
was the gown that was beautiful. Nevertheless, when
the women had undressed her to put her to bed, she
had laughed at their teasing with as much ease as she
might have done when she was a child. Like, and unlike
herself, this carefree person, half merry with wine; and
yet she was not so tipsy as not to be a little afraid, not of
Walter but of things she did not understand. She must
laugh more loudly so that the women would not guess
she was afraid.

She lay and waited. Presently they would all come in
to see her and Walter bedded. The warmth of the wine
was receding and she was left with a feeling of chill.
Soon, if he did not come, she would be cold and stupid;
she wanted him to come and yet she did not.

They were coming up now; she could hear their trampling feet on the stairs. This was a wedding, and it would help to make a home of this new house of her father's. A birth and a death, they needed now, to make it one. They had been jesting about the birth to-night; Patrick, the King's fool, with a bone from the feasting in his hand instead of a bauble, had made everyone laugh about it, and she had laughed too, as she and Walter were flushed with wine in any case and could not blush further. Did Walter understand this thing that was to happen now? Man enough, the Queen had said that day. Men were different . . . the Queen had tried to talk to her yesterday, but she had not wanted to listen.

They were here, with shouting and laughter bursting open the door into the chamber. Four of the young men bore Walter, crimson with laughter, along in their arms. Patrick's bone waved, still, among the crowd; he was singing. Everyone was jolly with wine and the women's headgear was askew; they mingled together, men and women and girls, and laughed and teased and sang. The King and Uncle Ned came, thrusting through the crowd with their great height, which made them easily seen from the door; the room was full. Amid a great surge of laughter Walter was thrust towards her, everyone kissed her, her uncle and father last; a stocking full of salt was flung, and then Walter must kiss her also. She could taste the wine still on his lips, and hear the shouts of joy this pledge of the bridal gave the watchers, who pulled to the bed-curtains. The sudden blotting out of the light made darkness soft and strange. She could hear the muffled shouts of well-wishers, thrust from the room by others until at last

they were left together in silence. Walter's hand reached
out for hers beneath the furred skins of the covers.
They were alone now, in the blurred dark with the
lowered flame of the crusie-lamp still burning by the
door, high among shadows.

"Marjorie."

The voice, low and loving, seemed to come from a
long way off. He must know she was afraid; his arms
were gentle, sliding between her body and the furred
skins. "You're cold," she heard him say softly. "Are
you frightened? They shouldn't have left you so long,
the noisy fools. Weddings are always like this, it will
be better after we leave to-morrow . . . and go home . . .
your home. May I come to Methven with you, madam
the wife of the Steward? Oh, Marjorie, how lovely you
looked to-day. . . ."

"But not now." She was trembling. "Walter, warm
me, I'm so cold."

She could feel his warmth surround and enclose her,
helped by his hands and the low loving voice; she might
have been a hurt animal that he tended, nursing back
to sanity with small words that meant nothing, only
delaying silence till it should cease to hold fear. Gradually she yielded, soothed by his voice and touch. This
was marriage that she had been afraid of, but the reality
was swallowed up in her recollection of that other fear,
the one that was not physical, that could not be ex-
plained by reference to ordinary things. Dimly, now
that he could possess her without awkwardness between them, she heard his voice telling her how he had
always loved her—"although of course I didn't call it
by that name, boys never do"—but he had thrown
away his leather gloves of Percy's gift that day because

she scorned them; "and you ran away from me then, and again since; don't ever run away any more, you're mine and you'll stay by me. . . . What is that you're saying, my darling? *What?* Oh, you heard her, then. . . ."

"Green fare," murmured Marjorie, drowsy with wine and her body's gift. What did it matter about the Queen? "Walter, if we have a son perhaps he'll be King. I don't think Uncle Ned will ever have any lawful children. He said something to-night about wanting to be King of Ireland, but I think it was only the wine. He can't be King of two places at once. Walter, I'm warmer now, hold me so till morning, will you?"

Walter laughed softly, with his mouth in her hair.

IV

The King went to the Isles that summer to receive homage of the chiefs, and Walter accompanied him. Marjorie saw them on board and watched till the ships, with the royal lion painted on their sails, drew away from shore and moved, growing rapidly smaller, into the silver distance. A haze hung over the water, persisting after nightfall; she felt as if it had swallowed them up.

Turning back with the other women to Cardross, she was silent. She had not wanted to return to Court life and would have preferred to go to Renfrew, even though the hangings were not completed and the new walls smelled of damp. But Walter had not liked the idea of her living alone and had arranged that she should go back to the Queen till his return, and they

had quarrelled and then made it up again. "You don't
know what sort of state the High Steward's wife must
keep yet, and I won't have you going to Renfrew until
I am there to show you," Walter told her. He reminded
her often of the dictatorial boy who had been set to look
after her at Dundonald, and in such moods he irked
her, and she let him know it. However—she felt a
little rise of triumph—it so happened that she would
have to go to Renfrew in any case, because her grandmother, the old Welsh Dowager of Mar, had chosen
this moment to come down from the north and visit
her, and she could not defer the visit if she would for so
stupid a reason as Walter had selected. "He can't say
I am alone when I am staying with my grandmother,"
she told the Queen, and Elizabeth shrugged lightly and
let her go. Now that Marjorie was off her hands, she
had no resentment left for her, but she made no offer
to accommodate old Lady Mar, who was an uncomfortable visitor.

No one knew how old Elen of Mar was. She had
lived in retirement these many years, and saw only
those whom she chose to see. Long ago, before the
English conquest, she had come out of Wales, whose
hereditary prince had been her father, to marry that
Earl of Fife who was dead now these thirty years.
Then she had wedded Mar and borne three children
to him, among them Marjorie's own mother, whom
scarcely anyone now remembered. Marjorie had been
reared on tales of the ancient great lady, but had
never seen her and had no knowledge of the reason
for her sudden decision to visit. She found herself nervously awaiting the old Countess at Renfrew, being less
knowledgeable of the hostess's part than most brides.

News was brought to her of the Dowager's approach, and she stood to receive her in the hall. The old lady was borne inside in her litter, which she never left except to enter her bed; and she asked to be taken to this immediately. Marjorie saw a pair of bright brown eyes regarding her from a face as wrinkled as a monkey's; later the Countess sent for her, and she went to her in her chamber.

"Your rooms aren't heated, your masonry's damp and the very logs are green," said a voice. "Well seen you're lately wed. Are you breeding?"

She was ordered to come closer to the bed so that the Countess might see her. "Not much of you," was the verdict, "and that gown's poor stuff. What ails that father of yours, spending money he has not got? Glass windows in his house, ships building upon the sea, and a wicked amount of waste at that wedding in Bergen."

"Father is not . . ." began Marjorie, and then fell silent. For she remembered Nigel's telling her once that this old lady would speak of past, present and future as though no veil divided them. Certainly the wedding of Aunt Isobel to the King in Bergen was long over; one must accustom oneself to disentangle the remainder.

Old Elen called for wine, and when it had been brought she drank it, slowly, holding the goblet in her two hands as a child would do. The eyes regarded Marjorie over the flagon's rim; they were dark as beads.

"When will the child be born, answer me? I do not ask questions for nothing."

Marjorie flushed a little. "Oh, grandmother, I'm only married less than a month. How can I tell you?"

"Then they should not have sent away your young

man until you are sure. That is Carrick again, very improvident. Why do you suppose I have come if it was not to see your child? I have been alive long enough but I will live longer than you." She set the flagon down. "There are so many dead young people. But I shall see your son. You can go now, because I am tired; I am an old woman and have come far." She called for her waiting-woman, who fussed forward with pillows; when Marjorie reached the door, she was already asleep, or appeared so, with her hooded lids drawn down over her eyes, and her tongue silent.

Marjorie crept away, feeling the place no longer hers and Walter's. Would the terrible old woman indeed stay until a child was born? No, Walter would never permit it, he would be much too angry.

Twisting, flatly glistening in the faint light from the turret windows, the staircase wound below. She could hear her own small footsteps tapping, tapping, slowly, in the time it took to descend from the chamber to the hall. What had the old woman meant, and why should the things she said be true, even though they were told to her by that ancient whispering blood that had come down from Arthur and forgotten kings? Yet the same blood ran in *her* veins too. . . .

Did old Elen mean that she would die in childbirth? Was that what her eyes saw?

The Countess of Mar never left her bed, and after a few days Marjorie became accustomed to the thought of her presence upstairs. She herself was not wanted, she saw, except for an hour every day; then she would go and stand by the old woman's pillow—although this was Walter's house and she was its mistress, she never felt free to sit in her presence—and answer questions. Sometimes the Countess would talk, showing a shrewd knowledge of present-day affairs; other times her mind would wander, and it became difficult to distinguish between her prophecies and her remembrance. Letters came from Walter in the north, saying that he was well; the King had received his homage, and would be sailing soon for home again. Walter had a gift for her, he wrote, but did not say what it was. She sat by the fire in the great hall that night, seeing the smoking of the green logs that Elen had condemned, and spelling out the words with care. She had learned to read a little between the days at Dundonald and the years in the convent, but seldom troubled greatly with it. If a woman could sign her name, that was as much as she need do, unless she wished to be a nun. Walter's letter now kept her from brooding too greatly on that old presence upstairs, or on the other things Elen said, day after day.

In spite of herself, Marjorie recalled them, feeling them unfold in her mind and spread themselves out so that they came between her and the page. There was a thing Elen had said about the King's son that she said he would have. "A poor worthless thing; better never conceived, he! He'll reign, the son of a fool mother, until they spit on his name; then *your* son will be king."

Always her son—her son! Was it indeed true that her father and Elizabeth would have a child at last, and that he would be such a bad king that it would be better if he had never been born? Surely not after all these years of aversion, of hardly seeing one another? "She'll serve," old Elen had said, on a cackle of laughter. "Not to her liking, or his, but what else can they do who would breed kings? If he had taken a switch to her back when he first brought her north, it would have been better. Women, dogs and children spoil for lack of a rod. I leathered all mine, and they respect me. My father . . ."

Her lips had parted then and her eyes grown cloudy. "The last Llewelyn fell in fair fight, but that murdering rascal caused his head to be struck from his body and paraded above the streets of London, crowned with ivy. There will never be any more Princes of Wales. Ah, never tell me that poor mammet is any of ours, carried out of Caernarvon Castle as he was, on the flat of his father's shield, with the thin weak legs of him waving and his mother's cord still on his belly, and his mouth demanding milk! 'I will give you a prince that can speak no word of the English tongue,' says the murdering rascal, his father. Certainly he could speak no tongue at all, and it would have been better if he had remained dumb, from what I hear of him now. Ah, but the brave leader, the sweet minstrel, the fairest prince of all, Llewelyn, is dead, and leaves no son behind him."

So she would ramble on, at other times telling of the long wooing of the last Llewelyn and Simon de Montfort's daughter, Eleanor; and of how in spite of the enmity of the "murdering rascal" Longshanks they were married at last in his presence, with great pomp, in Worcester Cathedral. Then Eleanor had died at the birth of the baby, Gwendolen, who was one of the ladies induced to take the veil at the Glastonbury convent Marjorie had heard of. She had tried to tell this to Elen, but the old woman never listened to anyone else's talk; returning at last, as she usually did, to Marjorie's son, or to the dead Princes of Wales. The two things seemed bound up in her mind inextricably; something she had said to-night seemed to link them, and Marjorie tried to recall it.

A prophecy there had been, Elen said. It had been made by a bard of her father's—"and as you will know the murdering rascal slew all the Welsh bards, so there are none any more"—and foretold the coming of a Welsh prince to the throne of England. "But it is you will bring back the line of Llewelyn to rule over north and south and west alike. From you in the end he will come, and not from your father and that woman, or that hot fellow with the red hair who will try to make himself King of Ireland, and will cause a lot of trouble before being killed. Mind what I say. You'll not see any of it, and no more will I." Then she had shifted in her bed, kicking at the covers which had grown too weighty for her feet, and demanding wine.

Walter came home again to find his wife seated small and pale by a smoking fire. Having forgotten his anger in finding her here in pleasure at seeing her again, he downed any blaze of wrath on being told there was a visitor. "How could you prevent it? I'll pay my respects to the old lady to-morrow; it's too late to-night. Saints in heaven, how glad I am to be back, and with you!" He stretched and yawned, thrusting out his mailed feet to the hearth; he had not changed since riding in. "The Isles are magic, though, and the people are fey; the King has more devotion there than anyone knows, and it was an experience I wouldn't have missed to see that horde of yellow-shirted, long-whiskered savages kneel as one man and kiss the steel to him, which is their inviolable oath and never to be broken. I brought you a gift, Marjorie; it's a feast-day dress such as their women wear—very grand, with a scarlet skirt and a bodice threaded with gold, and a plaid of five colours, because you are a King's daughter."

Her silence struck him, and although she showed pleasure at the news of the gift, her wan smile struck at his heart. Told of the Countess's peculiar sayings, Walter moved restively. "That old witch! Pay no attention to her. Old folk get like that," he said, and opened his mouth to call for the page to divest him. Marjorie watched, curled up in her seat by the fire, while this was done; when he was arrayed in his easy house-attire, Walter came over and sat down, pulling her to him.

"That's better, I couldn't hold you close before for fear of crushing you. And now forget this old hag with her weary tales; you're white as a little candle. What does the past matter now, and who can tell the future?" The present was enough for him, he added, kissing her. Beside them the fire blazed high although it was summer; damp in the new castle chilled the room and left mildew on the hangings if there were not constant heat.

Marjorie hid her face against his shoulder. "Oh, Walter, she foretold her first husband, the Earl of Fife's murder. She told him not to ride out that day and he would take no heed, and he was dead before night. And many other things."

"Happier dead," growled Walter, disposing of the Earl of Fife. "What else has she said that's so wonderful? I won't have her frightening you; she can get over her journey and then back she goes. I'll see to it." His mouth set grimly.

Marjorie fingered his surcoat. "But, Walter . . ."

He glanced down; she had been pale, he knew, but now the colour flooded her face and throat. "Walter— oh, don't be angry—she was quite right; I am going to have a child. I was not certain before, but . . ." She stopped, and smiled up at him. "She said our son would be a king," she told him. "Do you think that could happen? After Elizabeth's son and my father's is dead, although he isn't conceived yet—she did not say when he would be conceived—she said he would be a bad king, but our son's descendants would rule over north and south and west."

But Walter had not heard anything beyond his own delight at her news, and she did not tell him what Elen had foretold of her own death at this birth.

v

The child was to be born in spring, and during the time that she awaited the birth Marjorie spent, in spite of old Elen's sayings, the most contented time of her life. For one thing, the old woman had left Renfrew at Walter's insistence, and had been found lodgings in Paisley; go north she would not, until the birth was over. But the lifting of the knowledge that she was always in that room above, like a raven waiting for bad tidings, eased Marjorie's mind and made her able, if not to forget what Elen had said, to thrust it to the back of her thoughts.

There was enough to occupy them, as day followed day. For the first time since her return she felt herself beloved of the people for her own cause, not because she was the King's daughter. The knowledge of it gave her a shy pleasure, and hearing the blessings shouted after her as she and Walter rode out of the Abbey grounds, or followed the Court in the river lands about Dumbarton and Glasgow, was welcome; often a poor man or woman would come with a gift of baked stuff or cheeses, and they would ask how she was, and she would tell them. They had always come readily to the Kings of Scotland, who met them in the open way and heard their news, good or bad as it might be; her father told her of that.

He himself was so beloved that it was certain that any man raising a hand against him in Scotland now would not live long. This had at first astonished and pleased her, remembering the old days of the Comyn murder, with half the country rising thereafter in arms against Bruce. "Half our enemies were within and half without," he told her, "and I had to fight those within before I could make any stand against England."

He found leisure sometimes to spend an hour with her, at first on horseback, and later, as her pregnancy advanced, with the two of them in a litter. The King himself was not in good health and she noticed often that his eyelids and ankles would be puffy, as though water filled them. "It is since I took the fever in the north," he said lightly, and dismissed it as of no consequence. But she often had a fear that the hardships and privations of those years in the open had told on him more than anyone knew. Asking Will of it, he told her it was an affection of the water, which grew thick "and therefore it cannot pass out of the body. More I cannot tell you, for no one can." He told the King to eat red meat and the King laughed at him, "Keep your old wives' tales for those who need them," he said. He seldom took any heed of physicians.

One day they had made their way up to the heights above the King's palace, and leaving the litter by the roadside made their way forward towards the slope. Below them the silver river ran, broad as the sea at this place; shimmering far off in the distance was a great rock, and islands.

Marjorie sat on a spread cloak which the King had placed for her and clasped her knees with her arms and watched him. More than ever now he seemed to her like a giant figure, of metal forged in many fires till it was both hard and supple. He stood looking down at the water, one foot before the other, hands behind him; the river wind lifted the thick grey hair, casting it back from his face.

"He looks," she thought, "like a man who has laid aside his sword for a very little, and is pausing for strength, before he fights again."

The thought appalled her; surely, after all that had been, the war would soon end! It was true that Edward of England would even yet not recognize the title of King of Scots for her father; that the Pope still supported England; and that twice in the past year her father had made incursions into the South, since the English would not grant the recognition that would bring peace. And Uncle Ned had sailed for Ulster in the summer, and was fighting the Queen's brother now somewhere in the glens. "It is all trouble," Marjorie thought, "and he has had more than most men already."

As if he had heard her thoughts, he turned, and smiled at her. "I'm showing little courtesy in turning my back on you," he said. "Forgive me. It's a sign, though, of affection between two people, that they need say nothing to one another and be content."

"What were you thinking of?" she said. He laughed a little.

"Not what you might expect; not war at all. I'd forgotten Uncle Ned and his Irish throne, forgotten Philip, the Pope and Edward; forgotten even your child, for an hour. I was watching the river, and wondering where it led, beyond the sea to the west, beyond Ireland and the route that leads nowhere. Then I wondered what size of ship would be needed to sail to the further side of the world, and whether ships built on this river would ever attain it. It's broad enough, broad as the sea."

Suddenly he turned and came and dropped down beside her as though he had been a boy and talked, with outspread gesticulating hands, as he had been used to do in the days before the troubles came. Listening, she felt a great thankfulness that now, as on that night long ago in the forest, they were alone together; without Elizabeth, without even—there was no question of disloyalty in her mind—Walter; only herself, her father and the child, not yet born, to listen.

He spoke of many things and she realized, watching and hearing him, what it was that made men follow this man to the death, and obey his orders implicitly to the death, as at Bannockburn. The grey eyes shone; he was young again, having at the same time the wisdom of age and the courage of suffering; the mantle of Wallace lay on him. What would have befallen, or what he would have become, if Wallace had not died, she wondered, and could not know. The death of Wallace had forged steel in this man's gold; thereafter he could not be broken, only scarred.

Yet he spoke gaily enough of small things, their life at Court; the plan he had for a barge to be built, that would carry him up the river or to the Isles, if necessary; and then he began to describe the dark folk of the Isles, as Walter had done, only less from their appearance now than by the difference in their minds.

"Their loyalties are deep-rooted and very strong. They'll fight for a man because his grandmother was their chief's daughter, not because he has given them bread to eat. I found that out in the war with Buchan, dearly enough; they'd die for him." His brow furrowed, remembering how he had defeated Isobel's husband in the north at last, after a fierce war. "All of this nation is so many nations; that's where we differ from England. It was folly of old Edward ever to dream he could merge the two lands into one; they're separate, both in nature and by loyalties, and to attempt otherwise will mean failure, soon or late."

"If you'd sat and waited, the lands would be one now," said Marjorie. He shook his head.

"Not one; under one ruler, maybe. *That* may come; though not in our day. But to swallow up one nation in the other is not God's plan, though it may have been Edward's. Put any Englishman side by side with a Scot, and one will think one way, and one another—and that goes for the men of Lothian, and the men of the north parts, and the men of Kyle. Whatever old Edward may have intended to do, he's cemented, not annulled, the differences between us."

She did not answer; her mind was on old Elen's saying, that her son's sons would rule over north and south and west. Half in mockery of herself, she told him of it.

"An uncomfortable heritage," said Robert drily. He was still watching the light on the silver water.

Epilogue

THE LEECH OUT OF SPAIN

SHE spurred the horse, feeling pleasure in the response against her foot's touch, the instant long leap forward; as though in the mere act of physical command her spirit found constant solace. Perhaps for all her life now the feeling of sudden freedom would be strange.

Yet more than a year, a summer's fading, had passed since that time in England and the shadow of the cage, and the seasons that dragged slowly by without action and without news. The heather about King Robert's palace had flowered twice in the colour of blood and paled and died, and now again would be sending young shoots upspringing beneath the riders' hooves where Walter followed to-day at the King's summons. For it was spring, late as that always came in Scotland; to-day for the first time it had required no thought to ride out without warm coverings, for the air was mild. What did old wives say, about not casting a clout till May was past? Well, if she were to heed old wives she would not be in the saddle at all, so near her time as she was, but in a litter. Yet she hated litters, which made her feel shut in . . . and the child had taken no harm from her riding, though Walter would be angry with her. She smiled. There was a faint, delicious satisfaction still in the disobeying of Walter, as on that day at Dundonald long ago.

She raised her head, crinkling her eyes against the young sunlight. How far off that time seemed, another world between then and now, and yet yesterday! The child who had looked in Egidia's mirror and herself were the same; would have no need of speech if they met, understanding one another.

"I, I, am the same. Nothing that has ever happened, that ever will happen, will make of me a different being."

She thought with a curious detachment of the child in her womb, not seeing him now as a part of herself but separate, with his own thoughts, dreams, habits, hopes, desires. She must not try and order his life for him, to make of him another person than the one he would be . . . her son. He must be a son; she had not at any time, in her own mind, considered him as other than male, as if she and Walter could not beget women. Her mind and Walter's body; or would he resemble neither, being from the beginning only himself? Would the forces that had shaped him have no regard to anything that had passed, only blind chance making him what he might become, poet, dreamer, lecher, soldier, monk, or king, her son?

Her mind cast back to this morning's Shrove Tuesday Mass in the Abbey of Paisley, from which she rode. Very little remained of the grey stone buildings she remembered from childhood; Walter's reconstruction was well under way, and the familiar statues of the Virgin and St Ninian and St Columba and St Catherine, and Mirin the patron saint (who once caused labour pains to be sent to the King of Ireland at his Queen's confinement because he would not hear the Gospel), were new and garish in their niches of carved white stone. Marjorie had knelt among the scaffolding and wooden planks and prayed for a live child, to St Mirin particularly, as he was known to be careful of that kind of prayer. . . . Laughter, irresponsible and gay, rose to her lips as the horse galloped on, remembering the tale of one of the monks to whom she had spoken in passing through their wooded lands, drawing him up with his hawk on his wrist to enquire for the building, and he had enquired for her condition.

> *We bring forth a child of stone,*
> *You a child of flesh and bone,*

he had quoted, and called his blessing after her with all the more warmth because Walter, in imitation of his ancestor the old Abbey's founder, had just given vessels of silver gilt, and a great crucifix, to the new. Marjorie had seen them swathed in purple for Holy Week, the way the images at Scone had once been for the King's crowning. How everything harked back, by devious ways, to what had gone before! Always when she saw the Easter purple now she would remember that year. . . . She was not like Walter, who could feel for every ceremony its proper reverence only. To her the significance was more deeply hidden; remembering the weight of grief and death that had followed God's death for all of them, and the splendour of victory at last that was almost like resurrection. Did she blaspheme in so linking her country's fate, her father's, with the symbolism of Christ? Blind Wishart said she did not, and his eyes now saw only what mattered.

The flat road flung its grey length out before her as she rode. Her train lagged behind; now and again the ground rose slightly, and she would lose them till it subsided again. How long would it be before she could ride again like this? She felt almost sure that the child would be born very soon . . . and then for a while she could not leave her bed. So now, now, in this last hour's freedom, before solemnity took her, she would gather speed . . . she, the wife of the High Steward of Scotland, the Princess, the mother of the heir! How good to be no one again, only a girl with dark hair back-blowing; no one before her, the road glistening after late rain, and the upturned stones lying across the way. . . .

Faster! Faster! The castle of Renfrew would soon be in sight, rising solemn and heavy over its land-line, promising comfort, warmth, ceremony and respect. And so on, for days and years the same; down into middle age, old age, and peace. But once she had ridden away from all pursuers and had found in a hollow a man with strange eyes. Once, while the spring wind ranged the sky, as now; and ground and sky had come together, and present and future had merged into one.

So now there was this. For a brief space the joy of swiftness claimed her; the magic of the ground falling away from under her mount's hooves; the fluidity of grey and green that was earth and clouds mingled, the roaring in her ears that was the wind and the distant sea.

For this last moment, this brief last, she was herself, in her own possession.

Then the ground slewed about as her horse stumbled; a fall, bewilderment, shock, grinding pain, and night. The pain was so quick that she could remember nothing more; that instant was the world's end; then the night engulfed her.

The horse screamed and tried, with flailing legs, to right itself. Its rider lay still among the churning hooves. Presently the servants came riding over the slope; seeing, they hastened forward, making a group about the woman's body and the agonized horse. There was one, a tall fat pale man, who took command. Speaking curtly, wasting little time even for gestures, he told them what must be done.

Will of the Simples had travelled much since his sojourn in the land of Spain in the part where infidels were. From them and others his scholar's mind and enquiring methods had learnt much, and he had such skill with herbs it was said he could bring back the living from near death. But there was little he could do for the High Steward's wife, who was dead by the time he reached her; a feather placed before her lips made no stir, and her eyes stared openly at the sky. But a practice the Arabs had used did not desert him, and with the tears running down his face he called for his knife and his unguents; these last not for the dead Princess yet, but for her child, who might still live. Amid the terrified sobbing of her women he slit the belly of the corpse lengthways, plunging at last both hands in and extracting the child .It was alive, but "A few moments longer and I could not have saved it," said Will. He held the child, which was a boy, head down and tied off the cord; rhythmically, he slapped the baby till at last it cried. Wrapping it in his cloak, he gave it then to the women; later he would take his herbs and unguents to render the body of Marjorie Bruce fit for seemly burial. He mounted his horse again, leaving the men to carry the corpse and the women the child. He heard them rail after him for a vandal, a warlock; a heathen. Not heeding, he rode on; there would be no anger, he knew, for him from those who mattered. Neither man nor woman, he; his lips settled again into their melancholy smooth curve. Later the King would reward him with nobility and land, as for himself and his heirs. "What heirs will I ever have?" murmured Will to himself. "But this day I have brought an heir to Scotland."

She was dead, his lady. That she would have approved of what he had done he knew. Later, before her father and her lord the High Steward came, he would dispose her body as befitted a dead bride. Clad in white, he would leave her; no sign of any wound. It was too early in the year for the white flowers she had worn at her wedding; but the women should gather primroses that grew by the way. They would make a loving wreath to show against the dark cloud of her hair, and to place in her square brown hands.

Robert, the King of Scotland, stood and looked out to where the flat lands of Renfrew merged into their sullen skyline. All the sorrow of this day was outwardly ended, laid like Marjorie in a little hollowed space in the building Abbey across the plain. Later they would raise a stone monument over her. That would be all that was left, a monument of stone. . . .

He had lost so many through death. He had never had the leisure to love them; Isobel, his first wife, that dead girl's mother; the lads who had died so horribly, at Newcastle and Berwick and Carlisle; the rest, who had fought and fallen for him; the women who had loved him. Isobel of Buchan had died of her cage. The rest had been a night's solace, a brief snatched hour.

And Marjorie? He had scarcely known her. Her childhood had been forgotten; her girlhood forfeit. She had loved him, he thought; that one hour in Lorn forest, wrapped in his cloak, they had been close; for an hour.

And now she was dead. Why had she ever been born? To-morrow, by the world's reckoning, he must take his wife to him and beget an heir. He wanted no heir of her flesh; she was alien. But it was no longer the personal things that mattered since Wallace had died and he had set out on the task before him.

So now he must not grieve overlong or he would be a man again and no king. A man unfit for kingship, desirous only to weep.

Others might weep for Marjorie. He turned past where Walter stood red-eyed and silent, towards the place where the cradle lay. In it the new-born child slept, his face still crinkled lilac beneath dried downy hair. How frail a baby's life was, the King thought! There was no certainty that this heir would live. His strange and cruel birth had told on him, and there had been some injury to his eyes. They were inflamed now, with discharge beaded between the lids. He moved fretfully, as if that outrage chafed him.

"He may rule," said King Robert, and did not know he had spoken aloud. His voice and his mind had a like dun quality now, as if much striving had scarred them. Yet still within himself the spirit strove and would not be stilled. His eyes remained fixed on the child in the cradle.

Walter the Steward turned his head, but made no sound at all. It seemed that all his life that had begun was now ended. Whatever he might achieve henceforth would be impermanent, a marking of time till he could rejoin Marjorie at the far side of the grave. His strong inbred faith grasped at that possibility already, accepting it. In his mind already lay the image of Marjorie in stone, with one day beside it his own image carved, masses sung over their heads and their hands lying near, as it had been for all the High Stewards since the oldest Walter Fitzalan had founded Paisley Abbey for his soul's weal. Of the life that remained to be lived, Walter had no vision at all. As long as he lived he would follow the King. He would in time die for the King, or his successor.

This land that they had hewn again must be kept from the flood of change, from invasion or, worst of all, the creeping neglect of indifference, for the decadent to forget. . . .

His son would help to keep it. He and his son.

Under the King's eyes the child woke and shifted slightly, unaware of his great destiny or of anything at all except the moving shadows that surrounded his cradle. Their unfamiliarity struck at his mind and he began to cry, not conscious of loss or change so much as of a yearning for food. Presently his wet-nurse would come and he could turn to her largeness and be comforted. The gaunt man standing in his vision's range meant nothing to him yet at all.

"Why, Walter, hear him!" said the King, and smiled a little. "He thrives—there may yet be a Stewart King in Scotland!"

The new Robert Stewart wailed, and waved his feeble fists.

THE END

Printed in Great Britain
at Hopetoun Street, Edinburgh,
by T. and A. CONSTABLE LTD.
Printers to the University of Edinburgh

SONOMA
COUNTY
LIBRARY

to renew • para renovar

707.566.0281
sonomalibrary.org

SONOMA COUNTY

FREE LIBRARY